Odd Socks

David Clapham

To Naomi, with love and all good wishes from David   5 Oct 2013

iUniverse LLC
Bloomington

ODD SOCKS

Copyright © 2013 David Clapham.

All rights reserved. No part of this book may be used or reproduced by any means, graphic, electronic, or mechanical, including photocopying, recording, taping or by any information storage retrieval system without the written permission of the publisher except in the case of brief quotations embodied in critical articles and reviews.

This is a work of fiction. All of the characters, names, incidents, organizations, and dialogue in this novel are either the products of the author's imagination or are used fictitiously.

iUniverse books may be ordered through booksellers or by contacting:

iUniverse
1663 Liberty Drive
Bloomington, IN 47403
www.iuniverse.com
1-800-Authors (1-800-288-4677)

Because of the dynamic nature of the Internet, any web addresses or links contained in this book may have changed since publication and may no longer be valid. The views expressed in this work are solely those of the author and do not necessarily reflect the views of the publisher, and the publisher hereby disclaims any responsibility for them.

ISBN: 978-1-4759-8951-9 (sc)
ISBN: 978-1-4759-8952-6 (e)

Library of Congress Control Number: 2013908259

Printed in the United States of America.

iUniverse rev. date: 5/31/2013

To Lena, Eric and Sara
and to the memory of
Jennifer Newton

Acknowledgements

Andrew Sheer outlined for me his probability calculation round unpaired socks coming out of a washing machine, which led me to invent the characters and episodes of *Odd Socks*; and Mary Newton and Sue Melber explained some business basics for me. Ben Goldacre in *Bad Pharma* (Fourth Estate, 2012) has influenced the story by his discussion of the difficulties facing drug companies.

For editing the manuscript and for advice and encouragement, I am warmly grateful to Doug Watts and the late Jenny Hewitt of the Jacqui Bennett Writers Bureau, to the staff of iUniverse, and to Lena, Eric, and Sara Clapham.

Some of my forestry colleagues, particularly Tran Ho Quang and family, introduced Lena and me to Vietnam and made us feel at home, for which I give many thanks.

Frank Watson very kindly provided the cover photograph.

PROLOGUE

Andrew Carter's father had been a lorry driver for most of his working life, changing to taxis for the last few years. After he retired, he often related nostalgically what fun he had had with his lorries.

'I loved it,' he was saying one day, 'particularly during the war, creeping along in the blackout, with only the dim light that was allowed.'

'Steve and his lorry,' said Andrew's mother, 'just played and played all day, and sometimes well into the night.'

'But wasn't it exhausting, driving in the blackout?' asked a neighbour who had dropped in to their south London home.

'It didn't matter because people needed me; they were desperate for their rations.'

The neighbour, a friendly lady, turned to Andrew.

'What are you doing nowadays? Something I won't understand. And still at *Cambridge University*, so grand, even after your degree.'

'I'm doing something called analysis,' answered Andrew, warily.

'Sounds like chemistry. I thought you were a mathematician.'

'It's mathematical analysis. About systems of numbers, sort of.'

'Above my head, but I expect it's awfully exciting.' She paused. 'What *use* is it?'

'Often wonder that myself,' said Andrew's father.

'I'll get the tea,' Andrew's mother said and withdrew discreetly.

'At the moment, my supervisor wants me to keep my project very theoretical,' said Andrew. 'He prefers maths not to be useful.'

'Is he a snob?' asked the neighbour.

'Suppose he is, a bit. Actually, my area of maths might sometime become important for computers, though it's hard to know exactly how and when.'

The tea came in, and the conversation switched to television, still something of a novelty in that area of London.

'Did you see Morecambe and Wise last night?' enquired Andrew's father.

'For about twenty minutes, and then I got tired of them hopping about like that,' said the neighbour. 'What I really miss is *Face to Face*. I used to watch every time. What did you think when Gilbert Harding actually *cried*, in front of all those millions of viewers?'

* * *

Later, when he was back in Cambridge and walking by himself in a college garden, it occurred to Andrew that he wasn't a mathematical theorist by nature. He had been good at maths at school and then followed what his teachers laid out for him without deliberate decision. After he had finished his current research project, he should find the energy to change to something more applied and useful – something he could explain to his mother and the neighbours or, even, in the best tradition of physicists like Lord Rutherford, to a barmaid, not that he was often in pubs.

In his fourth term, a history undergraduate with a college room on the same staircase had happened to cross the court with him one morning and, to start a conversation, said, 'You're rather an isolated person, aren't you?'

'I don't see why you say that. I suppose I don't go to parties or pub-crawl, but I have quite a lot of friends really, far more than I had at school.' Andrew wondered if he seemed isolated because he was an only child. His parents had turned forty when he was born. He continued, 'I do some acting and meet a lot of theatre people.'

'What sort of roles do you do? Ever take the lead?'

'I prefer to take small parts; they're more fun and don't take so much time.' Andrew had early become typecast in walk-on, often working-class characters.

'The mathematicians I meet,' commented the other, 'usually have time on their hands. They say they can concentrate on their work for only two or three hours a day without mental exhaustion.'

Andrew didn't need to respond to this, as they had now reached the porter's lodge and separated.

* * *

One possibly useful thing Andrew did was assisting at the problem classes that were part of the special maths teaching for first-year undergraduates reading chemistry. Two girls who always sat together found the problems particularly difficult. Marge was small, dark, and rather plump. Cleo was blonde and wore blouses with low hemlines by the standards of the late 1960s; she had false eyelashes and applied make-up heavily round her eyes. The girls always arrived in good time for the lectures given by Andrew's professor, sitting at the front and taking notes meticulously.

Towards the end of the problem class after the first lecture, the girls summoned Andrew to their desk for special consultation.

'We hate differential equations,' said Cleo.

'Our maths mistress at school wasn't any good at calculus,' amplified Marge, indicating one of the problems in the book.

Andrew believed that it was important to remove the mystique from maths; solving the problems was a matter of following straightforward procedures that he could explain even to people who dreaded figures. He addressed Marge first and then shifted his gaze to include her companion. 'What's the first thing to think of when you see …' Andrew faltered as, from his strategic standing position, his glance fell on Cleo's expanse of minimally supported bare breasts. 'When you see a differential equation?'

'Tell us,' said the girls.

Andrew presented the straightforward procedures, continuing for a while after the official end of the class. The girls might be backward, but both of them were diligent, even Cleo, who didn't seem abnormally flirtatious. The revealing dress was a way of expressing her feminine personality, he decided.

* * *

'There should be a special place in hell for mathematically incompetent girls reading chemistry,' asserted the professor later in the day at the departmental tea break. 'I have two specimens in my class this year. One is dark and dumpy, to match her limited intelligence. The other dresses disgracefully. Somebody should tell her, I think.'

An elderly lecturer agreed. 'She has the general appearance of a …'

'Of a tart,' said the professor. 'Someone should tell her.'

'Why don't you tell her yourself, Alaryck?' suggested the reader, second in command in the department. 'It's the sort of thing you do *so* well.' He was about forty years old, a short man wearing unusually large spectacles, known as Freddie.

Alaryck Tomlinson looked at him coldly.

'I was only joking, of course,' said Freddie and gently touched Professor Tomlinson's arm.

The professor moved his arm away a trifle abruptly, Andrew thought.

'While I remember,' continued Freddie, 'did any of you lot see Joe Briesley on the telly yesterday?'

'You know I don't have time to watch television,' said the professor.

'Of course not, Alaryck, but occasionally the wife switches it on while one happens to be sitting in front of it.'

'If you really want to know, I had the misfortune to see the last ten minutes,' said the professor. 'I can't stand the man. If this is popularizing science, God help the people.'

It seemed that most of those present, including Andrew, had watched Joe Briesley survey the latest and largest computers and predict how the world was going to change over the next fifty years as a result.

'I have to admit he impressed me,' said the elderly lecturer. 'Briesley has a most engaging way of explaining what we can learn from handling vast quantities of data and how computers will move from numbers to words, become more powerful, and then get smaller and smaller – so that, soon, we'll all have our own handy computers.'

'He's vulgar,' said the professor.

'Don't you love his Newcastle dialect, Alaryck?' enquired Freddie. 'I always think Geordie sounds so musical. It caresses the ears.'

'Poppycock, Freddie,' said the professor.

Freddie peered up at the professor through his huge glasses, obviously delighted with the reaction to his teasing, making Andrew think of a frog sunning himself on a stone. *How can the two of them stand each other?*

Andrew wondered. Freddie, as a reader, was admittedly almost impossible to sack, but he had seen Freddie and the professor laughing together on occasions.

The elderly lecturer continued, 'Briesley says that, soon, computers won't have experts ministering to them like high priests; they'll be designed so that almost anyone can use them.'

'It'll be much better for everybody if computers remain under expert supervision,' said the professor.

'Alaryck wants us to return to medieval times, where he would be a high church dignitary contemplating mathematical aspects of the divine order,' said Freddie.

The professor ignored this.

'I hear Briesley's moving to a chair at North Lancashire. One of the new universities,' said the lecturer.

'A CAT with an expensive facelift prowling in the limelight,' sneered the professor.

'By "CAT," Alaryck means college of advance technology,' Freddie explained for anyone who was mystified. 'Alaryck is naturally opposed to upgrading them and calling them universities. He's allergic to their smell.'

Professor Tomlinson ignored this, too. He noticed Andrew sitting in the vicinity. 'Ah Andrew, while I think of it, you must apply for a grant for your living costs. You can begin by taking a chance on the Sloan Awards. They're intended to support more applied mathematics, so write a short sketch of your project with me, about two pages, briefly emphasizing its significance for the development of the theory of statistics, if only in the distant future.'

* * *

Andrew and some of his immediate circle at the department and in college were prepared to admit that they lacked close female company of their own age. They blamed this on the sex ratio of the undergraduates at Cambridge, which was seven-to-one against.

'At the beginning of the first year, a few girls were around in the class, and nothing special seemed to be happening; then suddenly they were all paired off,' a physicist expressed it to Andrew.

'Exactly the same phenomenon for maths,' agreed Andrew.

They assumed that the situation would improve after they graduated. To date, even after graduation, it hadn't.

'How is it with those two chemistry girls you're seen with at the problem class? Is the department paying you to continue with them after the official end of the teaching period?' asked a young departmental colleague one day. 'You must have given them a few hours overtime altogether.'

'It's pointless to ask if there's any extra money,' said Andrew. 'There wouldn't be. Actually, the exam is today. It'll be interesting to see how they do.'

'Oh well, they're nice enough girls. And one of them is really juicy,' said the colleague.

A week later, Andrew, out in the town, noticed Marge cross the street towards him. He waved and waited for her to come up.

She stood close to him. 'I've just read the results. Cleo and I both passed everything.'

'Oh good, you can have a long relaxed vacation,' said Andrew. 'What are you going to do? Will you travel around in Europe?' This was what many of the undergraduates did in the endless summer holiday, stretching from June to October.

'Can't afford it. Neither can Cleo. I shall be at home most of the time. I shall try to get a job, serving in a cafeteria, or perhaps at Woolworths.'

She moved even closer to Andrew. 'It's thanks to you we passed the maths.' She stroked Andrew's back, to his embarrassment. But he interpreted her touch as a gesture within the family to someone in loco parentis (Cambridge speak), rather than a sexual advance.

'Anyway, best of luck for the future,' he said. 'I expect we'll meet again next term.'

* * *

Andrew's project for the Sloan Awards was shortlisted, and he was asked to travel to London to appear before an interview panel.

The panel consisted of six experts. Five of them were dressed in dark suits and white shirts and displayed sober ties. The sixth, a man in his mid-forties, informally dressed in open-necked shirt and jeans, seemed familiar.

This was explained when he said, 'We agreed I should take this one, Mr Chairman?' in a pronounced north-eastern accent.

Andrew was not surprised when the chairman replied, 'Go ahead, Dr Briesley, I mean, Professor Briesley.'

Joe Briesley was not in a hurry. 'Mr Carter, you're at Cambridge.' The tone of his voice suggested that he was less than awestruck by Cambridge. 'Rather different from Camberwell, your home address. 'What makes you say that your project has applications to statistics and computing? Your supervisor, Alaryck Tomlinson, never displays the faintest mathematical interest in anything earthly.'

The chairman said, with a smile, 'Professor Briesley likes to get down to brass tacks.'

Andrew had anticipated this question, if in a less blunt form. 'I want to develop the analytical theory along lines that I think will be relevant for large-scale computing.' He added, 'I should like to do something that might be useful. Of course, it won't have any enormous effect in itself, but perhaps, together with what other people are doing, it might all add up to something eventually.'

The panel rustled papers and took notes. Andrew was afraid he had sounded naive.

Professor Briesley's next question was, 'What do you think of the current enthusiasm for Bayesian statistics?'

He and Andrew exchanged views on this topic.

Then came, 'I see you have some experience teaching classes at Cambridge. I expect you get the feeling at times that one or two in the class might be future geniuses.'

'Possibly, but it's teaching the backward students I find the most rewarding. They're so grateful that someone is taking a personal interest in them, even if they're not potential geniuses.'

Again, a rustling of paper issued from the panel, and again Andrew wondered if he had said the wrong thing.

* * *

'I've received a letter nominating you for a Sloan Award,' Alaryck Tomlinson was saying to Andrew a month later.

'Yes, I was pleased. I couldn't really tell how well the interview was going.'

'A minor oddity,' Alaryck continued. 'A note's been added for the special attention of the supervisor. It runs, "In the opinion of the panel, it might be more suitable for the candidate to pursue his studies at a more technical department." That fellow Briesley is certainly behind it. Damned cheek! You see what he's doing? He's trying to pinch my student. Silly fool! As if anyone would prefer his hole to Cambridge.'

And the next day, Andrew received a long-distance telephone call.

'Joe Briesley speaking. I want you to apply for a junior lectureship in my department at the Stephenson Technical University. Some of the staff thinks they should meet you before we make a definite offer, but you have a good chance of getting the job. You need only say you're interested – no paperwork needed. We already have all your details. In my opinion, you should apply for this lectureship if you're at all serious about developing the statistical side of your project. Alaryck Tomlinson is no use in that area. People in my department here are much better placed to help you.'

'Professor Tomlinson is taking it for granted that I shall want to stay in Cambridge,' said Andrew.

'He would, wouldn't he? But it's not his decision. You don't want to be stuck in Cambridge for another three years, do you? You must have noticed what lingering in Cambridge does to people. Alaryck, for example, used to be quite an engaging lad, I'm told. Look at him now. And don't imagine it's better at Oxford.'

Andrew conceded to himself that Joe Briesley might have a point. 'Could I have a week to think about it?'

'Yes, of course; two weeks, by all means, but not longer. I want to get the post filled, and there are other attractive candidates. Don't forget, I'm making you a good offer financially. You'll be much better paid than on a Sloan Award.'

'I don't want to offend Professor Tomlinson,' said Andrew.

'He'll get over it surprisingly quickly,' said Joe Briesley. 'Goodbye for now.'

* * *

It wasn't easy. Andrew had assumed he would continue at Cambridge into the foreseeable future, and if he failed to get a permanent job or if the supply of temporary positions began to dry up, he would move back to London, near his parents. Should he be more adventurous? He had never considered the north of England, which lacked prestige according to the people around him.

But wasn't it glamorous if an emerging television personality like Joe Briesley offered you a job? Or was Joe Briesley only a vulgar showman, as his professor said? Should he break with someone as influential as Professor Tomlinson? But couldn't a television personality be even more influential? Probably only in the media world, which was hardly Andrew's destiny.

On the last day, he rang back to Joe Briesley and said he'd like to apply for the job. He thought to himself that he could always look around north Lancashire and then say, no, he'd stay in Cambridge.

'You will be applying in confidence, so that you don't irritate old Alaryck before it's settled, I suppose,' said Joe Briesley. 'As I said before, you don't need to write anything formally; just roll up here for an interview at the department. How about the day after tomorrow, nine o'clock in the morning?'

Andrew looked up the trains from Cambridge to north Lancashire and accepted that getting to the interview would require a detour via London and take ages.

Towards the end of the next day, he had reached Manchester and was on the train to Presley, the nearest town to Stephenson Technical University. He passed through an extensive depressed industrial region, after which the countryside improved as he arrived in Presley; there, he overnighted in a bed and breakfast place. The next day he took the bus out to the new university, much of it still under construction as extensions to a red-brick Victorian building. He found his way to the Department of Mathematics, Statistics, and Computer Science, still in the old building, where in addition to Joe Briesley two other members of staff questioned him about his work and experience.

One of them was sceptical. 'You haven't yet taken your doctorate. You must make sure you do so in reasonable time, and we can help with that. What bothers me more is whether you can stay focused. After your maths degree, you spent eighteen months in the statistics department. Then you went back to pure maths.'

'I had some ideas about modifying Bayesian statistics, but they didn't work out, and when Professor Tomlinson offered me a place to read Part Three maths, I thought I should take it.'

'I can understand that it was flattering to be asked back by Professor Tomlinson. But now, a few months later, you're considering moving again.'

'For leaving Alaryck Tomlinson,' inserted Joe Briesley, 'give Andrew full marks.'

'But he hasn't definitely done so yet,' objected the colleague.

'Well, as soon as he definitely does, give 'im full marks. Andrew, we should like you to withdraw into the secretary's office, while we discuss matters among ourselves. We'll come out shortly and tell you what we've decided.'

Andrew settled down to read a weekly newspaper he had bought. It was a longer wait than he had expected and enhanced his feeling that the interview had not gone well.

Finally, Joe Briesley fetched him from the secretary's office into his private room.

'Andrew, two things attracted me to you when we first met. You wanted to do something useful. And you liked teaching backward students. We're putting you in the first place for the lectureship, despite applications from two strong candidates. We don't require your answer immediately, but we need it in the next few days.'

But Andrew felt that he was now perfectly capable of taking decisions in response to unexpected events. 'I can give my answer now. I accept.'

'Fine. Can you begin first of next month? While you're here, you can fix somewhere to live. Elaine here, our secretary, will give you a list of temporary places while you find somewhere you really like.'

Next month was sooner than he had expected, but it seemed a good idea; best cut the time in the vicinity of Alaryck Tomlinson to a minimum.

* * *

Informing Professor Tomlinson was not a happy occasion.

'You're making a disastrous mistake, Andrew. If you want to do something useful, you should help me thrust back the frontiers of theoretical understanding, not try to do industry's work for it. And don't waste your time teaching silly young girls but concentrate on the undergraduates who really matter. Instead, you've chosen to move away from me to a vulgar showman like Briesley – a man who can say that the desk computer of the future will be "just too-too!" And you're about to move from Cambridge to a disease-infested industrial wasteland submersed in the grime of northern England! The air there is not good. If you have to be more applied, you could have consulted the statistics department here. Well, you've made your bed, and now you must lie on it. I won't say I'm not disappointed, but we shall survive without you, needless to say.'

'It's hard to turn down a junior lectureship.'

'Only if it's at a proper university in a civilized part of the country. But enough, I assume that further discussion is pointless.'

* * *

Andrew's mother was alarmed by the news of Andrew's sudden departure, but his father took the news lightly.

'Stephenson Technical University? My pal's lad has been installing the gas there. Funnily enough, me and the lorry once popped up by mistake in that area of Lancashire. Turned right instead of left but didn't realize what we'd done for ages. Finally decided we might as well carry on through all that rundown industrial area and look around and came to really stunning countryside before turning homewards. Can be a nice surprise, taking the wrong turning.'

Part I:
Antonia

Chapter 1

Andrew bumped into him – another young man in his middle twenties – almost literally, outside Presley railway station. He regarded the man curiously; someone he had seen before and should recognize but couldn't quite place.

The other young man was clearly going through the same process, but soon said, 'It's Andrew, isn't it? Andrew Carter. Looking lost, much as when we were both new boys at a strange school in the middle of London. Do you recognize me?'

Andrew didn't answer at once, but memories of various kinds began to fuse together until he could say, 'Toby Morton. The voice is familiar, but you're so differently dressed from how I remember you, and your hair's changed. But the expression in your eyes is the same.'

'I'm in my painting clothes; that's why I'm a mess.' Toby was casually dressed in old sandals, worn-out jeans with traces of paint, an open-necked shirt, and an anorak. 'I slipped out to buy a paper at the station. Andrew, what on earth are you doing here? You've a mass of luggage as if you're moving in permanently.'

'I've taken a job at the Stevenson Technical University – it's new; you probably heard about it – in the maths department. Or strictly speaking, maths, statistics and computer science. For that matter, why are *you* in Presley?'

Toby explained that he was freelancing in the provincial art world. 'I might as well live in an inexpensive area, not too far from my family and not too near, either. The rest of the family moved from London into a large place some miles north of here a few years ago. Weird that the two of us should crop up together in Presley. Most of the boys at school, dyed-in-the wool London provincials, would have just as soon moved to central Africa as to the north of England. Anyway, what did you mean by the expression in my eyes?'

'They're searching and sympathetic. That struck me at school.'

Clearly, Toby was pleased. 'Perhaps they're artist's eyes. I do a lot of painting these days. Where are you living? Somewhere in Presley? We can load your luggage in my car, and we'll drive there.'

But first they had coffee together, in a little café frequented by working men dressed not unlike Toby. Andrew was pleasantly surprised by how easily he could resume relations with Toby after six years.

'Do you remember when we did *A Midsummer night's Dream* in the first year at school? I enjoyed that,' said Toby. 'I realize now that Jimmy Howard was good at theatre productions, however boring his teaching.'

'I still think the lines we had as mechanicals were really funny, in the context. "I see a voice," and all that. Incidentally, it was you who talked me into acting.'

'I wasn't sure I could stand being on stage, and I wanted to be with someone I liked. Also, you seemed so left out, and I really thought you might enjoy being involved in something, for once. I went to Tony and suggested that you should have the part because of your not-so-posh accent, just right for the character.'

'He didn't say anything like that when he asked if I was interested.'

'He wouldn't. I could tell at the time he was embarrassed by my bringing up class. And six months later, you were talking like the rest of us. You changed faster than most of the other County Council Scholars. Have you done any acting since?'

'I took it up as a student.' It was time to stop saying *undergraduate* now he had left the Cambridge world. 'Only small parts. I could have acted in more plays at school, except I was under so much pressure from work. What about you?'

'I've been sufficiently occupied with painting.'

'And it's your job now? How did you get into it professionally?' wondered Andrew. 'You read classics, didn't you?'

'Yes. Greats. Hated it.'

'Why did you do it?'

'Prestige. The classics are supposed to be good for you – make you a well-rounded man with a trained mind, all that stuff. And you get to know the right people. If there's one thing I've learned to perfection, it's never do anything because someone says it will be good for you. It never is.'

'But did you go to an art college? You liked painting at school.'

'Dad had died, leaving money I couldn't touch until I was twenty-one. When at last I could get hold of it, I left Oxford without taking a degree and used a large chunk of the money to attend the art college, much to Mother's disgust.'

'How was it at the art college?'

'Marvellous. And I was quite good at an old-fashioned, realistic sort of painting, complete with perspective. I still do a few pictures of that kind, and I can usually sell them, if only at modest prices. But something happened shortly after I'd finished there. I was at an exhibition of modern paintings and ran into a girl I knew from my time at Oxford. She asked me to recommend a picture for her to buy, and when its value went up fivefold, she told her father about me. Sir Oliver Laine, the Conservative MP.'

Andrew had heard of this MP; he was often on the news in connection with the latest deal he was involved in.

'Sir Oliver wanted to have lunch with me. I agreed, if only to see the inside of a London club. This proved to be in a side street near Leicester Square. The reception sent me up to a private dining room, and there he was.

'"Ah, Toby Morton, I'm Sir Oliver Laine, MP. Sit down at this little table, and you shall tell me about the art world while we enjoy together what I expect will be a rather good lunch. Help me to understand and love modern paintings and, incidentally, make money from them. My daughter Fiona says you were at my old college. So your judgment was irreproachable."'

Toby had reclined back, imitating an expansive grandiloquent man in middle age being ingratiating to a young visitor. He continued, 'The food arrived. Fixed menu, dishes with French names, including *coq de vin*, and an elderly waiter serving them off silver plate. Very conservative – chicken and fried potatoes – like a college lunch on a good day but with a fancy sauce. After that, Sir Oliver got down to business.'

Toby switched to Sir Oliver's style. '"The conversation we are about to have will never, in fact, have taken place. Do I make myself plain?"'

'Did he really say that?' asked Andrew. 'It's like a bad film.'

'Exactly. I said I was curious as to what would follow, and he leant back in his chair, tapped the tips of his fingers together, and said, "I intend to forward your name as a young, highly competent judge of modern painting to the hanging committee of the Tippin Art Gallery in Porterfield, near my constituency. As you know, I am a member of Parliament. It is, incidentally, pathetic that such a large industrial city in northern England should have only the one art gallery. This one awards a prize annually to a promising young artist. Part of the prize consists of exhibiting at the Tippin – three paintings by the winning artist and one each by the two runners-up. You will suggest suitable names to me at an early stage. My dealers will buy the entire output of at least your first choice. You will propose the names to the hanging committee. I also sit on the committee, and I shall strongly support your choices, which I am confident will be accepted by the committee as a whole. The resulting publicity will lead to a substantial increase in the value of the artist's paintings, which we shall arrange to sell at a suitable time. Your share of the profits will be 20 per cent. What do you say?"

'I told him, "I don't think it will work, but I don't mind trying, at any rate once. How legal is it?"'

Toby reverted to Sir Oliver's grandiloquent style. "'It depends on your lawyer. Mine is particularly well connected, an old college friend – a soulmate, as I believe you will shortly be. A true Lainista, a soulmate of Sir Oliver Laine, realizes almost instinctively that a rule that applies to the crowd need have no relevance for himself; the rule can be bent. Indeed, it should be bent. Of course, the provinces are relatively small beer. We must act on our experience in Porterfield as a stepping stone to the London and international scene. In a year or two, we shall hear of a big prize for modern art that will be called the Turner Prize. Infiltration into the Turner Prize establishment must be our objective."

'I couldn't help being curious about the whole crazy scheme. "I'm prepared to go with you on the first step, even if I'm sceptical," I said to him.

'Then he gave me an extremely powerful handshake, bordering on the painful, and hung on. "You won't forget, will you, that this conversation was strictly confidential? My friends tell me that I am basically a good chap. But some of them say I can be a frightful shit."

"'I fully understand the point you're making," I assured him, hoping he would let go. Which he finally did, and indicated that he would contact me again in the near future.'

'Weird encounter. So you went on with it? How were the people on the hanging committee?' wondered Andrew, who had been an attentive listener.

'Long story.' Toby looked at his watch. 'I'll tell you later. Let's get you moved into your new place.'

Toby collected his car and helped move Andrew and his luggage to his small flat.

'Why have you come by train? Don't you have a car?' asked Toby.

'I've had a few driving lessons. It goes slowly.'

'You need to practise with someone, in addition to the lessons; then you'll learn much sooner. If you haven't got anybody else, I'd love to drive around with you. I can show you things at the same time.'

'That would certainly be a great help. I could pay something.'

'Nonsense; wouldn't dream of letting you,' Toby said. 'Now I come to think of it, there is something you could do for me, and then it would be quits, to put it mildly. Come to the family place in the country with me next week, over the holiday. I need additional buffer against Mother. Otherwise, we shall just quarrel horribly. It will be hard work for you – you'll draw some of the fire – but it will be only for a short time. Do you remember Mother?'

Andrew did remember Toby's mum – an imposing woman whom he had once met over a weekend.

'I go home as little as possible, but next weekend, it's the birthday of Antonia, my half-sister. Quite an important birthday. She'll be fifteen. Do you remember her, too?'

Andrew could recall an eight-year-old little girl with a good deal of personality, much friendlier than her mother.

It was settled that Andrew and Toby would drive up to North Lancashire together the next weekend.

Andrew wondered what Toby would say to his mother about the extra visitor.

'We shall just turn up, the two of us. It's always best to present Mother with a fait accompli. She accepts faits accomplis with resigned, suffering good nature. Otherwise, one just lands in a mass of tedious argument.'

* * *

Toby and Andrew met again a few days later. Andrew had felt he should come with a present for Antonia and asked Toby's advice.

'Antonia likes paintings. We can have a look in a shop I visit regularly. Mostly rubbish there, but sometimes one or two really good things, at not too outrageous prices.'

Andrew learned that Toby made part of his income by collecting pictures from antique shops around the country and selling them in London.

The shop was away from the town centre. At the entrance on the ground floor, Andrew noted the cheap reproductions, posters, and popular sketches. The owner, recognizing Toby, took them up to a sort of attic above. 'Here's something that might be of interest, Mr Morton.' It was a watercolour from the nineteenth century. 'A shy young man and an eager young woman, talking confidentially in a rural setting. This is a sketch for a larger painting that's now in the Victoria and Albert Museum in London, though not usually on show. Notice how the girl has her hand on the young man's knee. In the final version, she is lightly touching his shoulder. Perhaps the painter decided not to risk offending the potential client's sense of propriety.'

The picture enchanted Andrew. He enquired about the price.

'The painter is not well known nowadays, and it is only a sketch, so I was wanting around twelve pounds. What do you say, Mr Morton?'

'I might come back about it,' said Toby, 'but now we are looking for something for my friend Andrew here to give as a birthday present for a teenage girl, my half-sister. Have you something smaller that might be suitable?'

They moved to a corner where three old paintings of postcard size depicting street scenes in China were hanging.

'This one isn't bad,' said Toby, 'and at a sensible price for Antonia.'

Andrew could see that it was skilfully done.

'Seems a good idea.' Andrew pulled out his wallet to pay, and the owner brightened up in anticipation of a sale. Then Andrew had second thoughts; wouldn't Antonia think it dull?

'Is there something larger in the same price range?' he asked.

'It will have to be a reproduction of an old master, sir.' The shop owner took them to a cupboard and opened a drawer with a pile of prints. 'I'll get back to a customer downstairs.'

Toby thumbed through the pile and took out a picture, with a cry of satisfaction. 'One of Monet's water lily paintings. That's something for Antonia. It doesn't need to be framed; she can pin it up direct on her bedroom wall.'

Andrew was impressed. 'It's a good reproduction, and it's a famous painting.'

They carried the print downstairs, and the owner brightened up again as Andrew drew out his wallet. Then Andrew began to have doubts. It was a painting you could see reproductions of all over the place; it wasn't a very personal choice. And flowers rather than people – for a girl in her mid-teens?

'Can I look at the picture of the young couple once again?'

Toby and the owner exchanged glances.

Andrew ascended the stairs and stood looking at the picture, first from farther away, then from close up.

After a while, when Toby joined him, Andrew said, 'I think I'll buy this rather than the Monet. I realize it's a generous present for someone I hardly know, but it's something I really like, I don't know why, and I won't have to apologize for its possible shortcomings.'

'You're crazy,' said Toby, 'but Antonia will love it. She's a precocious little thing.'

'Precocious in what way?'

'Oh, you'll see. Incidentally, Mr Briggs, the owner, expects you to offer him ten pounds, rather than twelve.'

Mr Briggs accepted ten pounds quickly. He was obviously amused. 'You're like an old professor, sir, the sort that takes an age to make up their minds.'

Chapter 2

The next Thursday, Toby and Andrew drove down in Toby's ancient Morris Minor, equipped with L-plates so that Andrew could be at the steering wheel.

'I chatted with Antonia over the telephone yesterday,' Toby said. 'She even remembers you from all those years ago. Do you know what she said? "Under the surface, he seemed to be good, solid material." Don't take that seriously. I'm not sure what she really meant, and I didn't ask her. She's not telling Mother you're coming, of course.'

'You had another sister, didn't you? A little older and rather quiet.'

'That's Janet. Her relationship with us is complex – so complex that she's no relation at all. She's my father's stepdaughter. He was much older than Mother and died years ago. Then my mother married the man who was Antonia's father, my stepfather. He was also much older, and he died a few years ago. I expect Mother wore both of them out. I'd probably die if I lived at home.'

Andrew contemplated this information. 'Did you get on okay with your stepfather?'

'Oh yes; he was an easy-going man. He was fond of Janet and tried to boost her self-confidence a bit, but without much success. Mother just despises her, poor thing.'

They drove through a wonderful countryside, along a river valley with the Lake District mountains occasionally visible in the distance. Then Andrew saw a large house in Victorian Gothic style – a little large to be practical, he thought, but not large enough to be called a manor house or a castle.

'Here we are – Enby Hall, for what it's worth,' announced Toby.

They parked the car and went in through a side door to encounter Toby's mother in the kitchen, standing over a casserole.

'I've come with Andrew Carter, who I bumped into unexpectedly in Presley after all these years. Do you remember him, Mother? He came home once when we were living in Richmond. Actually I asked Antonia to warn you he was coming this weekend,' he lied brazenly, 'but she may have forgotten to tell you.'

'Andrew, your name is? How do you do, Andrew?' Mrs Morton greeted him in the manner often adopted by 'county' people to make strangers feel at home, welcome even, while reminding them of their relatively humble place in the higher order of things. She gave him a cool handshake and looked him up and down critically, while Andrew stood by diffidently.

'What school did you go to?' asked Mrs Morton.

Andrew needn't have taken this personally. Mrs Morton was expert at making people feel like a trodden worm, as many in the neighbourhood could have testified.

'Mother, really!' exclaimed Toby, still in a good humour. 'Andrew was in my class at St Luke's, the whole time to begin with and then for general subjects afterwards.'

'What did your father do, Andrew?' Mrs Morton continued.

'First he drove lorries, then taxis.'

'Was he the director of a large transport firm?'

'Mother!' exclaimed Toby, already irritated. 'Andrew's father himself drove lorries. Some people actually do things themselves, rather than just get other people to do them. Andrew was very clever at maths and won a local authority scholarship to St Luke's – which is why he was there, even if his family wasn't stinking rich.'

Mrs Morton was now saying, 'You're very welcome, Andrew, of course, even if this is short notice, to put it mildly. I saw you were driving Andrew's car with those L-plates attached. I wonder why you never learnt to drive, with your father what he is.'

'We were living in London, and it didn't seem necessary. My father wasn't in the best of health.'

At this point, Antonia entered the kitchen. She resembled Toby in her eyes, searching and sympathetic, but her self-assured entry reminded

Andrew more of her mother. She gave a friendly smile toward Andrew and asked, 'Who's this?'

And Toby repeated what he had told his mother.

'Oh, now I remember what Toby said over the phone. Sorry, Mother, forgot to tell you.'

Andrew wondered if Mrs Morton noticed the theatrical element in this exchange.

Antonia continued, 'So you're with us again! Do you remember me?'

'Yes, but I wouldn't recognize you as the Antonia of six years ago. It's your birthday today, isn't it? Congratulations!'

'Yes, I'm fifteen. Well into my teens. You could say I'm now a mid-teenager.'

Her mother intervened to say, 'There will be a birthday meal this evening. I've made your favourite casserole, Antonia, and, fortunately, I had the foresight to make a large one so I shall have relatively little problem filling an extra plate for our visitor.' She glanced at Toby while she said this, but he gave no sign of listening to her.

'Where's Janet?' he asked.

'She's lying in bed with one of her headaches,' explained his mother. The way she rolled her eyes told everyone in the room what she thought of Janet's headaches.

Toby took Andrew upstairs with his suitcase to one of the spare bedrooms and suggested that they walk along the river in the late afternoon sunshine. They asked the ladies of the house to accompany them. Antonia readily agreed to join them, but Mother declined, indicating that she was too busy in the kitchen for purely frivolous walks along the river, however delightful the spring sunshine might be.

The three of them went out of a side door into a large untidy garden and then onto a path that abruptly descended through a pasture down to the river. Antonia was young enough to run spontaneously ahead of them. Andrew breathed in the fresh air and took in the scenery – the river valley, the hills in the middle distance, the blue sky, and the clouds. He shook off the chilliness of Mrs Morton's reception and felt his spirits expand.

They arrived back at Enby Hall in excellent humour for dinner. Janet had recovered from her headache and was as Andrew remembered her, a subdued young woman. The rest of the party attacked the casserole with relish. Mother, in a gap in the general conversation, spoke to the uninvited guest.

'Andrew, what is it you do exactly? Some sort of academic, I believe. I expect it's all very interesting, really,' she continued, making it clear that this was exceedingly improbable.

'I'm a mathematician. Here I shall work on computer theory, but earlier I was concerned with statistical genetics. Actually, your family would be excellent as part of a genetic study to distinguish effects of heredity and effects of the environment. Toby and Antonia are related, whereas Janet is unrelated but shares the same environment. Janet would belong to the control group.'

Andrew, who felt sorry for Janet, thought that this would bring her into the conversation.

'I can't be part of a control group; I'm no good at controlling people,' responded Janet, apathetically

Antonia said, 'You don't have to do anything if you're in a control group; you can simply go on being as you are, and everybody will be delighted.'

Janet seemed relieved and even faintly happy. Andrew was pleased that Antonia, at least, seemed to understand him.

Mother said, 'I wish you scientists could do something useful for once, instead of theorizing about things. For example, if you could only solve the odd sock problem. Why is it that whenever we housewives load the washing machine with socks that have been carefully sorted into pairs, we nevertheless always emerge with at least one odd sock?' It was impossible to tell if this was a joke or if she were deadly serious.

'Actually, I've given that some consideration,' said Andrew. 'I have a special problem for students. It's like this; you have put several pairs of socks into the washing machine, but you can't remember how many. You take out $2n$ of them, and (assuming that each pair is distinguishable) you pair them up as far as possible and find that you have p pairs and $2n-2p$ odd socks. On the basis of this, what is the most likely number that you put in? It's a problem in maximum likelihood, really. Actually the maximum occurs at the nearest whole number to n times $(2n-1)$ divided by $2p$. Surprisingly simple formula. It's a good problem for not particularly bright students in their second year.'

Mother sniffed; she wasn't impressed by mathematical formulae, particularly when they were out of place at dinner tables. 'I suppose we taxpayers have only ourselves to blame for the peculiarities of the state educational system.'

Antonia smiled at Andrew. 'You must explain how you work it out sometime. I like maths.'

Andrew wondered if Antonia was mathematically precocious.

Mrs Morton was reluctant to leave Andrew alone.

'When do you expect to become a professor, Andrew?'

'I don't really aspire to become a professor.'

'Why not? You should …dare to excel.' Both hands motioned broadly upwards towards the stars, her voice resonated to match the excellence.

'I should hate a professor's working day. Professors have to spend so much time on things I'm not good at, like sorting out problems with people, organizing everybody's activities, impressing the university authorities by pretending to know the answers to everything, and writing endless grant applications to research councils. I'm prepared to do my fair share of hack administration, but what I enjoy is solving problems and helping students.'

'You sound just like Toby. He's afraid of responsibility, too.'

'Mother means I refused to go into business,' interjected Toby.

'You were perfectly happy to live in Enby Hall so long as your mother was paying. When the time came for you to contribute to its maintenance, you decided you were too fine for business. You were an artist.'

'*Mother*, we've been through this loads of times. Can we give it a rest? It's Antonia's birthday; let's toast her future.'

Mrs Morton was prepared to accept this.

It was now time to hand over Antonia's presents. From her mother and brother, Antonia received cards with money enclosed. Her sister gave her a bottle of scent and some cosmetics. Andrew thought they were somewhat dull presents, although Antonia seemed glad enough. He fetched the picture, which the shopkeeper had carefully wrapped. Antonia realized, after various guesses while she did the unwrapping, that it was a picture and was delighted when she saw that it was a proper old master, as she put it, and gave Andrew a hug.

She examined the picture carefully, looking at it from very close up. 'You can see from his expression that the young man doesn't really understand what's going on, but the girl – she understands completely. Girls mature more quickly than boys. The artist knew that.' To Andrew she said, 'Let's go up to my room and see where to hang it. We can look at the view at the same time. From my room, the sun will be just right for seeing over the river.'

'I must say I don't think it's a very suitable picture for a young girl. Is it even much of an investment—?' began Mother as Andrew left the room with Antonia.

They carried the picture up two flights of stairs to a long, narrow room like an attic, with a superb view of the garden and across the river to the small hills beyond. The room hadn't much furniture, but it had a generous bookcase with plenty of books, a chest of drawers, and smaller pictures and a number of photographs and postcards. Antonia asked Andrew where the picture should hang.

'About here, don't you think?' he suggested. 'Even if you have to move the postcards.'

And Antonia put the picture on the floor at the place indicated.

'There's another thing I want your opinion about. I've just got my first grown-up bra. What do you think of it?' And she swiftly took off her blouse and stood two feet in front of Andrew.

Andrew gazed at her. 'You look wonderful,' he said, with feeling.

'But what about the bra? Does it fit properly? It's not too big?' and she moved her left breast around inside the cup.

'I'm not an expert,' said Andrew in his best scientific manner, 'but I should say it's exactly right.'

'I've been filling out the last six months. I was the first girl in my class to get her period.'

She put on her blouse. 'I'm glad we found a good place for the picture.'

They returned to the dining room. Andrew joined Toby, who was sitting by himself in the corner of the room.

'You've been a fair time up there. What did you get up to?' asked Toby.

'Antonia showed me the view' – Andrew was a stickler for telling the truth – 'and one or two other things—'

'Sounds like Antonia—'

'And then we had a short chat about maturity.'

'Sounds like Antonia *all over*. See what I mean about precocious?'

Antonia, who had been out of earshot, reappeared. 'What would be marvellous now, after that casserole, would be lots of lovely ice cream,' she declared.

'Ice cream is just empty calories. You know what I think of that. We shall have a fruit salad,' replied her mother. 'In fact, I should like you all to come into the kitchen and help me make it.'

Mrs Morton blossomed when she could organize people. The mood lightened. Andrew peeled apples and cut them up into pieces of approved size. The family chatted together amiably, for once.

'The Armitages are giving a fancy-dress party,' remarked Mrs Morton.

'Are you going?' asked Toby.

'Haven't been invited.'

'Hardly surprising, after what you said to Nancy Armitage about the vulgarity of the new rich.'

Mother was too absorbed with the details of the fruit salad to react to this. They went back to the dining room, and the company made delighted comments on the success of their efforts. It was now time for coffee. Janet said she didn't feel like coffee. She withdrew to take the dog for a walk.

'How are things going for Janet? Does she have a job?' Andrew asked.

'She likes animals, as you may have noticed. Mother's idea for a time was that she should become a vet of some sort, but she wasn't academic enough. She liked helping at a local stables. Mother decided that she should take expensive lessons in what they called equestrianism. The idea was that she should make a dazzling display on horseback and turn the head of some rich young man. Mother forced her to turn up at social gatherings, preferably the local hunt; but Janet refused to do that with an unusual display of character; she can't bear cruelty to animals. She did make it to one or two equestrian dos. She had good rapport with her horse and was quite touching with him. Sure enough, she turned somebody's head, but it was the wrong somebody, Mother thought. A local farmer, called Fred Arlington, fell head over heels for her. Alas for carefully laid plans.'

Mrs Morton had listened to this with obvious irritation. 'Fred Arlington is no gentleman. I cannot bear the thought of him gazing possessively at Enby Hall.'

'He wouldn't be interested. The land isn't suitable for his sort of farming.'

'He is so tedious, going on endlessly about farming technicalities.'

'Exactly suitable for Janet. She has no small talk either. On the rare occasions when they weren't busy about the farm, they would sit on the sofa, gaze at each other in silent rapture, and be devotedly boring together. Anyway, he's an excellent farmer, they all say, and you wouldn't have to worry about Janet's finances.'

'It's not enough not to have to worry about her. I need someone from outside who will restore Enby Hall to its former glory, as there's no hope of your doing it.'

'And impress the neighbours, especially the Armitages.'

Andrew wondered why Janet didn't simply leave home, to live independently.

Antonia had finished her coffee. 'You know what I'd like to do now?' she said. 'I'd like to rummage in the junk room. Are you two coming?'

Chapter 3

Andrew was curious as to what a junk room in a place like Enby Hall would contain. The three of them climbed to a room high up in the house, a sort of attic approached by a narrow, dusty staircase. Near the bottom of the staircase sat a large bucket. It was a third full of water.

Noticing Andrew looking at it, Antonia explained, 'It's standing under where the roof leaks – to catch the drips.'

'The leaking roof,' commented Toby, 'is a serious domestic problem here.'

'Can't it just be fixed?'

'It would cost a fortune to have it done properly.'

The junk room had accumulated a miscellany of items that no one had found the heart to throw away over the last fifty years. At one end, a small window overlooked the yard. At the entrance was a bust of a Victorian gentleman, who resembled a Roman emperor.

'His bust makes him a pompous old ass, but there's an early photograph where he looks almost human,' commented Toby. 'He brought the gas to central Lancashire and built Enby Hall on the proceeds so that he could be a proper landed gentleman. He's the only one of us who ever did anything much. My great-grandfather.'

Toby went to a dusty chest of drawers where he had put some of his old clothes. He took out what appeared to be a pair of dark socks, except that when he separated them, one was black and the other dark blue. Toby held them up. 'A sentimental memory of my boringly misspent youth. When I was an undergraduate, Mother constantly nagged at me to go to formal functions where the dress was dinner jacket, like college balls, "to get to know the right people, for your father's sake." I obeyed, just to keep her quiet. I hate formal dos. But I used to make one little childish act of defiance. This isn't any old pair of odd socks; it's a pair I kept specially for wearing with a dinner jacket.'

Andrew wanted to hear more about Toby's encounters with Sir Oliver Laine. 'How were the people on the hanging committee you were supposed to meet at the art gallery in Porterfield?'

'There were five or six who attended regularly. Two were local worthies, heads of engineering firms and the like, who didn't pretend to know much about modern art but liked looking at paintings. They used to take notes conscientiously and check up on the artists' credentials as best they could. Then there were the Tippin Art Gallery people. One of them was director of the gallery. He was a charming old man. Modern fashion art wasn't at all his thing. He tried to promote the more traditional artists but collided with Sir Oliver Laine, who thought there wasn't enough money in traditional painting styles. I tried to compromise by choosing a traditionalist for second or third place.'

'How did it work getting your suggestions through the committee?'

'When two members of a committee know what they want and want the same thing, and the other members are just waiting around to see what happens, the result is predictable. Sir Oliver dominated us. At the end of the first committee meeting, the director asked me, "Do you have any other interests in art, besides the moderns?"

'I replied, "Nineteenth-century English painting; I think it's better than people usually say it is. Does the Tippin have some good nineteenth-century work?"

'The director brightened up. "You must be the judge of that. Would you like to see them?"

'"Yes, of course. But aren't you closed now? It's quite late."

'"It's not closed if you've got the keys."

'The director took me into the museum via a side door. It was only a small gallery, perhaps eighty paintings, with a similar number in a storage room. They went to his favourite corner, with a group of fine pre-Raphaelite paintings. On a little table was a leaflet containing information about the artists, the background of the paintings, who the models were, what the critics had said, and so on. I read it through and saw the director looking at me questioningly.

'I said, "It's a thoughtful introduction, well written. I expect your visitors linger over it and then feel they look at the paintings with new eyes. Did you write it?"

'"Yes. Took me ages. What I'd like to do is to complement these with a painting by Alma-Tadema, but I haven't been able to get hold of one at a suitable price."

'"It's funny you should say that. When I was looking round the north-east last week, I saw a picture in an antique shop that could almost have been by him. It was that sort of style. I couldn't make out the signature. It was at quite an ordinary price."

'The director was excited. "I'd love to have a look at it. I know an expert who could pronounce on its authenticity."

'So we went off with the director's expert to Northumberland. They bought the picture, after some price negotiation. The expert wasn't prepared to say that it was definitely authentic; it could have been by a young apprentice working in the studio, which might explain the absence of a legible signature. They discussed it all openly, much to the credit of the director, I thought, even if it wasn't *his* money at stake. The owner was a dear old lady who naturally got excited about the possibility of it being a much more valuable painting. The director paid her well over the original asking price, and she was happy.

'It was a splendid nude painting, pretty sensuous. It made me think of *Olympia* by Manet. It was almost as good as *Olympia*. But that would cost hundreds of times more if it ever came onto the market. Is it just because *Olympia* is by a French painter instead of an Englishman, and everybody knows that the English can't paint? I don't think I could make a good job of explaining why *Olympia* is more original, if it is, and it was painted only ten or twenty years before the Alma-Tadema. It's so much a matter of taste. One wonders who decides what's good and what isn't.'

Toby was silent for a while, lost in memories.

Antonia had been occupied with going through the contents of a cupboard drawer but had listened enough to put in, 'Aren't you going to tell Andrew whether it worked? Fixing the prizewinner, I mean.'

'Oh yes, it worked. Sir Oliver, using various names, had already acquired several of the artist's paintings. Their prices rose considerably after the publicity. I had to admit that he had been correct over what would happen.

The proceeds, my 20 per cent, duly came along – a modest but useful-sized cheque. Even so, I couldn't believe it could happen a second time. Or perhaps I just wanted an excuse to continue, although I knew I should have stopped.

'In the meantime, the director and I used to meet independently of the committee work. We had pretty similar views about the sort of things we admired. He was unpretentious and confiding. We used to visit exhibitions together. I grew really fond of him and regarded him as a close friend. I couldn't go on deceiving him. I could have sent my two cheques to some charity, but they were tainted money, so it seemed more appropriate to send them to Mother. I thought she might even be appreciative. She spent them on minor repairs about the house but wasn't at all grateful; just told me it was a paltry sum and why couldn't I get a properly paid job in the City, instead of scrounging a living from teaching evening classes and selling a few pictures.

'The thing is, I worked hard at touring all the exhibitions in northern England and visiting various artists during the two years on the committee, often in the company of the director. I learned masses about the art market and, because of being able to discuss with the director, not just the modern art market. From all this experience, I learned what would sell and what the prices could be expected to be in a few months' time. I found I could make a useful additional income by collecting pictures from provincial antique shops and selling them later on in London.'

'So it was worth studying dead languages at Oxford and meeting the right people, after all?'

'I can't go as far as that, but I concede that some of the people I met in consequence have been a great help.'

During this conversation, Antonia had been busy rummaging among the clothes in various parts of the junk room. From time to time, she disappeared and looked at herself in a mirror. She now came with her hair altered and one leg in a red stocking and one in a green.

'Who do you think I am now?' she asked them.

Andrew thought for a bit and answered, 'Pippi Longstocking.'

'You've got it,' she replied and ran off happily, humming a tune.

Andrew asked Toby, 'Did you move on to the London and international scene?'

'After our first triumph, I was invited to the Laines' London house for dinner. It was in St John's Wood, an impressive Regency house with a balcony supported by Doric columns over the front door. I arrived a shade early and pondered whether to knock with the heavy ornamental door piece representing Falstaff or ring. The doorknocker didn't work – it thudded ineffectually – so I rang as well.

'A smartly dressed lady with an expensive-looking pearl necklace opened the door. She was welcoming without being gushing. "You must be Toby. I'm Oliver's wife. Call me Agatha; forget Lady Laine. Pleased to meet you. I've heard a good deal about you from my husband. Come and sit down while we wait for the others. Just a small gathering."

'I was ushered into a fine drawing room replete with period furniture, imposing but cosy, and left to look at newspapers while Agatha was busy in the kitchen. A few minutes later, the doorbell rang, and the next guest appeared; this was Arnold Smith, Oliver's political aide – a soberly dressed man of about thirty with a polite civil service manner. We discussed current events in the news, pretty boring, with Agatha popping in occasionally.

'Half an hour late, Sir Oliver arrived with the remaining guest, whom I could recognize as Sidney Hacker; his face is even sharper in reality than in the papers.

'Sir Oliver said, "Sorry we're late. Effy was detained by committee work in the House."

'"You'll have to explain 'Effy', Oliver," Agatha told her husband.

'"Yes, of course. Toby, this is Sidney Hacker, who we hope will soon be chairman of the Tory backbenchers, the 1922 Committee. He's a good friend of mine and advises me on money matters from time to time. He's always talking about the improvements that need to be made to his E-type Jaguar. It's presumed, I expect wrongly, that the new model will be called the F-type. So Sidney is known to his friends as the F-type, or 'Effy' for short. Arnold, you know him. Effy and Arnold, this is Toby, who acts as my invaluable consultant on artistic matters. We've recently had a success."

'Sidney Hacker shook hands with me. I must say, he's handsome – super set of teeth, shiny black hair.

'"What improvements do you recommend for the Jaguar E-type?" I asked.

'"Briefly, more comfort. The inside of the car is not in tune with the excellence of what's under the bonnet." He stopped smiling. His mouth in repose reminded me of pictures of Lenin, an element of cruelty.

"'Sidney, with a little help in the Commons from Oliver, has made a killing out of trust funds. That's why he's Oliver's financial adviser," remarked Agatha Laine.

"'Really, Agatha, the important point is that Effy had the vision to introduce a new kind of shareholding that spreads the risk for small investors. Many of us hope that this will herald a new era of people's capitalism," corrected Sir Oliver solemnly.

'They talked about politics awhile, real insider stuff about how Effy was scheming to discredit the Labour foreign secretary, George Forrest – get him to drink too much at a local party meeting and photograph him lurching around, peering at some lightly dressed young woman who will be one of their people, purporting to be Young Socialist. Next day in the papers, and on independent television, "Unseemly behaviour of a cabinet minister."

'Oliver was not enthusiastic. "Do we have to go for George? I have a soft spot for him." Effy wouldn't stand for this. 'We shall not wait for Labour to destroy themselves; we shall actively hasten this process. The obvious target is George, the party's Achilles heel. Don't be sentimental, Oliver."

'At the end of dinner, Effy proposed we play poker. I've only played it at school and never for money. The stakes Sidney Hacker was proposing were preposterous; I could easily have been ruined. But Effy said, "I'll lend you the money at no interest. You can pay me back when you can. Aren't you *man* enough to play for real stakes? Arnold has no objection, have you Arnold?"

'I was beginning to hate Effy and said I'd leave them to play poker by themselves. I got up, apologizing to Agatha.

"'I can understand how Toby feels," put in Agatha. "The three of you can play as long as you like. I'll see Toby into a taxi." She followed me to the door.

"'Toby, I want us to meet again very soon. I have a good deal to say to you, things you'll appreciate hearing. I can't say it now. How about tomorrow? Is that Okay?"

'It wasn't convenient, but I thought I owed it to her. "Where?" I asked her.

"'Harrods. Meet me outside the tea room at eleven o'clock. You can find Harrods, can't you?"

"'Yes, of course.'"

"'Good. And, Toby, be there.'"

The encounter with top people had astonished Andrew. 'I hope the rest of the story isn't going to be an anticlimax. Did you meet Agatha as arranged?'

'I arrived at Harrods far too early and caught a glimpse of a smartly dressed young woman in hat and dark glasses. I thought I'd buy some small item. I saw a pair of blue socks that weren't bad. "How much are these?" I asked the assistant, a pleasant-looking elderly man.

"'Seventy pence a pair, sir."

"'*How* much?" I asked incredulously. *The assistant must really have said seventeen pence*, I thought.

"'Seventy pence, sir. They are of excellent quality."

'A voice I could recognize came from behind. "We'll make a Harrods customer of him yet. Along with the quality of the socks, he's had the opportunity to glimpse Darling herself, if he'd care to notice. We're paying for that privilege and, of course, excellent service." Agatha had also arrived early.

"'Thank you,' the assistant beamed, "and yes, madam, our regular customers include a number of illustrious film stars, among them Miss Christie."

"'I'll think about the socks," I said.

'Agatha took me off, saying, "As you're early, too, and I'm peckish, let's go straight to the tea room." She ordered tea and cakes of her choosing and made it clear she would refuse to let me pay.

"'I'm sorry I broke up the party last night," I began off.

"'You shouldn't be. I was delighted."

"'How do you mean?"

"'You're lucky enough not to know Sidney Hacker as well as I do. He was hoping to bully you into losing heavily at poker so you were in his power. He would have arranged to meet you frequently while you were paying off the debt. On each occasion, he would have encouraged you to drink heavily, while he gloated over your drift down into helpless alcoholism. His hobby is slowly destroying talented young people."

'I tried to orientate in the world of the powerful. "Your husband isn't like that, is he?" I asked her.

'"No, thank goodness. Oliver has a list of faults as long as your arm, but relishing other people's misfortunes is not one of them." Agatha continued, "When the F-type was manoeuvring you into playing poker, my gorge rose. If you had given into his taunts, I should have stepped smartly across and strangled him." She held her cup in such a way that I could observe her hands in tight black gloves, ready to strangle if the occasion arose.

'"I suppose the rest of us would have tried to stop you."

'"Maybe. Anyway, I admired you immensely for standing up to him. And saving me from attempted murder."

'I wondered about the other poker player. "How about Arnold Smith? Is he in danger?"

'She said, "Arnold's too dull to interest Sidney. It's promising, talented young men that Sidney Hacker delights in dragging down."

'"Why did Oliver take up with the F-type?" I asked her.

'"He has a weakness for buccaneers and won't respond to warnings."

'Agatha then told me her proposition. She was intrigued over what sort of artist I was when she heard Oliver going on about me. She tracked down three of my paintings, ones I had exhibited and sold at modest prices and liked them all. She's interested in my other paintings and might even buy one sometime. She says she's aware I'm no Rembrandt or Monet or Picasso but thinks I'm a talented young person who deserves encouragement from the middle-aged. She said, "I know some rich people who can be persuaded to pay reasonable prices. One of them is influential in the art world and can arrange for your work to be exhibited in prestigious places. But there's one condition. You must give up your association with Oliver. Nothing good will come of it."

'I promised I would. I was intending to anyway.'

Andrew had listened attentively to Toby's account. 'So did you part company with Sir Oliver Laine, as you promised?'

Antonia reappeared. 'Tell Andrew about the toy soldiers.'

Toby explained that, one day, he was summoned to Sir Oliver's overnight apartment in central London. He was standing in front of a sort of miniature sandpit with old-fashioned toy soldiers placed in it. At one end was a mountain range with a peak carrying a flag marked 'Turner Prize.'

Toby adopted his authoritative Sir Oliver style. "'Here is your cheque from the aftermath of the second year of the Tippin Gallery memorial competition. We have now had enough of provincial small change. We must capture the Turner Prize. This will require meticulous planning, like a military campaign. You were, fortunately, too young to wear uniform, except perhaps in the school Cadet Force. I saw active service in the last four months of the war. I realized, of course, that this was supposed to be a formative experience and that I must draw attention to myself."

'He took off his jacket and rolled up his sleeve. He had a short ugly-looking scar on his lower arm. "I performed an act of heroism by exposing myself to enemy fire, admittedly unnecessarily, within sight of a bigwig. I sustained this shrapnel wound. It became infected. It was agony for three days. Naturally I went to the commanding officer and asked to be recommended for a decoration – at very least, mentioned in despatches. Unfortunately, he was a vulgar Yorkshireman without breeding. He just laughed. 'Dab some iodine on it', he said."

'I said, "I'm surprised it hasn't healed better after nearly twenty-five years."'

Toby imitated Sir Oliver leaning forward confidentially. "'As a matter of fact, I had it tattooed in crimson later on, to show how awful it was originally." He leaned back again. "Anyway I wasn't discouraged by the old Yorkshireman. I was bent on putting my army time to good use, even if we were some way from an important part of the front and the days were arse-achingly boring. And indeed I was to meet Field Marshall Montgomery personally."

'"What, in Germany, in the midst of battle?" I asked.

'"No, Salisbury Plain after the war. Territorial Army. He came down one day to supervise an exercise. He went through it at the end of the day, demonstrating tactics at the sandpit. Marvellous experience. All the young pseudo-officers were deeply impressed. I knew that, thereafter, I must have a sandpit to convey to my subordinates the niceties and significance of higher strategy.

'"To get down to specifics, the Turner Prize, as it will probably be called, will be a tough nut to crack. Enough razzmatazz will be surrounding it to make one's head swim. The great plus of the situation is that the prize will mostly be awarded for constructions rather than actual pictures; you know the sort of thing, a pineapple stuck in the back mudguard of a bicycle. No craft skills involved at all. What's considered good or bad is largely arbitrary. Positively an invitation to corruption. So I shall advance to the Tate Gallery in my capacity as an MP vitally concerned with the impact of the arts on the health of the nation …" He moved one of the toy soldiers toward the flanks of the mountain; it represented someone important, in splendid uniform, mounted on an elephant. He took a flag, wrote "Tate Gallery" on it, and inserted it in a flanking mound. "And insist that none of the judges have any direct contact with the world of the arts. Instead, they should be gossip columnists, television personalities, detective story writers, that sort of thing. I shall suggest the name of a suitable young woman. You will encounter her by chance when she is looking at an exhibit somewhere, just as you did with my daughter, Fiona."

'He moved a foot soldier representing me to the area of the Tate Gallery. The soldier had two stripes on each shoulder, so I was a non-commissioned officer. "You will chat to this young woman. Go to bed with her if necessary. That sort of person never has any morals. Get her to nominate the right person, just as before with the Tippin."

'"I'm flattered that you have promoted me to corporal, to keep you company when you're being Viceroy of India. But sorry, I can't go on with this any longer. I've lost my stomach for this sort of intrigue. Anyway I don't think it will work."

'But Sir Oliver persisted. "You said that twice before, and were you right?"

'"No, you were right on those occasions, I fully admit. But I can't continue deceiving people I respect and rather like."

'"Have you been cosying up with the director of the Tippin?"

'"He's one of the people I can't go behind the back of any longer. What I can promise is that I won't betray your confidences. Best of luck in your campaign to conquer the Tate."

'"This is sad. I thought you'd grasped that life is a series of intrigues – small affairs for little people, big affairs for people with ambition and spunk. You're like my daughter; you won't face up to the fact that you can lead the relatively comfortable life you both have only because other people have been prepared to carry out big profitable affairs on your behalf."

'"*You* sound like my mother. She won't understand that people like Fiona and me and, for that matter, the Tippin gallery people get our satisfaction by doing small, in themselves unspectacular, but at least mildly creative things, not by trying to be someone important and living in a tedious mock castle and owning a yacht we never have time to sail and meeting pompous people and all the rest of it. Well, I'd better get off. As I say, I have no intention of betraying you, and anyway, I couldn't hold my own against your lawyer. Best of luck with the Turner Prize. I shall follow events with interest, even if I have no way of knowing whether your interceptions have been successful. We'd better not shake hands. Last time, my hand ached for nearly three days afterwards. I suppose I ought to have been ambitious and tried to get recommended for an MBE for pain incurred in the course of duty, but the relevant authorities would only have laughed, like your commanding officer."

'Oliver Laine took this well. "I like you, Toby. Did I hurt your hand? I'm sure I didn't mean to. More than ever, I am convinced that you have the makings of a true Lainista. Maybe I overemphasized the bending of rules. More important is that the Lainista has no respect for conventional opinion, especially when it concerns the arts."

'I had meant to go but lingered to hear more about the Lainista's views on the arts.

'"Take music," continued Toby's impersonation of Oliver. "You must have heard countless proper-minded people declare that Beethoven is the greatest composer of all time, the Shakespeare of music, that there's more in Beethoven than any other composer."

'I nodded, and Oliver went on. "A few days later, an equally proper-minded music lover will say that, if you haven't grasped that Bach is the world's greatest composer, further discussion with you is pointless."

'"And then the Mozartians come along," I said.

'"Exactly. And you see the Bach lovers with eyes glazed over with boredom during some horrendous cantata—"

'"But later they're obviously enchanted by some popular pieces by Grieg or Rachmaninoff." I was entering into the spirit of the discussion. "If you ask them why the Grieg concerto is inferior to a Beethoven concerto, they're flummoxed."

'"Because judging is a matter of personal taste or one's feeling at the time or the influence of some fashionable critic or journalist, not of objective judgement. That's how it is with music. It's the same with literature. One endures left-wing jargon from solemn commentators claiming to make important statements about the nature of the human predicament as presented in great novels – chronically gloomy people, ill at ease with the present, pessimistic about the future, longing to return to a mythical past where, against all probability, they would be lords of the manor. Miles different from us Lainistas, who enjoy life as it is now and want others to enjoy it, too; we're on the side of life."

'I was aware that Sir Oliver was watching me intently. I had joined in the discussion too eagerly, so he knew he had baited his hook skilfully. He resumed insinuatingly, "It's not the money that attracts the Lainista to infiltrate institutions like the Turner Prize, though a little money dutifully earned is no bad thing. It's the opportunity to take the mickey out of the po-faced prissily dressed art establishment. If something goes wrong and we are discovered, the people of England will forgive us because we have debunked all that pretentious bollocks they hear from their supposed betters. We shall have contributed to the fun of everyday life, to the gaiety of nations."

'I was remembering my promise not to let Sir Oliver beguile me. "If things go wrong, I am not sure that *I* shall be forgiven. You will be because people regard you as an amiable old rogue."

'"Amiable old rogue, did you say? Sounds as if Agatha has got her claws into you. She's a naughty little pixie. I'll be negotiating with her."'

'Was that the last you heard from Sir Oliver?' wondered Andrew.

'Yes, essentially. Agatha rang the following afternoon.

'"Toby, a word of advice to those about to negotiate with Sir Oliver Laine, from one with extensive first-hand experience."

'"What's that?" I asked.

'"Don't."

'"I didn't."

'"I know. So far, so good. But Oliver thinks you wavered."

'"I didn't. I kept my promise to you," I pointed out indignantly.

'"Good. And don't waver in the future, either. Bear in mind the F-type and others of his kidney. But we can forget them for the moment. Have you been keeping up your painting?"

'"Yes, of course. I paint every day.'

'"How long for?"

'"Most of the day, most days."

'She was satisfied with that. "If you had said you painted all the time, every day, I shouldn't have believed you. Go on keeping it up." She rang off.'

All this was a lot for Andrew to take in, and he couldn't think of what to say.

Antonia, who had joined them after occupying herself in various parts of the junk room, asked Toby, 'How many customers has Agatha raked up for you?'

'Three so far. She's been a great help.'

'But she wouldn't have done as much if Sir Oliver hadn't first wrapped his tentacles round you. In a way, you owe your customers to him. Andrew, have you ever met anyone like Sir Oliver? How's your new boss?'

'Not remotely like Sir Oliver Laine. His name is Joe Briesley. He appeared on television about six weeks ago, to explain how people think computers will develop.'

'I didn't see it myself, but one of the girls in my class was talking about it. She thought Joe Briesley, it must have been him, was super. Wonder if Sir Oliver saw the programme. Perhaps he'll fasten his tentacles round Joe, too, if he has marketable ideas.'

Toby was now in an excellent humour, having enjoyed recounting his adventures with Sir Oliver. He and the other two went out for a stroll, inhaled the scented evening air of early summer, and retired contentedly for the night.

Chapter 4

The next day, the four young people decided on a longer excursion by car. Andrew would have liked to sit back, relax, and take in the countryside, but Toby insisted that Andrew should drive, at least to begin with.

The girls sat in the back. From time to time, Janet made nervous comments on Andrew's occasional mistakes; Antonia giggled happily and told her not to worry. They drove off towards the sea, stopping at a little village situated beside the estuary, a mile or two before the river reached the sea. They walked at leisure down a road that deteriorated into a path and petered out along the sometimes rocky, sometimes sandy shore.

They came to a little cliff, with woodland just visible at the top. Andrew could sense that it wasn't so difficult to climb as it at had first appeared. Antonia, noticing Andrew's interest, said, 'Up there's my secret place. I discovered it years ago when I was in third form.'

Andrew took it for granted that all of them would want to see the secret place, but Toby and Janet preferred to stay at ground level. So Antonia and Andrew clambered up alone, arriving out of breath at a broad ledge behind which the woodland began. It was far enough up to feel secluded from the shore and allowed a more extended view of the estuary. They sat down together and rested.

'What did you do here?' asked Andrew

'I read a bit, and dreamed, while the others were doing boring things like shopping.'

Her words painted a glimpse of a childhood that was more privileged than his own, which is not to say that his had been unhappy. But when he was growing up in London, he'd often yearned for more countryside than the over-trampled parks and commons.

*　*　*

At the bottom, they rejoined the others, who were now feeling more energetic. Toby said, 'It's a good enough day to go up the Knott. I'll drive us there. You can take it easy, Andrew.'

'What's the Knott?'

And Janet replied, 'It's a nearby hill, not so high, but quite a climb. We should have taken the dog. He loves it.'

Soon they had parked at the base of the Knott and were walking up through the limestone countryside to a sort of plateau at the top. From occasional glances over his shoulder on the way up, Andrew had begun to suspect that a striking view was awaiting them, and his expectations were fully rewarded. Far away in front, the mountains of the Lake District were just visible over the tops of the nearest hills, with a powdering of snow on the highest peaks. To their right, the railway viaduct crossed the estuary to a little town. To their left was the broad circle of the bay. Andrew felt this was the most magnificent view he had ever seen, and after only half an hour's steep ascent from the car. Around them were juniper bushes, yew trees, limestone rocks, and a mass of emerging wild flowers. They were out of breath and sat down in the sunshine.

A young couple climbed up to join them, laughing together and obviously enjoying each other's company enormously. The young man, perhaps eighteen or nineteen years old, was a tall blond with blue eyes; he could have made an excellent Wagnerian hero, except that he had the wrong general attitude; his bearing was incorrect, he slouched happily around with no hint of proud defiance, but he was a natural choice as the boy next door in a light comedy. The girl, also blue-eyed and blonde, was splendidly endowed and carried herself excellently but had a similarly wrong general attitude for a Wagnerian heroine – no sense of tragic destiny. It was impossible to imagine her in an act of self-immolation with the Rhine overflowing its banks. She seemed to Andrew an enormously attractive, uncomplicated young woman. The couple was wondering which path to take, with the girl saying to her friend, 'You are the man. You shall decide.' And they were off.

Andrew realized that Antonia had been watching him intently.

Toby, like Janet, had not shown any obvious interest in the young couple but was moved to remark incredulously, 'Did you hear what she said? "You are the man; you shall decide." And in a soothing voice straight out of *Mrs Dale's Diary*. The most unfashionable thing I've heard for months.'

They walked down the hill towards the little town, or 'growing village,' as it had been known since anybody could remember.

In the late afternoon, on the way back, they stopped at a general store to buy provisions, as instructed by Mrs Morton. It was at the edge of an industrial village, Screeside, and the car park had an attractive view over the fields towards the stony hills that had given the town its name. Toby and Antonia did the shopping, while Janet stayed near the car with Andrew, who they considered needed a rest after driving. They were looking around when a man in advanced middle age of military bearing and a plump lady in tweeds with a pearl necklace came up to them and greeted them affably.

'How good to see you, Janet,' said the lady. 'Isn't it lovely weather?'

'Good afternoon, Janet,' boomed the military gentleman. 'We're on a sunshine sortie to the stores to forage for suntan cream. And now I must *order* you to introduce us to the other member of the contingent, your good-looking young friend.'

'This is Andrew Carter, an old school friend of Toby's. And Andrew, these people are Colonel and Mrs Armitage.'

The colonel smiled affably at Andrew. 'Yesterday, we saw you and Janet's brother and sister walking down to the river – no, as you were – we saw you and Toby walking and Antonia running.'

They continued chatting, and Andrew concluded that, even if the Armitages' relations with Mrs Morton had cooled, they were careful not to take it out on the next generation.

* * *

The interior of the store was relaxing after the intense sunlight of early summer in the countryside. Toby attended to the shopping list, after arranging for Antonia to find a few of the more straightforward items, disappearing into the recesses of the store. Antonia soon finished. Boxes of sweets near the counter caught her eye, and then paperback romances, Barbara Cartland and the like, on the shelves beside. She opened one of them in the middle and read a few lines. She glanced round the shop at the few other customers, all middle-aged women. One of them had a question to the girl at the counter, whose voice sounded familiar. Antonia looked at her more closely. It was a friend's sister; Juliette, her name was, she recollected – a nice girl, but slow.

'Hello, Juliette, do you remember me?'

Juliette recognized her sister's friend, and they chatted while Toby tracked down the items on his mother's list. Antonia was sufficiently her mother's daughter to consider that standing at the counter of a general store, even if it was large and would shortly become the neighbourhood's first supermarket, was hopelessly unglamorous. She was sorry for Juliette and asked a few kindly questions. But Juliette was happy enough, and seemed unaware of any condescension in Antonia's voice. She attended to a customer, and Antonia returned to the bookshelf.

A boy walked into the shop. He was old enough, eighteen or nineteen, for Antonia to take an initial interest in him. Boys her own age were boringly immature. He was barely taller than Antonia and was dressed in a tatty shirt and old shorts. He had an expression in his eyes Antonia felt she had seen before but couldn't place. He ambled up to the counter, put his head close to Juliette, and said something too low for Antonia to hear that clearly startled Juliette. Then the two of them bent over the till; the boy was trying to open it, and Juliette was resisting. They were talking in low voices, apparently arguing over a purchase the boy had made earlier in the day; the boy was demanding money back, while warning Juliette not to attract the attention of the other customers. The two of them had an affinity, Antonia felt; both were faintly pathetic.

The boy stepped round the counter so that Antonia could see his face while he was talking to Juliette. She remembered where she had seen that expression – in the eyes of a mildly delinquent girl at school; special eyes, like those of a hunted animal or a concentration camp victim she had seen a photograph of. Pathetic really. The boy was making her feel almost maternal.

Juliette was arguing with him, and he was becoming impatient. He stepped back and, to Antonia's astonishment and Juliette's horror, pulled out a gun. Juliette screamed, as did one or two of the elderly women customers who were near enough to take in what was happening. Then silence engulfed the scene, while nobody seemed to know what to do.

In later years, Antonia wondered why she hadn't been more afraid. At the time, she was fascinated. It was like watching an old Hollywood B-film at the cinema. In fact, it was better than that – more like being on the film set itself. Perhaps it was because the boy was so pathetic; it was difficult to believe he was dangerous, even if he was waving a gun. Besides, she loved excitement.

What should she do? The other customers, including Toby, wherever he was, were paralyzed. She hated standing around, waiting for something to happen, with nobody doing anything. She should take part in the film, or was it an historic event really, if only in a walk-on role. In a proper Hollywood B-film, the hero would slug it out with the villain or jump on him from behind. She couldn't manage action like that, even if she was about as tall as he was. But this boy was pathetic. Perhaps he could be made to listen to the calm voice of common sense. So she stepped cautiously on to the film set from the side, walked slowly a few steps towards the till, and talked to him in her best relaxed, motherly style.

'I don't know what you think you're doing, but if you've got any sense, and I'm sure you have really, you'll put that gun down and quietly leave the shop.'

The boy was wavering. The silence was intense. Antonia nodded to him encouragingly. For the first time, she was afraid – that a disturbance, from Juliette or one of the customers would lead to panic and gunfire. Then the lad slowly put away his gun and disappeared through the door.

Nobody in the shop moved for an age in case he came back. Juliette was ashen-faced, as Antonia was later to describe her, but came out with, 'Antonia! You were fantastic!'

Toby and the other customers emerged from various corners of the shop, some full of admiration, others inclined to scold Antonia for taking such a risk.

Toby went out to tell Andrew and Janet of the events and related the story for the Armitages at the same time. Antonia's action rendered the colonel speechless, and he had to lean against the wall until he recovered sufficiently to say repeatedly, 'Jolly good show! Jolly good show!'

Three of the customers were eager to call the local policeman and knew where to find him at this time of day. He was at the pub, half asleep in a favourite chair with his feet up, holding a glass of ginger ale.

It was difficult to arouse him. His reaction was to deliver the statement, 'There is no crime in Screeside.' Eventually, though, he agreed to walk over to the store to investigate. He got out his notebook to write down the official version of events from Juliette, who was animated and full of praise for Antonia.

But the elderly constable was critical. 'You took a terrible risk, young lady. It could have ended really badly. You should never do that sort of thing. You should leave it to us.'

'But you weren't there,' pointed out Antonia, sweetly reasonable.

The policeman was not at his best when coping with irrefutable logic. He sat down and rubbed his head. 'I must say, you were a very brave girl.'

'Actually I didn't think about it at the time. It simply seemed the right thing to do,' Antonia said blandly. 'He's probably okay, deep down. But ...' –here she lowered her voice and looked straight at the policeman – 'his socks didn't match. You know, some of us haven't had the advantages in life that you or I have enjoyed.'

The policeman nodded. He had switched to being in awe of Antonia, having initially treated her as a kid. 'I must say, that's very true, miss.'

Andrew drove them home. In the general mood of elation, he did a running commentary in the style of Colonel Armitage. 'We're approaching crossroads, no panic, eyes right, eyes left, eyes right again, straight over – as you were – halt at the traffic lights. They're red; now they're green. Carry on! Jolly good!'

The foursome related the day's events for Mrs Morton. Predictably, she was disapproving of Antonia's action. But Janet, Andrew noted with interest, defended Antonia surprisingly strongly. Then she went off to lie down with another of her headaches.

After the evening meal, Antonia, as energetic as usual, wanted to go for a stroll out along the river, and Andrew and Toby accompanied her. They began to talk about Janet. Andrew wondered why Janet didn't defy her mother and go off with Fred Arlington. 'It's not only up to Janet.

Fred Arlington catches glimpses of her only when she's with Mother, gets the trodden worm treatment, and is thoroughly intimidated,' was Toby's explanation.

'Can't Janet go to his farm by herself?'

'We've tried persuading her to do that, but she won't make the first move.'

'Can't your mother be got out of the house for a while?' As Andrew said this, it occurred to him that his practised version of the military man could come in useful. 'I can lay on a phone call from Colonel Armitage in which I say to your mother, "What a rotten bad show; somehow Mrs Armitage had failed to send an invitation to Mrs Morton for the fancy-dress party. Thousand apologies. Can't you come despite the short notice? Won't be the same without you. I'm afraid we can't accommodate the younger contingent, but they'll be otherwise engaged in whatever young things get up to on a Saturday evening."'

'Wow! It's a long shot,' said Toby.

But Antonia was enthusiastic. 'It's worth trying. Andrew may well bring it off, and anyway, there's nothing much to lose.'

Toby was still sceptical. 'What about Fred Arlington? We'll have to arrange for him to come over during the party.

'I'll fix Fred,' said Antonia.

It was still only early evening. Andrew spent a while getting himself back into training for Colonel Armitage – the upright walk, and the arrangement of the mouth so that the speech had the right degree of relaxed self-confidence. Then he walked to the telephone kiosk in the village and rang to Enby Hall. Toby answered the phone promptly and called his mother. 'It's Colonel Armitage on the phone. He says it occurred to him that you might not have received the invitation to the fancy-dress ball, and he wants to apologize to you personally.'

Toby handed over the phone to his mother. He could make out the colonel saying, 'Rotten bad show,' and 'I told her, the ball won't be complete without Mrs Morton to give it style.'

'What on earth am I going to find to wear at such short notice?' Mother wondered over the telephone. But Toby whispered to her that they could easily find things in the junk room, and his mother was soon asking, 'What time will it be tomorrow evening?'

Fortunately, they had anticipated this question, and by discreet questioning of acquaintances, Toby had managed to find the answer. 'Around seven thirty,' Andrew's colonel said. Mrs Morton progressed from tetchiness into relaxed amiability, even chattiness. The colonel cut this short.

'Forgive me, Mrs Morton, but I must contact some other guests who might not have received their invitations. See you at seven o'clock – as you were – seven thirty tomorrow evening. And you will be so disguised that none of us will recognize you. Remember, not a word as to who you really are. Keep everybody on his toes, guessing. That's *very* important.' The colonel rang off.

'It's probably best if *I* go and talk to Fred Arlington,' Antonia had said to Andrew and Toby conspiratorially.

Early the next day, she went down to Fred's farmhouse to tackle him. It was a fine morning. A number of people were out, and she was aware that more interest was being taken in her than usual. A neighbour, a middle-aged woman she knew slightly who was out shopping, came up to her and said admiringly, 'That was a wonderful thing you did yesterday. We are all so proud of you.' They chatted for a while.

Antonia turned off the main street down a lane leading to Fred Arlington's farm. She found him in a field inspecting the wall near the gate.

'Everybody's talking about what you did yesterday. Fancy, a little slip of a girl like you taking on a man with a gun like that and persuading him to put it away.'

But Antonia wasn't interested in discussing this matter; she wasn't flattered to be called a little slip of a girl; she detected a touch of patronage. But Fred redeemed himself by adding, 'What a nerve you've got.'

Antonia got down to brass tacks. 'Are you still crazy about my sister?'

'Of course I am. She's got away with a horse. Who wouldn't be crazy about her? But she's always with your mum, who cuts me dead. I don't get a chance to begin.' He added, 'I don't have your courage.'

'You can get a chance this evening. Mother is going to be out. She's invited to the fancy-dress ball. You're to come for coffee at eight o'clock when Mother's left the house. You and Janet will be by yourselves.'

'I was going to the fancy-dress ball. As it happens, I've been invited, too.'

'You've now got a much more important engagement.'

'I suppose I can tell the Armitages I can't come.'

But Antonia wasn't having that. 'Don't tell them you're not coming; just don't arrive. Much better like that. Concentrate on being with Janet this evening. Think of the things you're going to say to her. Make sure you've got them properly developed in your mind. Think of how to counter any objections she might conceivably make, particularly regarding disapproval from our mother. Come to the house at the right time. And really, if you haven't got engaged before the end of the evening, I shall be bitterly disappointed in you.'

Fred was looking thoughtful. Antonia, concluding she had made sufficient impact, moved off home.

Preparing Janet for the evening's events remained as a challenge. Antonia enlisted the support of Andrew, and the two of them accosted Janet in her room. Janet had gathered that her stepmother would be off to the fancy-dress party but was otherwise her normal apathetic self.

'Fred Arlington is coming this evening. You like him, don't you?' Antonia believed in direct approaches.

'Yes, I think so.'

'He's in love with you.'

'Well, he told me twice I look wonderful on a horse.'

'That means he's in love with you. When he comes, the rest of us will make ourselves scarce and you can serve coffee to him in the drawing room. Mother seems to be out of the house, so this is a good time to decide on seating arrangements, what you're going to wear, things like that. You mustn't tell Mother about Fred's visit, of course.'

'Won't she be angry?'

Andrew, detecting incipient exasperation in Antonia's face, put in, 'We'll have to tell her afterwards, but don't spoil it all now.'

'Let's go into the drawing room and think out what needs to be done,' Antonia continued, leading the others off.

'Should we remove some of the chairs, so as to focus on the sofa?'

'Could be sensible. We'll do it as soon as your mother's gone.'

Toby seemed to be detached from the proceedings, so Antonia concerned herself mainly with Andrew.

'What do you think Janet ought to wear?'

This was a tricky question. Andrew had never understood why women attached such importance to clothes. He tried to remember the content of a newspaper column from ages ago, where advice was given on what a young woman should wear when being proposed to. He could only think of 'suggestive frilly underwear,' but this seemed unsuitable.

'Something informal, relaxed, and vaguely inviting, I suppose. Even jeans.'

'Exactly. I know exactly the thing – a blouse Janet got from somewhere last year which she only wears occasionally, and now is the right occasion.'

Further discussion was at an end because Mrs Morton's footsteps could be heard. She was soon saying, 'I wish you young people would take the trouble to advise me on how to disguise myself for this ball tonight. The idea is that no one shall recognize me.' She sounded martyred again.

Antonia put in promptly, 'One possibility is to appear as a man. Somebody famous. Perhaps historical. What do you think, Andrew?'

'How about Lord Nelson? Have a patch over one eye, but avoid being like a pirate.'

Toby, after a moment's consideration, said, 'Good idea, isn't it, Mother?'

'I don't mind dressing up as a military hero, I suppose,' said Mrs Morton magnanimously.

'Then let's go upstairs and rummage around in the junk room.'

'You mean, I've got to go up all those stairs?' Mrs Morton sounded plaintive.

'For goodness' sake, Mother, get into the right psychological mood,' urged Toby. 'You're about to become a national hero. Climbing up a narrow flight of stairs is something you do standing on your head if necessary. Remember, you've got Lord Nelson's personality, and you're going to enjoy yourself this evening.'

'Oh, I suppose I can sacrifice myself.'

They eventually got her up to the attic, out of breath. Antonia experimented tying a black stocking over her mother's eye and yanked out a dark suit that had belonged to Mrs Morton's late husband. The trousers were far too large, but her children hauled them up and safety-pinned them in position. 'Put this over and you'll look positively smart, even imposing,' Toby told her, attaching a resplendent, old-fashioned cummerbund. 'That's not bad at all. A little bare, though. Nelson would have had ribbons all over his chest.'

Mrs Morton directed Antonia, a trifle imperiously, to fetch her husband's insignia, an old civil service honour, from a cabinet drawer downstairs. She put it on and gazed in the long mirror.

'Why, shiver my timbers,' she exclaimed, pleased with her new self.

'You must deepen your voice and make it sound more masculine,' instructed Toby.

'Shiver my timbers,' repeated the emerging Lord Nelson. 'How was that?'

'Isn't that what pirates say, rather than naval commanders?' wondered Andrew.

Mrs Morton was happily preoccupied with growing into her new persona and did not respond to this directly. But she took sufficient notice of him to say, 'Andrew, my man, run my bath for me – there's a good fellow – while Antonia finds my telescope.'

Andrew went off obediently. Antonia pulled out a toy telescope from a cupboard. Toby remarked, 'They didn't have baths much in the eighteenth century. Nelson would have stunk. But we needn't overdo historical accuracy.'

Antonia said, 'Mother, after your bath, you don't have to use your usual perfume. You can borrow Toby's deodorant. That will help give a masculine flavour.'

At the appropriate time, Toby drove 'Lord Nelson' to the Armitages. He explained that he was stopping a bit away from the house, leaving his mother a short walk, so that no one would recognize the car and realize who Nelson really was. Then he drove back home to find the others making the final arrangements before Fred Arlington's arrival. Janet was not enjoying the occasion. She had pleaded to be let off the evening, claiming a headache again, but Antonia had dosed her with aspirin and refused to accept her excuses.

Fred arrived shortly afterwards. He was dressed in his farm clothes. He explained that he had a sick cow on his hands and looked stressed. Antonia, who had answered the door, made a strenuous, whispered attempt to talk him into the right frame of mind and pushed him into the drawing room, where Janet was waiting, still apathetic. Fred brightened up considerably on seeing her.

Antonia closed the door and left them to it. She whispered to Andrew and Toby, 'Now we'll withdraw and let nature take over.'

Chapter 5

Much later in the evening, Fred Arlington emerged from the drawing room and called after Toby, who went to meet him, followed by Andrew and Antonia. Fred noticed the grandfather clock in the hall, and a worried look came over his face, appropriate to a man contemplating acute agricultural problems. 'Ten o'clock! Must hurry off. Got a sick cow on my hands. I'll talk to you as soon as things settle down.'

Toby, Antonia, and Andrew found Janet still on the drawing room sofa. They were unable to interpret her expression.

'I must say, you were a long time together,' began Toby.

'We were talking.'

'What about?'

'Farming. Farming in general at first. Then about cows.'

'Cows,' repeated Toby. 'Anything more?'

'Horses.'

'Cows and horses. Did you touch on other matters, birds for instance, or even bees?' asked Toby.

Janet looked confused. After some sobs, she was heard to say something that could have been an affirmative.

'So he proposed to you?'

More sobs and a more distinct 'yes' ensued.

'Did you accept him?' demanded Antonia.

Janet was sobbing uncontrollably. Antonia repeated the question. Between sobs, another possibly affirmative answer emerged.

'So you've accepted him?'

'I've never been so happy … in my whole life,' could be made out.

Antonia asked Andrew, 'Can you go with her upstairs so she can lie down awhile?'

Andrew escorted Janet upstairs, leaving Toby and Antonia alone in the drawing room.

Toby was in excellent spirits. 'I look forward to informing Mother of recent developments. The arch-manipulator being outmanoeuvred.'

Antonia did not comment. She stood for a while alone with Toby, without saying anything. Toby lit a cigarette thoughtfully. 'I must say, nature has proceeded along thoroughly acceptable lines. There's more to nature than ecological this and unsustainable that and seriously threatened this and red-listed the other. Nature' – he took a reflective puff – 'is underrated.'

'I expect Janet will recover from the shock of being appreciated fairly quickly. Toby, now that Janet is paired off, I can't help wondering about you.'

'What are you wondering about me?'

'About the young man you're living with.'

Toby spun round. 'How did you know?' he asked sharply.

Antonia gazed at him for a moment. 'I didn't. But I do now.'

Antonia could see she had shocked him. Toby was surely aware that girls, at least as early as boys, talked about 'improper' matters. He had often referred, jokingly, to feminine intuition and to her own precocity; he accepted that she was a schemer.

Toby said resignedly, 'I suppose we deserve each other. It's Mother in us.'

'Toby, blame Mother if you must, but it's not all her fault. We're made like this. Anyway, does it matter? I like us as we are. And Toby, can't we meet your young man sometime? I expect he's rather nice. Even Mother would probably accept him in a while, though I quite understand you don't want her to hear about it right now.' She slightly emphasized the last word.

Toby grunted.

'And one last thing, Toby. We said that tomorrow the three of us are going out in the morning to have large ice creams in celebration of getting Janet attached to Fred. Janet will have better things to do. Can't you miss that occasion and drive off in the early morning before everybody gets up? Actually, I've got some things to say to Andrew when we're by ourselves. Can't tell you what right now. I've got a suggestion for the note you can write, saying you forgot about an important engagement. And here is the alarm clock, all set for five in the morning.'

'I suppose you're scheming again, Antonia.' Toby sighed deeply. 'Okay,' he said at last.

'Oh good, Toby. I knew you'd understand. And, Toby, an important thing – even if you think we sometimes bring out the worst in each other, we ought to stick together, whatever happens. Remember, basically I'm on your side, and you're on mine.'

* * *

Around midnight, a taxi drew up in the drive. Toby had stayed up to welcome his mother home.

She was in excellent spirits. 'Marvellous evening. And no one guessed who Lord Nelson really was.' She lay down on the sofa in the drawing room contentedly.

Toby asked her for more details of the evening's entertainment, and they chatted amicably for a while.

Toby lit another cigarette. 'By the way, Mother, one or two things happened earlier in the evening when you were out. Fred Arlington looked in.'

'What on earth for?'

'Can't really remember. Anyway, we thought we could be polite, so we offered him coffee in the drawing room.'

'Did Andrew look after him? That's something useful he could have done.'

'It was more Janet actually.'

'What on earth could those two have found to talk about?'

'One might well wonder. Both of them are a bit limited conversationally. Anyway, in between discussing the hay harvest and the high cost of nitrogen fertilizer and the amount of rust on the winter wheat, he seems to have proposed to her.'

Mother was amused. 'Proposed to her, for goodness sake! And I hope Janet jolly well sent him off with a flea in his ear.'

'One might reasonably expect her to do something like that, mightn't one?' Toby paused to puff on his cigarette. 'But actually, she seems to have accepted him.'

'What do you mean, accepted him?'

'Seems she said yes, she would marry him.' A cynic would have said that Toby was enjoying himself.

It took a while for Mrs Morton to take it all in. Then she stood up in fury.

'Toby! Can't I leave the house for five minutes without chaos descending? Those wretched children get engaged to each other as soon as my back is turned? I'm aghast.'

She put her hand to her brow and fainted theatrically onto the sofa. She lay sprawled out for a minute or two and then sat up abruptly.

'I'm in agony. What is this sharp thing I've fallen on?'

It was one of Andrew's books left on the sofa, *Applications of Set Theory*.

'Why are maths books so *knobbly*? Why can't Andrew look after them properly? One can't even faint in comfort in one's own home.'

Toby made no comment. She lay down again and relaxed.

'I must say, the positive feature of this wretched business is that Fred and Janet deserve each other. Little idiots.' She sounded almost contented. 'Besides, the important thing is that I really enjoyed myself at the fancy-dress party this evening.'

Chapter 6

Andrew had bought two large cornets at the local shop, which opened at nine o'clock, even on Sunday mornings, and he and Antonia were now sitting on a wall a little way outside the village, their legs dangling. They were preoccupied with their ice creams and sat in silence, at ease in the late May countryside and the morning sunlight. It was a still day with a cloudless blue sky, too early for more than a few people to be out and about, and Andrew was at peace with the world.

His cornet was at a critical stage, demanding concentration, when it was soft enough to bite rather than suck but with risk that bits might drop off messily. He looked at Antonia and noticed that she was at the same critical stage and was rather charming in coping with it. It occurred to him that this was probably the last occasion when he would see her as a young girl who regarded him as a family friend. Next time they met, she would have embarked on her own independent life with those of her own age, and Andrew would cease to be of concern.

After taking a precarious bite from her cornet, Antonia glanced at him and asked, 'Andrew, when I'm a bit older, will you marry me?' She sat still for a moment and then thoughtfully took another bite of ice cream.

As noted, Andrew had not been spoilt by young women's attentions; he was conscious of the years slipping by with little progress in this crucial area. The sudden question was preposterous but had not come completely out of the blue; it had developed with its own logic out of the weird events of the weekend. It demanded an answer.

He responded, with minimal pause for consideration, 'That would be a great honour.' Big decisions of this kind were easier to take than small ones, which could be bothersome. In his student days, he had spent ages wondering whether to choose tea or coffee when on offer in a friend's room.

'It's not a question of honour; this will be a proper, down-to-earth marriage.' Antonia licked her cornet and then took a large bite. 'I'm fifteen now, and we shall marry as soon as I'm eighteen. And we shall take the first important steps when I'm sixteen. That's only one year off. But you must keep away from other girls until then.'

'Okay, but you mustn't become too much like your mother in the meantime. Or something will shrivel up inside me.' He was making a deal.

Antonia considered this. 'The thing is, I like people as they are. I don't have to change them into something else, as Mother constantly tries to do. Though I might give them a prod. And besides, if I do try to manipulate people, I do it much more skilfully than Mother does.'

'Your mother won't be pleased at the idea of your marrying me.'

'No, she'll probably try to disinherit me, but does that matter? You're not marrying me for my money, are you? And I shall have a job. I shall be a marriage counsellor part-time, as I like helping people, and a divorce lawyer the rest of the time. Lawyers are well paid. Anyway, Mother won't manage to disinherit me; I shall outwit her. And I'm not especially interested in money either.'

She shuffled up to him along the wall, changed the cornet to her left hand, and placed her right hand on his knee. 'Why do you want to marry me, Andrew?'

'You're a wonderful young woman, and you'll blossom into something utterly marvellous. Who wouldn't want to marry you? What's more difficult to understand is why you want me.' They must have resembled the young couple in the picture he had bought for Antonia.

'It's because you're nice and thoughtful and stable and predictable and considerate and generous. And you're clever. That helps, even it's only maths.' She said this with momentary disappointment but quickly brightened. 'And anyway it isn't only maths; you understand painting, too. Actually, we're quite evenly matched in cleverness. You may not be ambitious enough for Mother, but you're an achieving sort of person. And you may not be exactly handsome, but you're not bad looking. And you like women; I can tell by the way you look at them, even if you are a bit shy. That's why you mustn't look at them too much until you're married to me. Nor after that, either. And you may not be exciting, but I don't need an exciting man. I provide enough excitement by myself, and more would be exhausting.'

She shuffled away and finished the remains of her cornet. The two of them sat in contented silence.

'It's going to be a gorgeous summer day. And it's been a marvellous birthday weekend. So much has happened. But I wouldn't like it to be like this all the time. I love it around the second week of the summer holidays, when I wake up one day and haven't a clue what to do. Nothing whatever planned. At first I feel bored. Then I think of things to do and can take my time doing them.'

She smiled at Andrew. 'Now that we've settled our futures, shall we have a *leetle* bit more ice cream?'

And they strolled off towards the shop. Andrew, on an impulse, put his arm round Antonia's waist and gave her a little squeeze. Precisely at that moment, Antonia put her arm round Andrew's waist and gave him an independent little squeeze, and Andrew was aware of a nearly mature female body pressing against his. Then they disentangled and walked sedately on.

Chapter 7

Later in the morning, with the sun getting hotter, Andrew climbed on the bus for the first stage of his journey back to town. He manoeuvred his way to one of the few unfilled seats, laid up his suitcase, and sat beside a middle-aged man.

'Going to be hot,' Andrew remarked, feeling the need to be polite.

The man glanced at him. 'You're from the south, aren't you? I can hear you're not from these parts. Why, you're the young man I saw this morning with the young lady from Enby Hall, aren't you?'

Andrew took a closer look at his neighbour. 'Now I see you're the owner of the ice cream shop.'

'That's right. And we sell not only ice cream but a comprehensive range of the items needed on a day-to-day basis for normal housekeeping, and at highly competitive prices.'

Meanwhile the bus had driven up a hill and turned so that they could look back on the village, which from this angle was dominated by Enby Hall.

'You been staying at the big house? What did you think of the family?'

'The son of the house invited me there, and he and his sisters were very hospitable.'

'How about the old lady?'

'More difficult with her.'

'I thought so. I've never had a problem with the rest of the family, but the old lady treats me as a servant. She reminds me that we're feudal round her. Actually, the family are not really aristocrats, no more than landed gentry; they've been living here for only a hundred years, since 1866.'

'I see you take an interest in these matters,' said Andrew.

'I like to find out about local history. And it connects with another matter of enormous interest – genes and breeding. I've got a book called *The Facts of Life*. Old families keep dying out. Do you know why?'

This was proving to be an unusual conversation, but Andrew thought he should humour the man. 'Inbreeding, perhaps?'

'Exactly! A few ancient families keep marrying among each other, and they become inbred and depressed. What makes it worse is when the son of the family marries an heiress who will inherit all the money because she's an only child. No brothers and sisters – that means, low fertility.

'The girl of the house I saw you with this morning – her name's Antonia, isn't it? Now didn't I see you and Antonia give each other a quick hug this morning?'

Andrew reluctantly admitted that he probably had.

'Of course,' continued the shop owner, 'she's very young, and I didn't take what I saw seriously. But she's already thinking along the right lines. She's taking up with you because you're not from these parts and you don't belong to the landed gentry – I can hear you're from somewhere in south London. She's going to improve the stock by cross-fertilization, across the country and across class barriers.'

'I can't believe that Antonia consciously sees it like that.'

'No, it's not conscious; it's more instinctive.'

Andrew was amused but was inclined to say, 'It's a heavy responsibility for the parties involved, having to rejuvenate the ancestral stock.'

'Don't worry about that, sir. From talking to you, I can tell you'd be the right man for the job. Funny I should call you "sir" when we're sitting on the bus together. It's partly a habit from talking to the customers in the shop and partly that, as I said, we're feudal round here.'

He leaned back and looked out of the window with satisfaction. 'It's a real summer's day. The hawthorns are still in full bloom; the roses will be coming next. It's going to be hot. Funny thing, you look out, and it seems tranquil enough. The occasional houses blend into the landscape. But underneath that placid surface, there's a lot going on you don't see. The countryside's riddled with tiny organisms, their genes seething with activity.'

He stood up. 'I'm getting off here, visiting a friend. It was good talking to you; I expect I'll see you around.'

Chapter 8

Andrew rang Toby a few days later.
'That was a weird and wonderful weekend; I won't ever forget it, for a heap of reasons. I have a lot to thank you for.' He hadn't yet told Toby about the events of the final day.

'It was certainly an extraordinary time. And I have plenty to thank *you* for, Andrew. You played a crucial part in fixing up Janet. I no longer have to feel so hopeless about her.'

'Could we make another trip to Enby? I really appreciated your efforts at teaching me to drive. More important, I am concerned about Janet. She may lose her resolution if your mother is constantly telling her how hopeless Fred Arlington is. I don't think we should leave countering your mother all to Antonia.'

'I know. I have been bothered about that myself. We should make another trip as soon as possible. By the way, how did it go with the ice cream?'

'We both had cornets. Rather good. One scoop of vanilla, and one of chocolate. Mind you, a bit more happened than ice cream. I'll tell you about it in the car.'

'I expected additional events.'

Andrew didn't feel like discussing subsequent developments over the telephone. 'Did your mother write a thank you letter to the Armitages? I hope that won't cause disturbances.'

'She did write a thank you letter, and Antonia very decently offered to post it for her. She went out with it and put it in the rubbish bin instead of the pillar box. There's nothing wrong with her nerve. Of course, if Mother found out in some way, Antonia would say she was thinking of something else and made a silly mistake. Mother would believe her. Young girls make thoughtless mistakes.'

'I suppose *they* do, but Antonia doesn't.' Andrew continued, 'I seem to be getting into intrigues. Makes me think of your Sir Oliver Laine.'

Toby sighed. 'I'm afraid so. What surprises me is that you take to it so readily. It seems to come naturally. No one would suspect it of you. You'll probably be effective as an intriguer.'

'Is this a temporary phase, or is this what real life is like most of the time? You thought you were opting out of intrigues, but now you're back in.'

'I hate it. But you seem to like it.'

'Our current intrigue together is making people happy, so why should we be ashamed of it? You aren't becoming like your mother, if that's what you're afraid of.'

Toby sighed again. 'You're stronger than I am. It's as if some of Antonia's toughness has washed out over you. You've been altered over that crazy weekend.'

'It's not only Antonia; it's that whole wonderful countryside, that huge river valley, the view from the Knott over the estuary, the mountains in the background.' And he added, half to himself, 'It's the genes coming to life.'

'What did you say about jeans? The line isn't good. By the way, I know an excellent shop in town to buy jeans, low prices and good quality. I'll show it to you when we drive out next Saturday.'

* * *

The lesson began with a warming-up trip into the countryside towards Enby, but Toby took his role sufficiently seriously to include hill starts and three-point turns. In future, they would tackle the even more serious business of positioning at roundabouts and tricky turns to the left in the midst of town traffic. Andrew was finding the lesson hard work, and he could tell that it was tough on Toby, too. After half an hour of tense practice, Andrew had moved off smoothly from the area's most notorious test of the hill start.

'Shall we have a little pause?' suggested Toby. 'Wondering whether we're going to slide rapidly down the hill backwards is trying on the nerves for me, too.'

Andrew parked at a point with a pleasant view over the surrounding countryside.

'By the way, there isn't something you would like to discuss with me, is there, while we have a little pause?' Toby asked.

'What, how I feel about driving?'

'No, how you feel about Life – Life with a capital *L*.'

'Antonia must have been talking to you. We decided she could tell you how things are better than I could. A secret engagement with an underage girl seems ridiculous to me, and surely to most people, but it doesn't seem to bother Antonia.'

'No, she started it all, as I understand it. I expect you're scared of Mother.'

'I have to admit I am.'

'You've probably decided that Antonia will handle her better than you.'

'I suppose I'm being cowardly.'

'In a way, yes, but Antonia isn't any underage girl. I think you're right to leave it to her.'

Andrew wondered how Toby himself had reacted to the news. 'You must think I'm being pretty silly and that I'm highly unsuitable for Antonia.'

'At first, of course, I was flabbergasted. But sooner or later, Antonia would have a first affair; in fact, as it's Antonia, it would be sooner rather than later. And why not with you? You're most unlikely to exploit her; you're certainly no fortune hunter. She could do a lot worse, even if on the face of things it is most unlikely to lead anywhere. That's how the fond, protective brother in me, what there is of it, argued.' He puffed on his cigarette. 'Antonia has always looked after herself. My influence is negligible, except as a co-conspirator.

'But there's also you to think about. The fact is, Antonia will be good for you, if I don't sound too patronizing. She'll draw a whole lot out of you that few people would think was there in the first place. That's fine by me, because I like you.' He smiled at Andrew. 'As we're talking about Life with a capital L, you probably realize that my tastes are those of a minority group, but don't worry, you're not my type, to use that ghastly term.'

Andrew had occasionally wondered about Toby's tastes but considered they were not his business. But he was sufficiently curious to remark, 'It can't make your life any easier.'

'Being young is difficult enough for most people. The middle-aged have no reason to envy the young, as they so often do. It's worse if you come to realize you have my inclinations.'

Andrew was sympathetic but could only say, 'At least it's no longer illegal. That should help a bit in future.'

* * *

Andrew and Toby arrived at Enby Hall, minimized the exchanges with Mrs Morton, and picked up Antonia. The three had a lot to discuss, and Toby quickly replaced Andrew at the wheel, to remove distractions.

'Question number one, how is it with Janet?' Toby asked Antonia.

'At first I thought nothing much had changed, and she seemed her usual apathetic self. I was really worried. So I egged her on to decide when she was getting married, whether they wanted a big formal wedding, etcetera. She said she supposed she would ask Fred what he thought. And I told her to fix it up with Fred without talking to Mother first.'

'And did she?' asked Andrew.

'That's the thing. Half an hour after breakfast, she slipped off down the road, and when she came back, she informed Mother matter-of-factly that she and Fred would be getting married in a couple of weeks' time at a registry office, with two of Fred's farmhands as witnesses and no reception afterwards.'

'Has she said anything about a honeymoon?'

'No honeymoon. Too much to do on the farm, where she'll move in straight after the wedding, of course. Fred will turn up at the hall the same day with tractor and trailer to take away her belongings. Mother was reduced to speechlessness.'

* * *

The trio spent most of the day in a variety of occupations – driving instruction, sightseeing, walking in the countryside, and shopping. This was the usual pattern for Saturdays over the next six weeks. Toby and Andrew had plenty of conversational start points, often the personalities of those they had known at school. Some of what her older companions said was over Antonia's head, but she insisted on their explaining themselves, and she vigorously inserted her own views when she didn't agree with them. For Andrew, an adult was emerging from the knowing, precocious little girl.

After a tough session of town driving, Toby would suggest a secluded spot where Andrew could park. Toby would then withdraw discreetly for a quiet cigarette while Andrew joined Antonia in the back seat. Their physical contact was of modest scope but enough for Andrew to regret that he had allowed so many years to pass without close female companionship.

Towards the end of one of these sessions, when Toby was expected back, Andrew remarked, 'Driving lessons are heavenly.'

Antonia nodded contentedly. 'I do agree. It's heaven. Driving lessons have brought out all the potential in you I knew was there, Andrew. You've come on greatly over the last weeks. Now you're as dexterous with your tongue as you are with the handbrake in your hill starts.'

* * *

It was a Saturday in early September. It was a bright day. Andrew had done his town exercises, and Toby had wanted him to drive farther into the countryside than usual before parking in a secluded spot. The late summer butterflies, the tortoiseshells, the red admirals, the blues, and the skippers were around them, and the heather was flowering on the slopes above. They were out of the car in the warm sunshine when Antonia decided that all three of them should climb over the heather moors to the top of a craggy hill on the nearby horizon. Andrew agreed readily; the moors looked marvellous, the crags irresistible in the soft autumn sunshine and still air. Toby had intended to do some shopping but was brought round after a little persuasion.

Antonia kept bounding ahead, and even if she waited periodically for the other two to catch up, the pace was fast, and they had soon made it to the top of the crags, out of breath. A fine view over the river valley confronted them, and they sat down to gaze at it. Antonia wanted to proceed down to the river, but the others couldn't face the prospect of climbing back up the hill to return to the car.

Toby said, 'You two go on down to the village and get the bus back. I'll collect the car and do my shopping; that's best.' And he left them abruptly.

Antonia responded, 'Come on, Andrew,' and started running down the hill. She jumped wildly into a peaty hollow, landing bottom first in the thick peat. Andrew, abandoning caution, jumped after her, landing similarly. They found a grassy patch and lay beside each other, at first laughing and then silent as they absorbed the September sunshine, the occasional bird call, and the scent of heather. They relaxed after the exertion of climbing the hill too rapidly. Andrew dozed off for a minute or two.

Waking, and feeling Antonia at his side, it occurred to him that he was happy, a feeling almost of revelation. He tried to remember when he had previously felt as happy as this. It was an unconscionably long time ago, when he was ten, nearly eleven. He had been playing an improvised game of cricket with the other boys in the school yard, and unusually, it had gone well for him. The other boys, too, were satisfied with the game, even those on the losing side. Andrew had gone up to the boy who had organized the game, who was tall and dominating but subtle enough in his ways to be genuinely popular. 'Tim,' Andrew had begun and realized that he had committed a frightful breach of decorum in using a first name. 'Sorry. I mean Norbury.' But Tim Norbury had laughed; he didn't mind. 'It doesn't matter. Call me Tim.' This was a high point of Andrew's childhood.

Within two years, the problems had set in. In a woman's magazine to which his mother subscribed, he subsequently read an article about the various ages of childhood. That week it was about ten-year-olds. It was the happiest age, psychologists said, a period of equilibrium of body and mind before the disturbances of adolescence.

He said to Antonia, 'I'm very happy.'

'I am, too,' Antonia said, and rolled across to give him a hug. 'This is the beginning. There'll be lots more.'

* * *

Antonia's school term had begun. She concealed her age and saw a number of romantic X-films, not for children under the age of sixteen, with Vanessa, her closest friend at their girls-only school.

Their friendship had developed through discussing school homework. One morning, a group of classmates had assembled early in the classroom and discussed the assignment that was to be handed in that day.

'In 1512, Henry VIII ascended the throne—' began Antonia, reading from her essay.

'It was 1509, not 1512,' interrupted Vanessa.

Antonia altered the date. 'Okay. To continue, Henry VIII's religious views remained *essentially* unchanged throughout his long reign—'

'How can you possibly say that? First he was Catholic and then Protestant,' protested Vanessa.

'But that was purely tactical – to get rid of his wives and grab church land. His *personal* religious views didn't change.'

'Perhaps, but you ought to get your dates right,' persisted Vanessa.

'And you ought to consider the reign of Henry VIII in terms of his personality, instead of as a succession of boring dates,' returned Antonia.

Officially, the school was against the pupils discussing assignments, but Antonia had heard the history teacher say, 'They learn at least as much from going through their homework together as they learn from me.'

For Vanessa, history as ideas and personalities rather than facts was something new, and not entirely unwelcome, Antonia sensed. She would reinforce this by referring to people who were in the more immediate neighbourhood than Henry VIII. In the morning break, Antonia asked her, 'Why do you think Podgy Rogers is so bossy?'

Miss Rogers taught French.

'I don't know. I suppose because she thinks she's so clever,' said Vanessa. 'What do you think?'

'She has an inferiority complex because of her appearance. She tries to compensate by being brisk and authoritative.'

Miss Rogers had a French mother, had grown up in France, and corrected her pupils' language automatically without allowing queries.

Over the next few weeks, Antonia and Vanessa went through all the other teachers and all the other girls in the class and enjoyed themselves immensely. Vanessa was punctilious in correcting Antonia's facts when necessary, while both agreed that Antonia was better on psychology and the interpretation of human behaviour.

Antonia invited Vanessa home, telling her in advance that Enby Hall was not as grand as it looked from a distance; it was in a bad state of repair and the roof leaked.

Vanessa greeted Mrs Morton warmly. 'Hiya, Mrs Morton. It's real nice to meet you, 'specially with me and Antonia being such great friends. Fancy, just the three of you living in this huge castle! It's magnificent, even if it is a bit run-down.'

'How do you do?' said Mrs Morton.

They had coffee in near silence, after which Mrs Morton said, 'Antonia, see to it that Vanessa doesn't miss the last bus, I wouldn't want her parents to have to pay for a taxi,' and left them.

The visit would have gone better, Antonia realized too late, if Vanessa had come unprepared, fallen for the outer grandeur of Enby Hall and the high bearing of its mistress, and kept quiet.

'Does your mother have a superiority complex?' Vanessa wondered, being well into complexes by now.

'She *knows* she's superior; she doesn't bother to have a complex about it,' said Antonia. 'Next time, it's best we go to your place.'

Vanessa lived in a cosy little Victorian terrace house. It was pretty cramped, but the family, who included Vanessa's older brother, seemed to get on with each other easily enough. Antonia liked sitting with them in the kitchen in a run-down easy chair.

Vanessa's brother worked as an electrician in a local firm. Various friends of his turned up at the house, and one of them fell heavily for Vanessa, four weeks before Andrew came on to the scene for Antonia. So Vanessa was the first to acquire a boyfriend. Fortunately she was too good-natured to gloat to Antonia over this. Even so, it was unfair that Vanessa, less expert in human relations, had been the first to cross this important threshold. And Antonia hadn't even been involved in setting it up. Then came the weekend when Andrew arrived on the scene, and they were quits, but Andrew was a secret, and remained so till the end of the school term.

Antonia and Vanessa met seldom and only briefly during the summer holidays, but they resumed their friendship in full when the new term began in September.

Vanessa's boyfriend's name was Ed. Antonia persuaded Vanessa to personalize this to Eddie.

'I'm really curious to meet Eddie. Can it be at that coffee bar place that's just opened in town?'

Vanessa was happy to arrange this, and one afternoon after school the three of them sat down together in a secluded corner on the ground floor of the coffee bar. Eddie sold X-ray film in the northwest of England, mainly to hospitals. He made it clear that the firm was pleased with him; that very morning, his boss had told him that he was virtually the managing director for the northwest.

'Does that mean you will be promoted into management?' asked Antonia.

'No, not promoted. I'm too valuable as I am. My firm is afraid of promoting people above their ceiling, instead of leaving them to carry on what they do well and often like.'

To Antonia, this made sense. At the same time, she was pleased because the young man seemed even less dashing than Andrew, while pleasant enough. She put away any tendency to wonder if she had impulsively taken up with Andrew on the rebound from hearing about Eddie.

Vanessa and Eddie were beginning to get absorbed in each other, and Antonia felt redundant. Vanessa was sufficiently sensitive to disentangle and remark, 'Antonia doesn't have a boyfriend yet, but she will soon, won't she, Eddie?'

Vanessa was sorry for her; Antonia was appalled to realize this. The injustice of the situation stung Antonia into losing her caution and saying, 'Actually I have one.'

Vanessa was startled. 'Why didn't you tell me? What's he called?'

'Andrew. He's an old school friend of my brother, Toby. We haven't told anyone'; it has to be a secret.'

'Why?' asked Eddie.

'It all happened suddenly, after a strange weekend at our house, and … people would think we'd gone crazy.'

'If it happened at your house, I bet your mum was really horrid to him. How old is he?'

'Nearly twenty-five.'

'Twenty-five! That's middle-aged!'

'Steady on, Vanessa! I shall be that in a few years,' objected Eddie.

'Almost middle-aged. Why do you like him?'

The emerging adult in Antonia found it hard to explain. 'Because he's dependable. And clever. And considerate.' She added, 'And he's open.'

'How do you know he's open?' asked Eddie. 'You can bet he doesn't tell you everything.'

'I mean, he's open to suggestions.'

'Aha,' said Eddie, a trifle too knowingly. 'Such as what?'

Antonia was irritated. She could vaguely think of a number of examples of Andrew's openness, but they were perhaps not sufficiently striking, so she said, 'When I proposed to him, he accepted, even though I was only fifteen and he'd known me hardly more than two days.'

Vanessa was astounded and reduced to silence.

'Whew,' said Eddie, and sank back into his chair, in mock exhaustion.

Vanessa recovered sufficiently to say, 'He must be a dream prince.'

'He's nobody's idea of a dream prince, but he's …suitable.' Antonia, conscious that this was unromantic, added insistently, 'It's a secret engagement. You mustn't tell anybody. Promise not to tell anyone. Put your hand on your heart and swear.' She looked around to check that no one was in earshot, but they were alone on the ground floor.

The others, amused, did as they were told.

'Mind you, I'm no dream prince either,' said Eddie. He refrained from pointing out that Vanessa was no one's idea of a princess.

'Can't all four of us meet some time? Four ordinary people,' suggested Vanessa.

'Correction, at most, three ordinary people – at *most* – plus Antonia,' said Eddie. 'By the way, what does your mum think of Andrew?'

'She's snobbish about him.' To her annoyance, Antonia was close to tears. She felt that events had unfairly forced her to grow up too hurriedly; for a moment, she wanted to return to being fourteen. She tried to concentrate on the memory of relaxation beside Andrew on the moors.

Vanessa was obviously ravished by the idea of a secret engagement. She was moved to kiss her boyfriend warmly and lingeringly.

Antonia was shocked that she had been needled into revealing her secret engagement, particularly as it had been made to seem ridiculous. She should regain control of events, and of herself.

* * *

Three weeks later, Antonia was sitting in the doctor's waiting room, well-rehearsed for her visit after careful discussion with Toby. As usual, the doctor was running late. Antonia was sufficiently relaxed to read in the magazines about the carryings-on of the celebrities until she heard her name being called by the secretary. She was soon sitting in the patient's chair and confronting a comfortably built, genial man in late middle age.

'Why, it's Antonia Morton, how *very* good to see you again. It's been some years since I came to that marvellous house of yours, Enby Hall, to treat you for all the little childhood complaints – mumps was the most nearly serious, I seem to remember. What a fine young woman you've blossomed into.'

'Thank you, Dr McCready; you're not half bad-looking yourself. Some men get better and better with the years. Many female hearts must be set a fluttering under your disciplined, professional hand.'

The doctor took this in his stride; to judge from his smile, it went a little to his head. 'I expect you're here for more than an exchange of compliments, Antonia. But I can hardly believe there is anything seriously wrong. You are a picture of health.'

'Why, Doctor, you too look full of vim, I'm pleased to say. But I am sure you're a busy man, so I shall come straight to the point. In a few weeks' time, when I'm sixteen, I shall be sleeping with my boyfriend. Naturally, I need to go on the Pill. Attention to small, fiddly private things like contraceptives is not my boyfriend's strongest side. I certainly do not intend to have my schooling broken off by unfortunate events.'

Dr McCready was taken aback, despite a reputation for being liberal and willing to move with the times, but he recovered quickly. 'I'm delighted to hear that you take your responsibilities seriously. But you're very young – not sixteen yet. Have you discussed your feelings for your boyfriend with your mother? If not, I think you should do so before taking the matter further.'

'That would be ill advised. Don't you remember what Mother's like?'

Dr McCready's expression indicated that he remembered Mrs Morton sufficiently well to accept that Antonia had a point. 'You place me in a difficult professional position.'

Antonia guessed that he was wondering how he could possibly be talking like this to a girl of fifteen.

She was only partly right; he was recalling that she had always talked in a surprisingly grown-up manner. 'Of course, my young patients must feel their confidences are safe with me. On the other hand, I have obligations to their parents. They must not consider that their family doctor has let them down by failing to inform them of their children's drug habits or sexual misbehaviour.'

'I am hardly misbehaving if I sleep with my boyfriend. It's perfectly normal.'

'It is difficult to know where to draw the line. Much depends on the age of the child. Suppose you had been only twelve years old instead of fifteen? I should surely be justified in informing your parents.'

'I'm nearly sixteen.'

'Even sixteen is a borderline case.'

But Antonia, with Toby's help, had gone to a lot of trouble to inform herself on this point. 'I have talked to the National Council for the Protection of Civil Liberties. They say they would be prepared to sue a doctor who betrays the confidences of a sixteen-year-old girl.'

The doctor considered this. Antonia and Toby had settled for Dr McCready partly because he was notorious for being liberal; he enjoyed teasing people who maintained he was ushering in the permissive society, still new in the 1970s, to a quiet rural area, thereby causing its downfall. But he liked discretion where possible. 'May I suggest an alternative approach? Many young girls are troubled by heavy and irregular periods and find going on the Pill excellent for relieving the disagreeable symptoms.'

'Dr McCready, you're a genius! Why didn't I think of that myself? We can forget about the boyfriend side of things and concentrate on the purely physiological. And we can agree we shouldn't worry Mother about such a small matter as a troublesome period now and then.'

* * *

Antonia was considering her recent successes and failures in the field of human relationships. The incident of Vanessa and Mrs Morton had suggested that she couldn't always manage on her own; it was best to discuss with others and have a division of labour, even if this meant a kind of conspiracy. Objectively speaking, there had been a number of successes lately. Marrying off Janet was an excellent example of successful conspiracy. And Toby had been really helpful in laying up strategy over Dr McCready. And most important of all, she had joined up with Andrew, with the best still to come.

Conspiracy implied planning. How important was planning? Andrew had arrived out of the blue, and despite some doses of conspiracy, most of that crazy and wonderful weekend had developed unpredictably, unplanned.

She was sitting by herself in the favourite coffee bar, evaluating the need for planning and waiting for her bus home when Andrew and an older man entered. They were clearly on friendly terms. She could see that Andrew was initially uncertain what to do but finally said, 'This is Antonia, the sister of an old school friend of mine. Shall we sit down with her for a while? I expect you recognize Professor Briesley from his television programmes, Antonia.'

'Hello, I'm Joe.' He and Andrew placed their coffee cups on the table and seated themselves opposite her. 'Andrew and I have been discussing how to develop an idea about computers, and we went out for some refreshment. We've reached a point where we need to contact someone from the business world to get support.'

'Will that be difficult?' asked Antonia.

'It will be what they call a high-risk project, so we shall have to approach someone with the funds to back a number of such projects and spread the risk.'

'My brother gives art advice to that Tory MP called Sir Oliver Laine. He's into high-risk projects all right. Toby could set up a meeting, couldn't he, Andrew?'

Andrew waited to see how Joe Briesley would react. Joe was clearly amused. 'If you can fix a meeting with Sir Oliver, that'd be interesting, wouldn't you say, Andrew?'

Andrew was aware of Antonia looking at him eagerly. 'Toby meets him every now and again over some painting project, as Sir Oliver's constituency is only an hour's drive away. Perhaps the next time they meet, he can come over to our department.'

'I'll fix it with Toby,' said Antonia.

'Have a go, by all means,' said Joe. 'Your friend's sister here seems to be quite a character, Andrew. Sir Oliver should meet her, as well as us. Or has he met you already, Antonia?'

'I've never met Sir Oliver, only heard Toby talk about him. Can't you take him here after he's seen the department, at about this time?'

'Peculiar place to take an MP, but he's no cabinet minister, no security problem,' said Joe. 'We can provide him with dark glasses if he doesn't want to be recognized. I must say I fancy relaxing with him in a modest little place like this, after discussion at the department. Mind you, it'll be a hard call trying to get money out of him.'

It was time for Antonia to catch her bus home, and she left them. The same evening, she rang Toby and related the recent events.

'I'm supposed to be seeing Oliver at his flat in his constituency a week on Saturday. I suppose I can suggest instead he comes up the day before to hear about the project from Joe Briesley,' said Toby.

'And from Andrew.'

'And Andrew. Hope they understand what they are letting themselves in for, associating with Oliver. Anyway, Joe Briesley can surely look after himself.'

In a subsequent telephone call, Toby could report that Oliver Laine had agreed to visit the department. He had said, 'Joe is much better fun than most of these scientific technical chappies, from what I've heard. Could be interesting, talking to him at his Department of Mathematics, Statistics, and Computer Science. Incidentally, what a mouthful!'

Friday found Antonia sitting in the now familiar secluded corner of the coffee bar, in good time, wondering if the others would turn up or if Oliver Laine had pleaded urgent business elsewhere.

But only five minutes after the arranged time, she heard a loud confident laugh from upstairs, more laughter on the narrow stairs down, and soon Sir Oliver was saying, 'So here's Toby's sister, I presume, the one who has a way with delinquent boys. Delighted to meet you.'

They sat down with their coffee.

'What exactly have you been discussing?' asked Antonia.

'We have plans for a home computer,' said Joe. 'It will be the size of a large box, rather like a bulky television set, and it will quickly do calculations. Even more important, we think it can be used like a typewriter. You will be able to write a letter or a document on it. In fact, it'll be better than a typewriter because it should be possible to correct mistakes, before printing the document, but there's a lot of work to do there. Andrew has done some calculations and has convinced me that a computer with just sufficient capacity, four kilobytes of information in the jargon, can be housed in a box of large television size.'

'If it's to be a sort of typewriter, why call it a computer?' reacted Antonia. 'It will put people off, unless they love figures.'

'Antonia has a point there; we can think of a better name,' said Andrew.

'It should be the name of a person, perhaps a film star,' said Antonia.

Oliver Laine liked this. 'You'll have to give it a voice.' He switched to a robot style. 'The …name is …Bond …James …Bond.'

'No,' objected Antonia, 'that's too macho. You want a more feminine name. Like Ingrid. And if it's to be at home and women are to use it, too, it should be shapely and elegant, not a heavy square boring brown box.'

'By Jove,' said Sir Oliver, 'I do believe this young woman is a person after my own heart, someone with ideas and drive, an instinctive Lainista. I'd love to go on talking, but my chauffeur will be waiting in the square. I'll have to see if I remember how to get back over there.'

Andrew offered to show him the way, leaving Joe Briesley with Antonia.

Joe took another cup of coffee.

This was an opportunity to find out how Andrew was getting on at work, but she wasn't sure how to ask. She began, 'How did it go with Oliver Laine?'

'Rather well. He was interested. He'll fork up if we get an equal sum of money from elsewhere, a matching grant. Also he wants big control over the business side.'

Antonia came out with, 'Do you like Andrew?' which wasn't altogether satisfactory, she realized.

But Joe didn't seem surprised by the question. 'It's a new department, and it was important to get good people for it. I have a knack for picking the right people. I can recognize them based on a few clues from what they say and how they behave, without prejudice about background or education. I give them plenty of responsibility from day one. Naturally, they make mistakes, like everybody else, but if I allow them to make their *own* mistakes, they grow into the job. I've had some disappointments, but Andrew won't be one of them. I'm telling you this, young as you are, because I think you can understand.'

'That means you like him,' Antonia laid out as a feeler.

'You could put it like that, yes.' Joe regarded her with a trace of amusement. 'Actually, I've rather got the impression you like him, too.'

He glanced at his watch. 'We'd better go off now, if you're going to get your bus.'

* * *

Two weeks before Antonia's sixteenth birthday, Andrew received a message that the following Saturday afternoon he was welcome to arrive at Enby Hall. He had recently passed the driving test and, two days later, had acquired a car of his own, a somewhat newer Morris Minor than Toby had but sufficiently like what he was used to.

Antonia opened the door. They embraced, and she said, 'I expect you're tired after the drive. Come into the kitchen and get revived over a cup of something.'

'Tea will be fine.'

'Or a glass of something. I might be able to dig out some sherry,' Antonia was inspired to suggest. 'Do you like sherry?'

'I'd rather have tea. You make a good pot of tea.'

They sat in the kitchen. Antonia poured out rather small cups for both of them.

'Congratulations on passing the driving test. And buying a car immediately afterwards. You must tell me all about it and about your car, but not now, some other time.'

'The examiner passed everybody that day; he was in a good mood. So am I, complete euphoria. And refreshed with your tea.'

'Good, because I've got something really interesting to show you. Come upstairs.' She took Andrew up to her room and motioned him to a chair along one wall, while she stood by the long mirror on the opposite wall beside the picture he had given her on her birthday. She took off her blouse and then her bra while she looked at herself in the mirror. Andrew watched her in silence, half inclined to laugh. She undressed completely in front of the mirror, without ceremony, untheatrically and not at all in the manner of a striptease artist as has become familiar from numerous films. Then she faced Andrew.

'How do I look?'

'More wonderful than ever.' The words sounded unreal; events had proceeded too quickly and smoothly; again, Andrew felt suspended in an unserious Neverland.

The nude Antonia stood motionless with one hand on her hip, the other by her side. 'I am that quintessential figure of the 1960s and 1970s, the girl on the Pill – liberated, available, and safe. The first girls of our kind in history.'

She came over to Andrew, who was more than ever suspended in Neverland, and sat in his lap.

'You aren't sixteen yet; it isn't legal.'

'My birthday is in two weeks. No one worries about two weeks.' She kissed him, and he felt a rush of excitement. 'Except the lawyers, perhaps,' she added.

Andrew was brought back to earth. 'You never miss an opportunity to get people in your power, me included.'

She reacted to his distaste by putting her arms tightly round him. 'I know, Andrew darling, I can't help manipulating people. You must take me away from Enby Hall, and then I might stop.' She added, 'But you rather admire my manipulations. In a way, you enjoy them, don't you?' She wriggled in his lap. 'Remember, driving lessons were heavenly. This will be even better – perhaps not the first time; it will take a little practice. So forget the lawyers – I shouldn't have brought them up – and relish my availability, especially as it wasn't so easy getting round Dr McCready.' She kissed him again. 'Let's get you out of your clothes, so that we can kiss properly, with bare bottoms.'

* * *

Toby was spending a weekend at Enby Hall. His visits were less infrequent nowadays; he felt sorry for his mother, who was more isolated living in the large house now that Janet had left and Antonia was growing up and was out of the house or occupied with her own things during much of the day.

Mrs Morton, in turn, was more accommodating than earlier; she was less inclined to provoke quarrels. This weekend, Antonia was away on a school trip, her mother had been informed.

During dinner in the evening, Mrs Morton enquired after Andrew. 'How's his driving progressing? His lessons seemed to go on interminably.'

'Takes a long time learning to drive these days. The examiners have got fussy. But he passed the driving test a while back.'

'Thank heavens for that! He won't be wasting your time anymore.'

After dinner, Toby made a telephone call. On returning to the living room, he suggested to his mother that they should have a little drink. 'How about gin and tonic?'

He mixed a glass for each of them. 'Living in Enby Hall, don't you sometimes feel, as I do when I'm around, that you're taking part in a sort of Victorian melodrama?'

'Not at all.'

'Anyway, in a Victorian drama, the heroine or her mother is commonly offered smelling salts when something disturbing or unusual is in the offing, so that she doesn't faint.'

'Toby, you're talking in riddles. What on earth makes you bring up smelling salts?'

'I was thinking that now the First World War is in the distant past, and even the Second World War seems ages ago, things have changed. The heroine is revived with a gin and tonic, rather than smelling salts. I've mixed a good gin and tonic this time, don't you think?'

Mrs Morton took some sips. 'Yes, thank you, Toby. A bit stronger than I usually have, but it's good.'

Toby chatted some more. 'On the subject of Andrew, I expected you noticed that Antonia rather liked him.'

'Yes, ridiculous; it was almost as if she had a little crush on him. Harmless enough, but it could have turned into something nasty. Then I would have put my foot down of course. But I was glad for her sake when she hardly mentioned him again after that awful weekend when he was here and Janet suddenly got engaged.'

Toby moved towards the drinks. 'Antonia may not have mentioned it, but she subsequently met him every now again. She used to ride in the car when Andrew was having his driving lessons. She likes seeing the countryside, you know; mind you, we were mostly in town. Have another drink? You only live once and all that.'

'I shouldn't really, but actually I think I will.'

They chatted some more. 'To return to Andrew a moment,' continued Toby, 'he was rather impressed with Antonia, too. They both became rather fond of each other.'

The second gin and tonic was strong, too. Mrs Morton was beginning to feel light-headed. 'Andrew's too feeble to do more than worship from afar. I don't think we need worry. Mind you, the young are so *active* these days. The contraceptive pill is a very mixed blessing. As regards appropriate suitors for a girl like Antonia, with her almost aristocratic family background and upbringing, I am nevertheless realistic enough not even to dream of the second or third son of say the Duke of Devonshire; I'd settle happily for the son of a dog biscuit manufacturer, like that boy in the neighbouring school I tried to interest her in, but Andrew, the son of a lorry driver! I can't bear the thought of Antonia coming into contact with the clammy, sweating naked body of someone of that kind.'

Toby contemplated resignedly that delicate arena where class meets sex. 'For goodness sake, Mother, you must know as well as anyone that sex isn't beautiful, but it isn't repellent; it's ordinary, often boring, even if it's with the Duke of Devonshire himself – not that I speak from experience. Anyway, Antonia has been having it off with Andrew for a year now; she had a little talk with Dr McCready and went on the Pill at sixteen.'

Mrs Morton, outraged, sat bolt upright. 'Impossible! Dr McCready was an old and trusted friend of the entire family. He would certainly have informed me if that were true, which I don't believe for a moment.'

'Antonia fixed it somehow; I expect she tried blackmail.'

'Antonia wouldn't attempt a thing like that.'

'Of course she would! She's her mother's daughter – just as I'm your son.' A hint of affection had crept into his voice.

Mrs Morton sighed. 'One blessing is that they're not married yet and can't be until Antonia's eighteen, even if they're' – she wrinkled her nose – 'having it off or whatever you called it. They'll need my permission. We've got time to influence and control events.'

He mixed some more gin and tonic. 'Mother, one of your amiable and enduring qualities is that you don't mount a last-ditch attack in pique when the situation is lost and you don't get what you want. We have now reached the point I was building up to with the aid of smelling salts. You noticed I had a telephone call immediately after dinner. Antonia called to say she and Andrew drove up the road for a weekend trip. Short distance into Scotland.'

'They're having a whole weekend together! In public! I'm aghast!'

'I'm afraid there's worse to come. Brace yourself. They've got married at a registry office. Very quiet wedding, couple of witnesses, friends of Antonia. Sixteen is the age of consent in Scotland, without parental permission.'

Mrs Morton uttered faintly the dread name of the village associated with countless stories of underage English lovers escaping to the nearest Scottish place to formalize their romance: 'Gretna Green!'

'Not actually. Antonia thought Gretna Green was too corny. Proceedings were at a little town, forgotten its name for the moment, farther along the Galloway Peninsular. Drink up your smelling salts, and we can discuss the matter further, in a spirit of calm relaxation.'

If she had been sober, Mrs Morton would have followed her normal practice of crying out theatrically and fainting on the sofa. But after the smelling salts, she was weepy and self-pitying. 'Why wasn't I warned what was going on? Why didn't you tell me, Toby?'

'Because Antonia asked me to stay out of it. She's old for her years, and she's perfectly capable of running her own life.'

'Where are they going to live? As you say, I have a forgiving nature, but I'm not so saintly that I can stand having Andrew around here.'

'They'll live in Andrew's flat in Presley, to begin with. The idea is that she'll leave school and continue at the technical college. The school will be happy to get rid of a married girl. Mother, as I pointed out, one of your virtues is that you accept a fait accompli – you might make a frightful fuss to begin with, but if the event happens anyway, you accept it with good grace. You can do the same now. Give Antonia a chance to be happy with Andrew, whatever you think of him.'

'But what about *me*?' cried Mrs Morton piteously. 'What's to become of *me*? Shall I be left to wither away in Enby Hall, while the old stone building slowly collapses round me?'

'There I have a good suggestion, if you'll bear with me,' said Andrew calmly. 'Do you remember that restaurant we went to a few weeks ago? A dark-haired young man who cooked at the table and chatted with you? You rather liked him. You described him as dapper.'

'Yes, he talked *beautifully*. And he was so knowledgeable, too. He knew that Enby meant "Juniper Village" in Old Norse.'

'He'd like to rent a room here at Enby Hall. He says he'd love to potter about the house, making repairs and renovating it. He's skilful in such things. Here's the suggestion. I need space for my studio, more than I can easily get in a Presley flat. If I set up the studio here, with us living together in proximity, we'd get on each other's nerves—'

'But I've been much better recently, and so have you—'

'But if Albert, the dapper little charmer, moves in too, you'll have someone sympathetic to talk with. He loves cooking things in the kitchen, even outside his job; in fact, he'll try out his dishes with you. You'll be able to cook as much or as little as you please. You won't have to worry about leaking roofs and the like because Albert will fix whatever needs fixing or arrange for someone else to do so at low cost. Isn't that a good suggestion?'

His mother seemed to agree with this. Toby mixed a concluding portion of gin and tonic.

'Not more smelling salts?' asked Mrs Morton anxiously.

'No, a celebration,' said Toby. 'But perhaps one small additional point, to fill out what you've probably understood – you will be able to show guests around without embarrassment. Albert and I both prefer separate rooms and will be most discreet.'

Part 2:
Cathy

Chapter 9

One day, early in the new millennium, Andrew, who was living in London again, received a telephone call from someone's secretary. 'Dr Andrew Carter? Please hold the line while I put you through to my employer.'

The next moment, a loud confident voice was saying, 'Andrew. This is Sir Oliver Laine again. Long time since we last met, back in Joe Briesley's days. I have something important to discuss with you, best in private rather than over the telephone. I wonder if you could oblige me with a meeting for lunch at my club in the near future, as soon as possible. I can send my man to pick you up in one of my cars over at your university.'

They settled on a date for a few days later. Andrew considered ringing to Toby in the meantime to keep him abreast of events but decided to wait until after the meeting.

So the next Wednesday, Andrew was sitting in the same room at the same club as Toby Morton had thirty years earlier, equally curious as to what Sir Oliver had up his sleeve. Sir Oliver was not far short of eighty but, from his appearance, could have been ten years younger. In response to comments, he would explain that he kept himself young, like Winston Churchill, by never harbouring grudges against those who had wronged him.

'Before we get down to business, Andrew, let me show you a recent acquisition.' From a box beside his chair, Oliver took out an old-fashioned black top hat. 'I've long wanted the title of doctor. The question has been where to obtain it at reasonable cost. The answer – Sweden. For only about one million pounds, one endows a chair in something or other at one of the numerous new universities mushrooming in provincial towns nowadays, to refill the military quarters after defence cutbacks. In return, they give you an honorary doctorate. This really quite elegant hat goes with the doctorate.'

Doctor Sir Oliver Laine reclined in his chair with considerable satisfaction. 'Which is better value for money – a British knighthood or a Swedish doctorate – is a topic for serious discussion. Both give a useful title. The knighthood opens more doors, but it is far more expensive, even if it is mostly the firm that pays. The honorary doctorate is cheaper, but there can be initial problems with charitable tax deduction.

'So much for doctors' hats. Now, to get down to the case at issue. I'll summon Francisco, so we can talk over lunch.' Sir Oliver rang an old-fashioned hand bell.

Andrew looked round the room with interest. Clubland was foreign territory. Two dreary pen drawings in thick wooden frames depicting life in the streets near the club, prominently dated 1812 and 1818, but surely modern prints, hung on the walls. A fine old table set for lunch stood in the middle of the room, together with four period chairs, elegant and comfortable but in doubtful condition. At the side of the room were the chairs on which Andrew and Sir Oliver sat facing each other. In stunning contrast to the other furniture, these were black plastic, and it now dawned on Andrew that the lower parts were shaped like a lady's bottom. They were out of place in a respectable London club, Andrew felt.

'Lovely chairs, aren't they?' said Sir Oliver, following Andrew's glance. 'They were bought at my suggestion some years ago.' He delivered his chair an affectionate slap. 'I couldn't let them get rid of the ladies when they redesigned the room. Originally, it was "contemporary," but when the wallpaper developed cracks in the middle of the economic downturn last decade, they redesigned it in Regency style. Interior decoration is a question of contributing to an atmosphere, or *gestalt*, as the architectural intellectuals will explain to you. Bare-bottomed ladies of any description are splendidly at home in a Regency *gestalt*.'

They sat down at the table, and the waiter, Francisco, arrived with an effusive, 'Good day, my friends!' He carried a silver tray with bottles of beer and a decanter of iced water. 'You are both happy with the day's menu? Traditional English.'

Francisco handed Andrew the printed menu, which indicated Lancashire hotpot followed by bread-and-butter pudding.

'I assumed that would be okay,' said Sir Oliver. 'Toby told me you ate most things.'

They began on their beer, while Sir Oliver got down to business. 'I don't need to remind you that the world is changing and that we must change with it,' stated Sir Oliver, as if addressing a public meeting, adding sotto voce, 'while giving a shove or two in the right direction, of course.' He resumed his grandiloquent style. 'Britain must look for new markets in emerging nations. One of the most promising of these new countries, often overlooked here, is Vietnam. But our contacts with Vietnam have been neglected. Sweden has been far more sensible. Thirty years ago, that chap, prime minister what's-his-name, begins with an O …' Sir Oliver wrinkled his forehead in an effort to recall and then turned to welcome Francisco, who had arrived with the Lancashire hot pot. Sir Oliver tasted it thoughtfully.

'Excellent as usual, Francisco,' said Sir Oliver with enthusiasm. 'I encourage Francisco to do a southern variety of Lancashire hot pot. He zizzes it up with paprika, garlic, tomatoes, and olives. He takes the word "traditional" with a pinch of salt.'

Andrew agreed; the stew was definitely zizzed.

'Last time I had this, it was with an EU official I was supposed to be softening up. He wanted to have something English, and Francisco obliged with the hot pot and bread-and-butter pudding routine. The EU chappie drew the line at beer though – insisted on wine. Where were we? O something, as I remember.'

'A Swedish prime minister, you said.'

'Oh yes, Olof Palme. Eventually got himself assassinated, poor chap. He was miles ahead of his time. He grasped the export possibilities to Vietnam and pretended to be a communist. Marched with the Vietnamese ambassador in protest against the American war in Vietnam. Fooled a lot of people who thought he was anti-American. Had to make private trips to America to explain to the Yanks that it was only a show to impress the Swedish public at home and please the Vietnamese and other developing countries. Of course, all the time, Sweden was busily cooperating with NATO while passing herself off as neutral. Palme's idea was to become secretary general of the United Nations in due course. President Nixon should have understood these simple domestic and personal ambitions; he really had no need to refer to Palme as "that Swedish asshole."'

Andrew was aware that this was not a strictly orthodox account of the historical events.

'Anyway,' continued Sir Oliver, 'the important point is that Sweden has excellent relations with Vietnam, which we must exploit to improve our own exports. We must bear in mind that, even if highly placed Swedes are, like us, unusually hypocritical by international standards, ordinary Swedes aren't a bad lot at all; they speak good English, too. Have you ever wondered which European country is most like Britain?'

Andrew considered this. 'No, I can't say I have, really.'

'It's Sweden. For historical reasons, mostly, stretching back before the Battle of Hastings. Right back to Beowulf, an English poem, Anglo-Saxon anyway, that's all about Swedes.' Sir Oliver stretched out his arms in an expansive gesture to indicate the vast canvas on which he was sketching the course of history and then placed his hands behind his head and leaned back. 'And on to modern times. Sweden, like Britain, was never occupied by Napoleon, by Hitler, or by Stalin. It was never even sat on by Stalin after the war, like Finland was. It's never been under the heel of a home-grown dictator, like Portugal, Spain, Italy, and Greece. What other European countries can one say that of? There's Iceland, but that's too small and far away to be worth bothering about unless there's a nasty volcanic eruption. There's Ireland, which personally I've never been to. It's Catholic and rather eccentric. Actually I never think of Ireland as abroad or even as a jumped-up former British colony but rather as a dearly loved member of the family who's grown up and left home.' As an afterthought, he added, 'The same applies to America, of course.'

Sir Oliver quickly returned to his tour of Europe. 'There's Switzerland, but that's a very peculiar country; she's neutral and hypocritical and with the same *Sw* at the beginning, but she's much less like us than Sweden is. It's to do with the geographical position in the middle of Europe. The Swedes are on the outside and even talk, like we do, of the continent to mean the rest of Europe; in many ways, they are a sort of island people. Naturally, Sweden was very late to join the common market and has a proper currency with the king's head on the coins; no nonsense with euros or whatever they're called.

'You will be wondering, Andrew, how we fit into this global perspective. We shall attach ourselves to the Swedish aid programme in Vietnam. This will give us a base from which to launch our company, A to Z Pharmaceuticals. I have proposed to the Swedes that a British company should augment the funds that the Swedish International Development Agency awards to medical projects in Vietnam. Actually, both the Swedish and the Vietnamese authorities responded enthusiastically to this idea. Always hard to say no to money donated altruistically. This will facilitate our company's entry into the Vietnamese drug market. The name A to Z Pharmaceuticals encourages helpful confusion with the existing well known Anglo-Swedish firm, Astra Zeneca.

'You will now be asking yourself, Andrew, "What can I do for the Vietnamese people and for A to Z Pharmaceuticals?"'

At this point, Francisco entered with the bread-and-butter pudding and hung around while the dinner guests tasted it.

'Excellent, Francisco, oodles of zing,' pronounced Sir Oliver and explained for Andrew, 'Francisco omits the bread from bread-and-butter pudding.'

'It's a worthy successor to the hot pot,' said Andrew.

Francisco withdrew, delighted.

Sir Oliver asked Andrew, 'Where were we?'

'You were saying I should be asking myself, what can I do for A to Z Pharmaceuticals?'

'And equally important, what can I do for the Vietnamese people?' Sir Oliver reminded him.

'I should certainly like to hear your answer,' said Andrew.

'You will advise young Vietnamese medicals on the design and statistical analysis of their medical experiments, including clinical investigations of new drugs. This will form the bridgehead for the launching of A to Z Pharmaceuticals in Vietnam, although you will not be personally involved with our commercial company. You will not encounter any ethical problems.'

'I presume you will be announcing the position and suggest that I apply for it,' said Andrew.

Sir Oliver wrinkled his nose. 'I hate formal job announcements. I secure the right chap by discreet enquiry from appropriate quarters; so much more streamlined. I remember you from our collaboration together with Joe Briesley all those years ago. Pity he retired and is out of it now, even if he is still alive. Anyway, I enquired how things were going with you from Toby Morton, your former brother-in-law, who warmly praises your personal qualities. Furthermore, colleagues have confirmed your professional competence in your present field to my complete satisfaction.'

Sir Oliver paused. 'As you doubtless know, Toby and I have long collaborated on artistic matters. At one time, we were going to act together from the side to bring a common-sense meaning and purpose into the razzmatazz surrounding the Turner Prize. Sadly, that fell through, but Toby has served as court painter to the family and our circle of close friends for many years now.

'But to return to the matter at hand, my one reservation about your duties abroad is that it could involve excessive times in a difficult climate. I have heard of too many good men going quietly to seed during terms of duty in the exacting tropical climes of the old empire. I, therefore, propose that you spend half your time abroad and half your time as a supernumerary fellow of Hereford College at Oxford University. What do you say about my Vietnamese suggestion? The emoluments will certainly compare very favourably with your present earnings.'

'Could I have two or three days to think about it?'

'Naturally. Why not talk it over with Toby Morton, who has long experience of sharing my thoughts and adventures?'

'Yes, I'll do that.' Andrew glanced at the empty plates and the remnants of their meal. 'Thank you for an excellent lunch. I'm glad I don't have to do the washing up.'

Sir Oliver smiled. 'That reminds me of a conversation I had with Margaret Thatcher the other day. Margaret and I rather like each other. Sadly, she never offered me a cabinet job, but I kept contact with her even after she gave up as PM. As a matter of fact, she liked the way I called her Margaret, never Maggie. Anyway, there she was at home with her plastic gloves on, clearing up after lunch when I came along and she said to me, "A woman's work is never done." "Best not to start," I said. I never do the washing up.'

(Mrs Thatcher had then looked out of the window and asked, 'Is that your old car?' On being told that it was a Jaguar E-type, borrowed from

Sidney Hacker, Mrs Thatcher had remarked, 'It needs a good wash, outside and no doubt inside, too. And when you give it back to Sidney, tell him he must do the same for his business management. Denis says the prospects for his funds are alarmingly iffy.')

Sir Oliver and Andrew were on their way down the stairs. Andrew couldn't resist asking more about the EU official. Had he been softened up sufficiently by the bread-and-butter pudding, and all the other goodies, to be more amenable during the subsequent negotiations?

'Things went quite well, actually. He was in a good mood. He said that he had come to England almost every year since 1970, and each time the food was a little better, admittedly by only 1 or 2 per cent but that, accumulated over thirty years, this made an appreciable difference.'

* * *

'The first question,' Toby was saying over the phone a couple of days later, 'is whether you like the idea of going to a Third World country like Vietnam and seeing it from the inside, over periods of six months at a time, rather than travelling out as a tourist and obtaining fleeting impressions.'

'Yes, of course it will be a fantastic experience of a kind I've never had before.'

'Good. The next question is whether you can trust Sir Oliver.'

'Exactly. That's why I've come to you; I thought you might know the answer.'

'I've known him long enough,' said Toby. 'He's a risk all right; he's a scoundrel, as he makes abundantly clear to everybody. But he's an amiable scoundrel. He loves his adventures, and people whose everyday existence seems grey and humdrum decide he will brighten things up for them. They try him out and conclude that he does nothing definitely illegal. And he can be surprisingly sensitive to people; even if he uses us, he doesn't exploit us ruthlessly. But if the worst comes to the worst, call in Agatha; she can often fix things.'

Andrew felt adequately reassured about Sir Oliver but had lingering doubts as to whether he would fit into the senior common room of an Oxford college. But Toby was reassuring over that, too. 'You'll meet some weird specimens at Hereford College; that's for sure. You'll be able to compare them with the Vietnamese to see who are the more exotic; you'll enjoy that. And in Oxford you'll live in marvellous comfort – a big plus of the whole proposition, if you ask me.'

Andrew was inclined to agree.

* * *

Hereford College was of respectable age, even by Oxford standards, but was not currently enjoying high status. At one of the meetings of the fellows, its future was being discussed.

'By appointing this chap Carter to a visiting fellowship,' the head of the college was saying, 'we can kill no fewer than four birds with one stone. First, he is of impeccable working-class origins, so that we can disarm critics of our alleged social exclusiveness. Second, he is a sort of scientist, applied mathematician anyway, so that he will help to redress the leaning towards arts subjects that our critics complain of. Third, he will be working within an overseas aid programme, so that we shall gain brownie points for Third-World altruism, with the additional advantage that he will be absent up to half the year in some Asian country, Cambodia or Laos or something, one of those places, I've forgotten exactly which—'

'Wasn't it Vietnam?' queried the chaplain.

'Vietnam, perhaps. He won't cost anything, even when he is staying with us; the business world will be paying for his food and lodging. Finally, even if he is hardly top-notch academically, he is well thought of within his admittedly unglamorous research area, statistical analysis of medical studies. He will add usefully to the length of our publication list, if not its weight.'

The trouble at Hereford College was that the fellows, although many of them had been wonderfully promising for years, experienced difficulty in getting their thoughts down on paper. They were inclined to look in the mirror and ask themselves, *Am I absolutely first class?* These existential doubts inhibited them from publication in case their supposed enemies pounced on possible shortcomings. The rector himself (the head of Hereford was called the rector) was known to be writing a book on the problem of evil in the non-Shakespearian Elizabethan drama. Some close friends had been shown certain chapters and pronounced them brilliant, but the book had never emerged in print.

One of the fellows enquired languidly, 'How solid are Carter's working-class credentials?' He belonged to that small select company, each member of which claims to be the only right-wing sociologist in the country.

'His father was employed as a taxi driver.'

'That's lower middle class, not working-class. I keep meeting academics who boast of their working-class origins when they are really only lower middle class. We are in danger of blurring an important conceptual distinction.'

'But he was a lorry driver before changing to taxis, apparently.'

'Ah! Point taken, rector. But you should have said that from the beginning.'

'*Must* we have another scientist?' queried the college's medieval historian, pathetically.

'You know my feelings about scientists,' said the rector. 'They'll be the death of the Oxford we grew up with and love. A scientist is rarely a good college man – his loyalty is split between his college and his department. I economize by deciding he doesn't need his own room in college, since he has one at his department. Despite these efforts of mine, scientists are ruinously expensive. They're forever insisting on new gadgets for their research and wanting to put up hideous new buildings to house them. Think of that biochemist some years ago. He wanted to erect an extravagant high-rise brutalist monstrosity in the middle of the Parks—'

'It was the professor of zoology, actually,' corrected Hugh Brenton, the young medical fellow.

(It can be said that, professionally, the rector was considered to combine brilliance of vision with a curious lack of exact scholarship.)

'Zoologist, then; much the same thing. How can we catch glimpses of a scholar gypsy, with legends going back to medieval times – he who loves retired ground – with a skyscraper complex sprawling over North Oxford? But scientists have no feeling for legend, no grasp of the supernatural; they insist that everything must be verifiable by evidence. Their publications are directed towards a tiny band of extreme specialists. I looked at a biology paper recently, about some gene sequence. It was a mass of a's and c's and g's and e's—'

'T's, not e's,' corrected the medical fellow.

'The point is that they should be more concerned with putting across the mystery and significance of life to a new generation of boys and girls. By all means penetrating study, but directed to universal questions. But usually they're not interested in teaching; they spend their time fussing over technicalities for the journals. One of them even said he couldn't care a shit what happened to his students after they'd left him. And most of them are married, more or less, and don't eat their college dinners properly; they say they're needed at home.' The rector, softening, added to the medical fellow in a less plaintive voice, 'Don't take this, personally, Hugh. We're very fond of you. You're cultured, even. Besides, you hardly count as a scientist; you're a doctor.'

Hugh giggled appreciatively.

'You say he was an applied mathematician originally? I hope that doesn't mean he is incapable of civilized conversation, like most mathematicians,' was the reaction of one of the fellows. (The mathematical fellow was absent on this occasion).

'It should be made clear that this new chap's no longer married, so there won't be any wife-and-children trouble,' resumed the rector. 'He will naturally attend our college dinners. One should never underestimate the civilizing influence of regular attendance at college dinners. Think of Tommy Shaw. When he was appointed a Junior Fellow at Christ Church, he was a wild young sociologist from whom one expected the worst. Yet after only three months of college dinners he was fully House-trained.' (The initiated at Oxford refer to Christ Church College as 'the House'.) 'He not only put on his gown without having to be begged to do so by the presiding college servant, he was circulating the port symbolically to his left' – the rector demonstrated this with his hands – 'even when the only people remaining at the end of dinner were sitting to his right.'

Thus, Andrew Carter came to be a fellow of one of the more idiosyncratic – some would say reactionary – Oxford colleges.

* * *

Andrew had been living in London again and, having gotten rid of his car, arrived at Oxford by train. He was to be met at the station by the chaplain of Hereford College, who made a point of welcoming new appointments to the college.

Andrew, without giving much thought to the matter, had vaguely expected the chaplain, whose name was Mark Noland, to appear in a black suit and dog collar. But he was greeted by a man of average height with a light-coloured jacket, open-necked shirt, dark blue trousers, and sandals, who approached Andrew abruptly saying, 'Andrew Carter? I'm Mark,' and then took up the luggage. He pointed to his car standing in the station yard.

Mark noticed a man in a dark suit and a dashing black hat walking in the same direction. 'There's Clemmie – we'd better pick him up, in a spirit of loving one's neighbour. Clemmie's a short-term fellow with us at Hereford. He's halfway in his career between school prefect and senior civil servant. Inevitably, he's said to have leadership potential.' His voice hinted at distaste, mollified by the fair-minded addition, 'Even so, he's not a bad chap.'

Clement Hargreaves accepted a lift, while indicating that he could easily walk, which would have been good exercise. He squeezed beside Andrew's luggage in the back seat. Andrew noticed his immaculately polished black shoes, in addition to his startling headgear.

Mark drove off briskly. 'The car's a wholly happy Hyundai now the garage has fixed his engine pains. He can feel the wind in his sails.' He turned off into the main road.

Clemmie was holding onto the back of Andrew's seat. 'That was a halt sign, Mark.'

'Was it?' asked Mark innocently. 'I always look very carefully at crossroads and check that nothing's coming before I drive out; otherwise, there might be an accident. But *stopping* at halt signs – isn't that for wimps?' He pressed his foot on the accelerator.

Clemmie sighed and talked politely to Andrew, to confirm that he was the newly arrived fellow.

'That's an interesting hat you've got,' remarked Andrew.

'My velour fedora? Glad you like it.'

'It's a Kojak imitation thing Clemmie ordered on the Internet,' explained Mark and accelerated sharply in low gear.

They parked near the college, and the three of them proceeded to Andrew's room with his luggage, where he was left to unpack. The room was on the top floor and one of the smallest in the college.

* * *

In the early evening, just before seven o'clock, the chaplain knocked on the door of Andrew's room and escorted him to dinner in the college. Andrew, as a new arrival, would ordinarily have been seated next to the rector at the head of the table. But the rector was away on holiday – or vacation, as he would have put it. Instead, he was placed in the middle of the central table in the huge dining room next to the chaplain, who asked him politely about his research. Having to explain maths to a non-mathematician was something that Andrew had accepted was unavoidable, and he had acquired some dexterity at it. He stressed it was applied maths and diverted into the medical matters it was applied to. The chaplain, to his credit, had made an effort to understand Andrew's brief exposition, had grasped an inkling of it, and had uttered noises expressive of interest. So Andrew had followed up by asking politely about the chaplain's theological interests, which proved to be the book of Jonah.

'Everybody knows that Jonah was swallowed by a whale. Curiously, though, it wasn't actually a whale, but a "great fish.".'

'A whale is not a fish,' put in Andrew, who was under the influence of a small glass of sherry, a large quantity of unremarkable but homely food, and a glass of excellent wine, combined with the fellows' sympathetic friendliness to a newcomer to the college.

'And God wasn't punishing Jonah by having him swallowed by the fish but was saving him from the storm. The fish vomited him up on dry land, as good as new.'

The young man seated opposite them – the medical fellow, Hugh – commented, 'I do agree about a whale not being a fish. I recognize another biologist, even if you're disguised as a mathematician or statistician or something. The fact is, a whale is a completely different kettle of fish, from a fish.'

'Don't mind Hugh,' said the chaplain, frowning resignedly. 'He can't help it. He's a psychiatrist. Anybody who thinks you needn't necessarily be off your rocker to be a psychiatrist, and fellow of an Oxford college to boot, should meet Hugh and get disillusioned. All the same, you're not a bad chap really, are you, Hugh?'

'Hugh seems very nice to me,' said Andrew shyly. 'Is he so peculiar?'

'You should see the way he steals into other people's rooms and reads their letters,' said the chaplain, good-naturedly.

Hugh didn't deny this. 'I take a friendly, gossipy interest in other people. What's wrong with that?' he asked. 'Anyway, I have a strict code of honour. I read stuff only if it's lying around open on someone's desk.'

'He means he never actually breaks open sealed envelopes,' amplified the chaplain, who had had abundant experience of Hugh peering over the top of his letter before he had time to bring it closer to his chest.

'One development that really is a godsend for people like me,' mused Hugh, 'is the printer for the computer. Papers laid out for me in the corridor. I can hang out for hours while folk print out their stuff – oodles of fascinating documents. Also, while we're on the subject of weird fellows of Oxford colleges, you should consider the chaplain,' continued Hugh. 'You must realize that he's of a generation that prides itself on not taking anything seriously. Seriousness is public enemy number one for them.'

'But,' intervened the chaplain equably, 'even if we're never wholly serious, nor are we ever entirely frivolous.'

The conversation paused while the three men finished their soup.

'Another interesting thing about Hugh,' resumed the chaplain, 'is that his patients like him. Even the professor has commented favourably, and that endearing old man seldom notices anything outside himself. He's complimented Hugh on his excellent clinical manner. Naturally, I've wondered how this was possible.'

Andrew glanced at Hugh, who seemed unconcerned.

The chaplain continued, 'Initially, Hugh, as a bright school-leaver, was going into management training. Inevitably, he went on courses and met business high-ups who had to be impressed. He asked them searching questions, without realizing that the last thing they want is discussion. Their idea of intellectual activity is watching sport on television. Hugh even uttered the hated B-word; instead of saying, "Yes, of course, will do, ASAP," he would begin off, "That sounds a good idea, but …*but* …" In short, he made himself impossible with the high-ups.'

'When a suitable occasion arises, I shall tell you about the chaplain's brushes with authority,' put in Hugh, equably, to Andrew.

'Now comes the good news,' said the chaplain. 'Hugh had the sense to give up his business administration studies and switch to medicine. The patients, unlike the tycoons, loved being cross-questioned, particularly the psychiatric ones – at last someone was taking a real interest in them. Of course, some of Hugh's patients are nearly as crackers as he is.'

Andrew, beginning to feel sorry for the medical fellow, said, 'It seems to me that the patients are right to like Hugh.'

'Thank you, Andrew,' responded Hugh.

The conversation reverted to the chaplain's special interests. Andrew, who usually called himself an agnostic, ended up promising to read the book of Jonah and discuss him further with the chaplain.

* * *

In search of a Bible, Andrew had looked in the senior common room where there stood a bookcase with an assortment of literature, mostly standard classics such as *Pride and Prejudice*. He was surprised that the choice was not more esoteric. Anyway, he found a Bible with reasonably large print, in which he managed to track down Jonah, while regretting the absence of an index.

'Got you on Jonah, has he?' commented the medical fellow, who was passing by.

A few days later, Andrew was again at dinner sitting near the chaplain, who began, 'I understand you've been reading Jonah.'

'Yes, I have.'

'Excellent. And what did you make of him?'

'First, I was surprised how short it is – only four chapters. I read it in five minutes. At the end, I felt much better informed but none the wiser. One reads such odd bits.'

'Such as?'

'At the beginning, God tells Jonah to go and cry against the people of Nineveh. And he refuses, though God has told him to, and professionally he's a prophet. I can sympathize with Jonah; his mission wasn't likely to achieve anything, and he was presumably taking a big risk. But to refuse to do what he was told, and then try to run away from God, seems extraordinary. God is supposed to be omniscient and omnipotent.'

'The thing is,' explained the Chaplain, 'Jonah was written comparatively late on in Jewish history. The Jews were beginning to get disillusioned with their prophets. The opening of Jonah reflects this.'

'And then, a really odd thing. Jonah, after the whale or whatever has sicked him up, eventually does what he was told and travels to Nineveh and tells them that awful things are in store for them – after which they are repentant and God forgives them – which makes Jonah go off into the desert and sulk because God shows him up as a lousy prophet. That's okay, I can sort of understand that. It's the next bit. God first tortures Jonah with the hot desert wind and then relieves him by having a castor oil plant grow up at fantastic speed overnight that provides shelter and sustenance. And Jonah is glad for that. Then God sends a worm to eat up the gourd so that Jonah is back under torture. Why?'

'I do agree that's a difficult passage. I think it's partly that the author is filling out the story. Jonah resents that God has been merciful to the hated Ninevites but allows Jonah only one day's release from the hot wind of the desert. God demonstrates His cosmic powers, His divine freedom to spare the citizens of Nineveh from destruction if He so pleases. Also, Hebrew literature often works in parallels, and here the first half of the story finds a parallel with the sequence when Jonah is under the plant in the desert. But the incident refers, in a complex way, to bigger issues such as God's relationship with Israel. No easy matters, and I'm working on them.'

Andrew rarely contemplated the cosmic. The chaplain's interpretation of Jonah made him think of Antonia. He could not see how her sudden removal fitted a divine purpose but found the idea stimulating. 'I'm beginning to see that Jonah is a pretty good story, even a gem of a story, perhaps partly because of its obscurity.'

Hugh put in, 'Or one might say, whale of a story – sorry, I mean, great fish of a story.'

The chaplain was obviously pleased with Andrew's reactions. He said nothing for a while and then suddenly asked, 'Andrew, do you believe in the supernatural?'

Andrew had recently decided that he would, in future, avoid polite evasions, so he said, without regard to the chaplain's presumed personal feelings, 'As a scientist, I am required to explain the natural world without invoking the supernatural, so, no, I don't. I don't see how believing in God is compatible with being a scientist.'

'Is it different for, say, journalists?'

'No, I don't think it is; nor for car repairers and garage mechanics, for that matter. I should not be impressed with a mechanic who said, "The devil has got into this car." What do you think about the supernatural?'

'As a matter of fact, I agree with you.'

Andrew was astonished. 'Oh for goodness' sake, what are you doing as a chaplain in the Church of England?'

'If I were still a parish clergyman, I should find life difficult. But this college is thoroughly sympathetic. Oxford colleges have their faults, but at least they believe in free enquiry.'

Andrew, having conceded that the story of Jonah held a certain fascination, was curious about the chaplain's relation to it. 'Why did you settle for Jonah in particular?'

'That's a complex story. Briefly, it's like this. You might have noticed that the God of the early Old Testament, including most of the famous passages, is pretty much a nasty old man—'

'I suppose that hadn't escaped my notice, but it's a surprise hearing that from a clergyman.'

'But Jesus is utterly different. The "love your neighbour as yourself" sayings of Jesus don't connect with the stony-hearted, punitive old man of the early Old Testament. I'm following how the one evolved from the other. I started with the late books of the Old Testament, including Jonah, which has the merit, if you're going to search out all the Hebrew references, of being mercifully short, as you commented.'

'And yet they're both joined up as God the Father and God the Son, together with the Holy Ghost – even if the son rebelled against the father,' put in Andrew

'Jesus's sayings evolved within the Jewish tradition. Jesus is, of course, a Jew through and through. I want to get at the original, historical Jesus, before the early church took Him over. It's probably impossible, but I'm having a try.'

Andrew could agree that the Jonah had something. You could hardly guess the consequences of planning a long-distance boat trip. 'I shall look at him with renewed interest. Thanks for getting me on to him. And for putting up with my silly questions, which must make me seem like one of your most backward first-year students.'

'Not at all. Anyway, I like backward first-year students who ask silly questions, if they learn something from asking them and are friendly.'

'In which case I have one more question – how did you get into this in the first place? Why didn't you settle for a life as a C of E clergyman?'

'I started out that way in a delightful southern English parish. But I met too many comfortably off lay Christians with tedious attitudes. They said to me in effect, "I've got most of the good things life has to offer, a well-paid job, a beautiful wife" –they always talk about their wife as if her alleged beauty reflects some special credit on themselves, a sort of shiny new car in good taste – "two children away at school, a place in the country. What more do I want? Well, eternal life – that would look good on my CV. And it's not especially difficult; I only need to believe on the Lord Jesus Christ, as I understand it. Perhaps you can help me there." But I couldn't help them unless they showed more interest in the values of the Sermon on the Mount.'

'What did you say to them?'

'Once, I began reminding a particularly earnest solid citizen of the Gospel story about the young man of exceeding riches who has led a good life but feels that something is missing and wants to know what more he should do. And he was told to take all that he had, give it the poor, rise up and follow Jesus. The earnest chap I was talking to got all thoughtful and told me that you couldn't read the Gospels in a straightforward way like that. "When Jesus talked about a rich man, He didn't mean a rich man as we understand it; He meant a *very* rich man – much richer than you or I can conceive of these days." I was disgusted by this; as if it matters whether the man was rich or very rich or inconceivably rich.'

'Sounds as if you were in the wrong sort of parish.'

'I suppose I was. I should have gone to an industrial parish in the north, but I don't think I should have made good there; I doubt I should have been accepted by the parishioners.'

Andrew was amused. 'So you went off sorrowfully like the young man in the Bible and took a job at Hereford College, Oxford.'

'Something like that.' The chaplain took this in good part. He continued, 'Will you come with me to my room? I want to show you a picture. We can take our coffee there.'

Andrew followed him to his room. He noted a mass of old books, many of them open, in disordered piles on a centrally placed desk. But the most striking object was a sizeable print on the wall showing Jesus with a collection of children. It was a type of religious painting that Andrew had often noticed through the window hanging in religious shops and in the study of a clergyman who had been a near neighbour. It was not, on the face of it, a sophisticated painting.

The chaplain noticed Andrew's interest. 'What do you think of it?'

'If nothing else, the artist was open-minded. You see a child of every imaginable shape, size, and colour.'

'Exactly. Even a mentally retarded child, if you look where I'm pointing. This picture is for me the quintessence of Jesus's message. I can't express it better.'

On the wall to the left of the big painting were additional, smaller ones. Andrew could make out Abraham about to sacrifice Isaac, with God looking on, and then Jonah and the great fish and then another prophet whom Andrew couldn't recognize. 'What you're investigating is how Jewish thought, represented in the picture on the left, could grow into what is represented in the big picture on the right.'

'That's right.'

'You need a space on the wall for the missing pictures, when you've found them, or got someone to draw them.'

'I shall move the Jesus picture towards the right.'

They drank their coffee and talked of more frivolous topics. But Andrew was conscious of the continued presence of the big picture on the wall.

* * *

The next day, Andrew was again in the chaplain's room for coffee and returned to the subject of the chaplain's unorthodoxy. Wasn't he exceptional among his fellow clergymen in his scepticism over what were surely the fundamentals of Christian faith?

'How about Jesus as the Son of God?' asked Andrew. 'Don't you have to believe in that, if you're the chaplain?'

'I don't think so,' said the chaplain, 'even if C. S. Lewis did. He was tired of people like me who think that Jesus Himself never claimed to be divine. He said you had to choose – either Jesus was the Son of God, or He was mad. He apparently meant that, if someone tells you to love your neighbour as yourself, he's either God or bonkers. Interestingly enough, I've met C. S.

Lewis's neighbours, a married couple. The wife planted out a mass of bulbs in the garden one spring – hours of work. C. S. Lewis's dog crawled through a hole in the fence and uprooted them all in twenty minutes. She replanted with fresh bulbs, a mass of work, and the same thing happened again. So the couple called on C. S. Lewis to discuss what should be done. He went all theological. "Dogs before flowers." Dogs must be allowed to have their fun. His neighbours weren't too pleased.'

A knock on the door interrupted the chaplain, and Hugh walked in.

Mark greeted him briefly. 'Good you turned up, Hugh. I was meaning to point out, *Columbo*'s on television tomorrow evening. It clashes with college dinner. What do you say if the three of us skip dinner in college, buy hamburgers and chips, and sit and watch *Columbo* in my room? I expect you like him too, don't you, Andrew? It's only an hour and a half. I *love Columbo*. I sometimes dream I have an authentic *Columbo* raincoat.'

'Mark has to outdo Clemmie's Kojak hat. Clemmie thinks headgear is important for enhancing an aura of leadership,' explained Hugh. 'Mark dreams of owning a *Columbo* raincoat and then wakes up and remembers he already does. And a crummy *Columbo* car, too, all messed up, like the raincoat.'

'Not really a *Columbo* car. There's a world of difference between an old Peugeot and a Hyundai. Actually, we could invite Clemmie to join us over hamburgers, to show there's no ill will. Surprisingly, he's also a *Columbo* fan. He admires Columbo's professionalism. It should be said in Clemmie's favour that he realizes the raincoat and car are aimed at inducing the suspects to feel superior and drop their guard.'

* * *

Clement Hargreaves was pleased to accept the *Columbo* invitation. The college kitchen was warned that, the following day, they'd be serving four fewer high-table diners. And the next evening found the four absentees duly squashed up in front of the television set in the chaplain's room. They were quietly preoccupied with their hamburgers and the adventures of Lieutenant Columbo, the most brilliant detective in the history of the Los Angeles police force.

In a brief pause in the story, the chaplain remarked, 'I must say,

Clemmie, you're eating up your hamburger without fuss, in a thoroughly creditable fashion.'

'I have to admit to a weakness for unhealthy food, and besides, I am completely absorbed in Lieutenant Columbo's *wonderful* performance and penetrating analysis.'

'Which is unhealthier, hamburgers and chips and Zingo, or college food with all that alcohol?' wondered Andrew. 'The number of calories must be much the same.'

* * *

Clement Hargreave's good humour continued the next day. Andrew was sitting opposite the chaplain and next to Clement Hargreaves at dinner. Clemmie was more politically interested than most of the fellows and liked to make comments on the news and current topics.

'How are we to interpret all this talk of climate change? I thought the greenhouse effect was supposed to make things warmer, but now the scientists are saying that the greenhouse effect can change the gulf stream so that it no longer warms us up and our winter climate will become positively Canadian.'

Andrew and Hugh both agreed that that they had heard something similar.

'That's the thing about the greenhouse effect,' said Mark. 'Anything can happen. It can get warmer. Or it can get colder. Or more variable. Or, most insidiously of all, it can remain much the same. In fact, whatever the weather is in fifteen years' time, I shall say, I told you so.'

It was difficult to proceed after that. Clemmie took up a new subject. Recently a leading EU politician had been praising the medieval Roman Catholic Church; he had been particularly lyrical about the unity of Europe under the universal language of Latin. Clemmie, with high church tendencies, related this with respect. Andrew remained silent, intrigued as to how Mark would react.

'To praise the medieval Catholic Church is political illiteracy,' stated Mark.

'Don't you admire the magnificent cathedrals?'

'Any old dictatorship can put up striking buildings. Even Hitler's constructions would have been impressive enough.'

'At the very least, it must have been a relief for a mass of people to have the authority of the Church opposing their despotic medieval rulers. And isn't it a boon to have order in our lives?'

'Mark would never admit that; you need only look at his desk,' put in Hugh, from his place opposite Mark. 'But actually, Mark rather fancies himself as Pope. Deep down, he knows he's infallible, about everything, not least climate change, but he would like official recognition of that fact.'

'Has there ever been a pope who chose Mark as his official name?' wondered Andrew.

'Only once, and for less than a year, in 326,' said Mark. 'Pity, really. St Mark is my favourite evangelist. He has a cheeky sense of humour.'

'Examples?' asked Hugh.

'There was the woman who had the blood disease for twelve years. St Mark says that she suffered many things of many physicians and had spent all that she had but was nothing bettered and, rather, grew worse. St Mark makes her grow worse as a result of seeing doctors. Shows a sense of humour,' enlarged Mark Noland.

'Cheeky, anyway,' said Hugh.

'Oddly enough,' continued the chaplain, 'that passage helps explain why St Luke is supposed to be a doctor. St Luke is an educated man. He knows Greek. So he has to be a priest, a doctor, or a lawyer. He's too unorthodox to be a priest. He makes Jesus say, "Woe unto you, lawyers!" so he can't be a lawyer. What about doctor? St Luke bases his account of the woman with the blood disease on St Mark's but removes the bit about her getting worse instead of better after seeing doctors. So he must have been a doctor.'

'That's very interesting, Mark,' said Clemmie. 'Now I shall go off and see the Olympics on television. How about the rest of us? I was watching the hurdling yesterday. Marvellous how skilfully they do it – a truly aesthetic experience. Incidentally, something Britain does well.'

'Talking of aesthetic experiences, is wrestling in mud included in the Olympic Games these days?' asked Mark. 'Sport is almost innocent amusement when you see two attractive young ladies wrestling in mud together – particularly if it's healthy, organic mud.'

'Mark's having his fun, Clemmie,' said Hugh. 'Take no notice.'

But the school prefect in Clement Hargreaves was irritated. 'Mark, I realize you're pulling my leg, but you must understand that there are certain things about which one does not joke. The United Nations is one example; the Olympic Games is another. Even the most wildly unorthodox priest can surely grasp that some things are sacred.' He walked out stiffly.

Chapter 10

At another college meeting, near the end of the long summer vacation, the head of college was saying, 'Hiram Stambrooke's widow, Mary, is in England on business and wants to look in.' Hiram Stambrooke had been an important donor to the college.

'Is she that awful woman from a small town in the Midwest called something like Moose Droppings?' asked one of the fellows.

'Wasn't it Texas?' suggested another fellow. 'I never understood how Hiram could put up with her, even when I was bending over backwards to be charitable.'

'I trust you didn't overdo it and fall over in an untidy heap?' asked somebody.

Before this could be answered, the rector commented, 'I had some difficulty in understanding their relationship myself, but actually, when you get to know her, she's not a bad sort. That's good, because we have to humour her in view of Hiram's donations to the college. One of us needs to take care of her while she's here – sit next to her at dinner, take her on a walk round Oxford, that sort of thing. It's next week.'

The five fellows present all claimed that they were unavailable the next week. Clement Hargreaves declared, in his authoritative manner, 'I propose we follow the usual procedure and delegate it to someone who hasn't attended the meeting. I suggest Andrew Carter. In fact he's perfectly suitable – he's talkative with someone he can feel on level terms with socially.'

So Andrew was landed with Mary Stambrooke. He had thought he wasn't a permanent enough member of the college to attend all the meetings.

*　*　*

Mary Stambrooke arrived by train in the morning a week later, and Andrew met her at the station. She was on the tall side and stylishly dressed, with colours chosen to fit her light brown hair and blue eyes. She gave an impression of relaxed self-confidence; she would easily hold a school class. She shook hands warmly and thanked Andrew for meeting her. The words were accompanied by a hug. Andrew interpreted this as American demonstrativeness, which he found congenial. He took her and her modest belongings to her rooms at college in his car, arranged to meet her for lunch, and left her to unpack and rest.

They had a light lunch in college. Mary was easy to talk to. She had kept up a career in the management of small businesses – restaurants, clothes shops and the like – despite her marriage to a rich industrialist.

'Are you going to show me around the colleges? It's been a while since the last time.'

'It's such an attractive day. I thought we could begin by a walk I'm fond of near the river. It's partly through a less prosperous area of Oxford, where we can see the buildings. You get a different, less conventional impression of the place than the usual one. I think you'll like it.'

They wandered off, along the river, by the gasworks, alongside a region of small houses and narrow streets, almost like a city in the industrial north. Then a heart-warming view of the Oxford skyline opened up. Mary had shown a lively interest in the scenery all the time; now she was as openly enthusiastic as Andrew.

Mary's pleasant drawl – she was indeed from somewhere in Texas – reminded Andrew of another striking city vision. He related how he had been on a plane bound for New York at the end of January, for a three month stay for work. After six hours in the air, the passengers were told the plane couldn't land in New York. A freak snowstorm had left a deep pile of snow. The plane was diverted to Georgia, in the Deep South.

The airline paid for taxis to take Andrew and the other passengers to a smart hotel in the centre of the city, where they could stay for one night without charge. The sight of the skyscrapers in the centre of town, silhouetted in the darkness by rows of tiny lights, had entranced Andrew. He felt he had entered a magical kingdom in a modern fairy tale. Together with the friendliness of the American people, the Atlanta skyline warmed the rest of Andrew's three-month work trip on that side of the Atlantic. It was a marvellous time, not least because it was unexpected, after years of exposure to what Andrew now regarded as the chronic adolescent anti-Americanism of the European press. Why didn't journalists explain that America more than made up in imaginative modern architecture, for any lack of historical buildings? And how else had the newspapers been misleading him?

Mary had been genuinely glad to see the Oxford skyline but was now restless. 'C'mon, Andrew; let's go shopping.' They were nearly back in the high street region.

Andrew was only a moderate enthusiast for shopping but was intrigued to watch Mary cast a professional eye over the wares on display and hear her judgments. She began with clothes shops. The assistant in the first place was a young woman, not talkative. They went out quickly. In the next shop, Mary enquired about belts. The saleswoman, in her early forties, showed a few belts and added, 'The stock is depleted at present; we'll be getting more belts next week. Would you like to see the handbags? We've just obtained some from Belgium, and the customers are most appreciative.'

Mary perked up at the prospect, and chatted contentedly for the next ten minutes. 'I like this – like how she shows me all her stock; it's the American way. Much better than in the first place.'

Finally, they got on to dresses. Mary was interested in buying dresses to sell in America, and she began to negotiate prices. Andrew could understand that she did this highly professionally. He was curious how Mary decided what was suitable to buy.

'You have to guess what your public wants. It's not easy to do, and I can't explain how I do it. But I discovered late in life that I have that faculty.'

For the rest of the afternoon, Andrew was off duty while he watched Mary at her work, with a pause for refreshment at a teashop. Finally, he thought he ought to show Mary some of the colleges and took her into two of the gardens that he liked walking round, first at New College and then at Hereford College itself. There they saw a very young-looking undergraduate, probably a freshman, walk across the lawn. A middle-aged man in green overalls, emerging from the bushes, met up with him as he stepped onto the path.

'The next time you walk across this lawn, I'll shoot you,' said the man, his mild manner contrasting with his words.

The undergraduate apologized. 'Won't do it again; I was in a hurry,' he said, and ran off.

Andrew presented the man in overalls. 'This is Tom, our gardener,' said Andrew. 'He's very expert, everyone says.' He introduced Tom to Mary.

'My, the lawn's looking smart. How d' you fix it?' Mary asked Tom.

'Nothing special – mow, roll, water, mow, roll, water, and carry on like that for three hundred years. Those are the basics. Give it love. Then we add some subtle tricks of the trade, like shooting anything that runs across. See you around.'

* * *

Mary Stambrooke was seated next to Andrew at dinner in college that evening. She took in the chandelier surroundings with appreciation and relapsed into thought. 'You're not married, Andrew?' she asked.

'No. I used to be, but my wife died in childbirth.' Andrew often had to explain this for people, and he did so without sentimentality.

'I'm sorry. It must have been a great shock, especially since it's uncommon for women to die in childbirth these days'. Mary touched him on the shoulder. 'Was it a good marriage, if you don't mind my asking?'

He wasn't used to such a direct question. He remembered an occasion when Antonia and he were going out to a party together. He had changed into a suit and presented himself for Antonia's approval. 'Andrew! That shirt, the collar's worn. It's too late to do anything about it now. S'ppose you didn't notice, as usual. You're *hopeless* about clothes.' Her voice softened. 'But it doesn't matter. I love you even so, somehow.'

He said to Mary, 'It was just an ordinary, down-to-earth sort of marriage. But we were fond of each other.'

'Sounds like it was a good marriage. I was head over heels for Hiram to begin with, and quite fond of him all the time later. But he could be such a pain in the ass.'

'Did I hear you mention Hiram?' enquired a fellow sitting nearby. 'He was a very good chap.'

'Mary was saying that he was a bit difficult at times,' remarked Andrew.

'I didn't say *a bit difficult*; I said a goddamn pain in the ass,' corrected Mary, going over to a more pronounced Texas drawl.

A momentary silence was interrupted by a loud popping noise when the old college retainer, unnerved, had removed the cork too abruptly.

'But I also said I was fond of him,' continued Mary, reverting to her normal voice.

Andrew couldn't resist adding, '*Quite* fond of him, at any rate,' and wondered, again, if he had been drinking too much.

Mary said loudly, 'You know, when I first saw Andrew, I thought, they've fitted me up with Mr Chips – the old fuddy-duddy if lovable schoolmaster in *Goodbye Mr Chips*. It's going to be deadly. After a while, when he started showing me round Oxford, I did a complete hundred and eighty. He gave me a really good time. Perhaps he was humanized by his wife, like Mr Chips. I shouldn't have said that, and I'm really sad Mrs Carter died in childbirth – like Mrs Chips in the book, strangely enough, and that was really sad, too. Anyway, I want to say that, because of Andrew, I'm increasing the donation to the college by a million bucks.'

Her short speech engendered a startled silence. The rector was smiling broadly. 'I think this calls for celebration. We have a special port we keep for such occasions. Do you like port, Mary?'

'Not much, but let's take a gander at it.'

High spirits prevailed for the next hour. Late in the evening, Andrew suggested that Mary and he should take a short walk down High Street. They encountered various groups of young people from abroad, whom Andrew presumed were on language courses.

'Are you envious of young people?' enquired Mary.

'Not really; I thought it was difficult being young.' Then apropos of nothing in particular, he said, 'The rector thinks that the college should have more women fellows.'

'Yes, I know.'

This surprised Andrew. 'How did you know?'

Mary said calmly, 'The contract for the donation wasn't signed at the time Hiram died, and I had to sign it in his place. I made it a condition that

15 per cent of the fellows should be women by 2010. Do you think it's a good idea?'

'Yes; if nothing else, the women will liven up the furnishing of the Senior Common Room. At the moment, it has that last outpost of empire look, like most men's clubs.'

'You're not really one of them, the other fellows, are you?'

Andrew was uncertain how well he fitted in. 'Most of them are cleverer than I am and seem to know more. Collectively, they can be difficult; they can go completely bonkers. If you get them on their own, though, they're all right, in fact thoroughly likeable.'

'I'm inclined to agree,' said Mary. 'The rector can be a real charmer, a dear old...confirmed bachelor. And even the guy who's all hat and no cattle, as we'd say back home, is dandy in his way.'

'You mean Clemmie.' Andrew liked Mary's description. 'I suppose you've seen his velour fedora. Mind you, people expect Clemmie to acquire his cattle in due course.'

They walked on in silence for a while. Then Andrew asked, 'What are you doing after your visit to Oxford?'

'I'm going to Vietnam on business. I shall be concerned with some clothes shops there.'

'Extraordinary thing. I'm going there myself.' Andrew explained how he was helping in the design of some medical tests.

They discovered they were both going to be in Hanoi at the same time a few weeks before Christmas and arranged to meet each other there.

Back in college, a few of the fellows were still lingering in the common room, absorbed in languid, companionly chat over the remains of the special port. The atmosphere was relaxed and voices low meld. Then against the background murmur could be heard advancing footsteps in the corridor.

'Here comes Clemmie,' said the chaplain, in a mixture of collegial affection and resignation.

Clement Hargreaves, with the leadership qualities already noted, always wore thin-soled heavy black shoes to accompany his customary dark suit. He could be heard approaching at a distance of up to fifty yards in favourable conditions – inside the august buildings of Oxford or outside in the streets at quiet times on Sunday mornings. This, together with an impeccably upright carriage, a commanding voice, and distinctive headdress for street wear, signalled a man who was destined for important duties. He was expected any day now to announce his transference to a fast stream in the civil service.

Clemmie entered imposingly during a lull in the conversation and, noting the port still in use, put in, 'I can't resist saying that I do congratulate myself on my choice of Andrew Carter for showing Hiram's widow around, not an obvious decision.'

'What should we do without your astute judgement, Clemmie?' asked the chaplain.

The man with leadership qualities continued, 'Mind you, a million dollars with no strings attached, even if it sounds a lot, will hardly do more than pay for the wine for a couple of decades.'

The medical fellow, hearing this, remarked quietly, 'I must say, as regards securing long-term financing for the really important college matters, this is not our century.'

Clemmie did not respond to this but announced, 'I don't know about the rest of us here, but I've a busy day ahead of me tomorrow, even if it's Saturday. I shall be getting a good night's sleep. I recommend the same for you good people. You look as if you need it.' Shortly afterwards, his footsteps could be heard slowly disappearing down the corridor.

'Indeed, what would we do without people like Clemmie's wonderful gift of leadership?' wondered Hugh, leaning back with his eyes closed.

The chaplain's own mantra for improving the quality of university life, uttered in confidence to close friends and colleagues as on the present occasion, was, 'You know my views on leadership, Hugh. Reread *Parkinson's Law*; then cut the leadership by 95 per cent; cut the administration by 60 per cent; and get the professors back into research and teaching – after which, it will be confirmed that all that leadership and administration was unnecessary. It shouldn't be so difficult; the professors are always saying how they wish they had more time for their real work. That offers a measure of hope, even if admittedly they aren't usually being sincere.'

'Why are you cutting the administration by only 60 per cent, Mark?'

'Because some administrators,' explained the chaplain, 'are positively useful; for example, the ones who fix a lecture room at short notice, when you've forgotten to do it yourself. It's the ones who have *visions* that cause the trouble. Somebody should tell them that one or two visions are usually harmless enough and can safely be ignored, but if you are repeatedly having visions, you should see a doctor – someone like Hugh, scraping the barrel a bit.'

'While I think of it,' intervened the college's medieval historian, a heavily built man slumped in his armchair, 'what did you think of that team-building course the bursar arranged for us, after Clemmie prodded him? I never got round to asking you. Tell us briefly.'

'One word will do. It was hell,' said the chaplain. 'What did you think of it?'

'I endured it through positive thinking, as recommended on this sort of course. I try to see the potential of the situation, rather than dwelling on the problems.'

'Same here; I do my best to concentrate firmly on the potentials of each situation but, in the process, mainly see potential for problems. Sadly, that doesn't seem to count.'

'Anyway, when we did the exercise in which we were bound to our partner round the legs and blindfolded and then told we must cooperate as a team by jumping up and down together on the wiggly platform so as to press two high-up buttons simultaneously, after which, in the best case, the platform would blessedly stop wiggling and a hidden cassette radio begin to play "Thank You for the Music," I was naturally reminded of torture under the inquisition. But I bolstered myself up with positive thinking; I felt that our chaplain, obliged to debase himself over this ridiculous exercise, might attain some level of Christian humility. Also, if I shall be charitable, Clemmie was loving every minute of it. He was shouting excitedly, "Come on, pair three! Don't give up now! One more heave! Both together now, jump!" and I was pleased for his sake. Needless to say, we were supposed to compete with the other couples, to see which team was the fastest.'

'I hear Clemmie's telling the bursar he should order our very own wiggly platform to install in the garden, for the benefit of the undergraduates' team-building proclivities,' said the chaplain. 'God help them!'

'What I don't understand,' put in one of the younger fellows, 'is why you didn't both blankly refuse to go on the course, like Tom, the gardener. By the way, where are Andrew and Mary?'

'They're out for a walk to see Oxford after dark.'

'Hmm …' the historian murmured, sinking contentedly back in his chair. 'That's a subject for positive thinking, Andrew and Mary walking together amidst the happy giggling youngsters from the language courses, pausing from time to time to gaze in wonder at the ancient stonework of the Bodleian and St Mary's all lit up and shining in the floodlights. Best to focus on that delightful scene. Makes me sentimental—whereas thinking about team-building makes me violent. Fond as I am of Clemmie, at least up to a point, I do hope when, in the near future, he moves on to higher things and shapes the nation's destiny from the treasury, he takes all his leadership away with him. He mustn't leave any behind. The bursar is so susceptible to unhealthy influence.'

(In later years, when an outsider enquired about his feelings for Oxford, Clement Hargreaves would explain that Hereford College was inured to a long slow downward slide, like Britain in the 1960s and 1970s. 'It needs a Mrs Thatcher, not Margaret herself, of course, but someone with her determination, to reverse the decline.' If the outsider wondered if Clemmie himself was such a person, he would regret that he had proved unequal to the task. He was more hopeful of advancing Britain as a whole from a senior position in the civil service than of influencing the dons at Hereford College.)

Chapter 11

From October till December was term-time, and Andrew's teaching obligations were unclear. He was officially attached to Hereford College, rather than to a department. It would have been natural for Andrew to give tutorials for at least one or two of the undergraduates reading maths, since these were organized by the colleges. Each tutorial was an hour's individual teaching and was crazily extravagant – an Oxford tradition that most of the undergraduates appreciated. But Hereford already had a maths fellow, a married man who showed little interest in college affairs, rarely appeared at dinners, regarded his undergraduates as personal property, and was generally difficult. Nobody expected Andrew to take over any of this man's tutorial pupils.

Then a lecturer from the recently reorganized Department of Statistics contacted Andrew. 'Hate to ask you this, but can you organize an optional course in introductory statistics this term, Friday mornings, for about fifteen to twenty undergraduates reading agriculture or forestry? They're most of them hopeless with figures, but after a while they get to see the point of simple tests of statistical significance, what control groups are, etcetera. Our chap who has had the course up to now said enough was enough; teaching biologists was beneath his dignity. He thought you might be a way out. He says that, as you were at Stephenson Tech for many years, you must be used to that kind of student. By the way, if you're going to take in genetical studies, your speciality, you'll need to explain the most basic principles, as most of them have forgotten anything they ever knew about genetics. Do say yes, you'll take the course; it will help a lot.' He seemed harassed.

The prospect would be like a repeat of where Andrew had come in more than thirty years earlier, but figure-shy biologists instead of chemists.

Andrew didn't like to refuse. He had become used to lecturing to much larger classes in London and thought a small class would make a pleasant change. The schedule was hardly daunting; he would have a week to prepare each lecture and the problem-solving class that followed.

The following Friday, he met the class for the first time. It consisted of twelve women and eight men, and despite the original information, six of them were master's degree students from abroad, rather than undergraduates. The women arrived in good time for Andrew's nine o'clock lecture; the men dribbled in later. Like old times, though, the late arrivals from overseas were apologetic. But there was one big change from old times; nowadays you had to suck up to your students, so that they gave you a good report. You didn't say, for example, 'This topic is tough, but you'll have to learn it if you want to pass.' You said, 'I know this is tricky; everybody thinks so. Am I explaining it clearly enough? If it is altogether too difficult, we shall consider leaving it out of the course next year.'

In Andrew's undergraduate days in the 1960s, it was unheard of even to allow, let alone encourage, undergraduate assessments of courses. Shortly afterwards, though, an undergraduate newspaper provoked outrage by printing an anonymous opinion of individual lecturers' performances.

Andrew outlined the topics the class would be studying. He had better make genetics sound relevant to ordinary life; and he should involve the class by putting questions to them. He had decided to ask in this introductory first lecture, 'Why do you think the Catholic Church forbids cousin marriage?'

The young men at the back giggled to each other; the women looked serious. One of them said, 'Isn't it because there's often something wrong with the children when the parents are cousins? They're half dotty, or infertile.'

'Why should that be?' Andrew asked her.

The discussion turned to inbreeding, depression, and deleterious recessives.

'But can societies become accustomed to cousin marriage, without obvious ill effects?' Andrew asked the class.

The question was met with more giggles from the back of the class, and serious but blank expressions from the girls in the front. Then the same girl as before mentioned the Mennonites, and Andrew talked briefly about tiny isolated religious minorities before moving on to the Indian caste system. (No problem here; no Indians in the class.) He finished off by mentioning that Kurds often married their first cousins.

He looked to see how the class was reacting. His eye fell on a small dark girl sitting by herself in the very first row. She had come in at the last moment before the start of the lecture when the preferred second row of chairs was already filled. She was left-handed, and Andrew had noticed her taking notes, writing slanted across unlined paper in green ink. A bothersome thought occurred to Andrew.

'Are you Kurdish?'

She smiled. 'Yes I am. I used to live in Iraq.'

Why did he allow this sort of thing to happen to him? It was as clumsy as taking up the inheritance of eye colour; notoriously, one of the students would have received the wrong eye colour from his supposed parents, and you would have to explain that the genetics was more complicated than was usually presented.

He'd redeem the situation the best he could. 'Isn't it true that Kurds often marry their first cousins?' he asked her.

'Oh yes. Actually I'm going to marry *my* cousin next summer, and my sister is marrying his younger brother on the same day.'

There was a stir of interest in the class. Andrew returned to more strictly statistical matters.

After the class, the girl who had mentioned the Mennonites lingered and talked while Andrew took care of the computer he used for the presentation. She was one of the master's students, Miranda, from Germany. Andrew asked about her project.

'Experiments with barley that will need a lot of statistics I shall have to learn about even if the computer does most of it. What's your research on?'

'Among other things, assessment of drug tests, how to get an overall impression of a drug's effectiveness when the results of different tests differ and you have to take side effects into account. Is the new drug really better than the one it's supposed to be replacing?'

'How far can you trust drug tests? I've heard that some of the doctors who carry out the tests get paid by the drug firms not to report unfavourable results.'

'That may happen occasionally.' Andrew was reluctant to appear cynical, especially in front of the young; but to completely deny the existence of murky areas was to collaborate with the wrong people.

It was best to get Miranda back on barley, which he succeeded in doing.

* * *

Two weeks later, at the beginning of November Andrew received a telephone call from Sir Oliver Laine.

'Only a month to go before you set off for Hanoi. I expect you're busy preparing for it.'

'I've been reading about the various projects, yes, and finding out if I need any inoculations for the trip, or a visa. Doesn't seem to be problematic.'

'Good, that's the right attitude. While you're at it, you might read about our new antidepressant, the latest from A to Z Pharmaceuticals.'

'What's it called?' asked Andrew.

'For the moment, it's only got a hard-to-remember number. More informally, we call it Feelgood-Two. Between you and me, the clinical trials have been mixed. Sometimes the experimental group of patients responds no better than the control group. But both groups always feel better after taking the pills, even the blank ones. Actually, our man at A to Z has given them a subtle, satisfying sort of flavour the patients like – particularly important with psychiatric medicine, where the placebo effect is crucial. One should push the drug hard at the start, while the placebo effect still works, and not make a fuss about the trials that don't give really positive results. Often one can't tell if those trials have been properly carried out.'

This was miles from Andrew's professional opinion, and he was wondering how to reply, when Sir Oliver continued, 'Feelgood-Two is based on old herbal remedies from the South Pacific; it's undoubtedly safe and didn't require years of research, it can be manufactured very cheaply, and it should be ideal for a country like Vietnam. You might mention it to the good folks at the medical centre in Hanoi when you're there, as soon as it's available under a proper name. I'll be emailing the info.'

Sir Oliver rang off.

* * *

Andrew's Friday lectures continued. He was taking examples from the evolution of crop plants to illustrate effects of genetic selection. As a diversion from the more mathematical side, and with so many women in the class, he talked about the role of women in the evolution of crop plants.

'Take maize as an example, a cross-pollinated, genetically highly variable species. The early farmers planted their fields with a wide assortment of seed. In primitive farming communities, it's the womenfolk who have the sense to save some of the seed over the winter so that there's something to plant next spring. The most productive individual plants contributed the most seed, so there would be repeated selection for plants carrying genes for high yield. This would happen even if unintentional. It can be called unconscious selection. It changed cultivated maize so completely that it is hard to know what the original maize plants looked like. The women created high-yielding varieties that are the basis of settled agriculture and, you can say, of the whole of civilization.'

He thought the girls would be pleased.

After a thoughtful pause, Miranda said, 'Can't you give women credit for *anything* unless they do it unconsciously?'

Andrew felt this was comically unfair. 'I gave women credit for thinking about the future, saving some of the seed instead of living only for the day. "Unconscious selection" is Darwin's term, I could have mentioned.'

He returned to statistics and finished the hour's lecture – after which there was a ten-minute pause, and then a problem class, organized as 'cross-group discussions'. The students sat in four separate groups of four to six, at different areas of the lecture room and in the adjoining corridor, and discussed among themselves how to solve the problems that Andrew had selected from the coursebook. Andrew himself moved among the groups to answer questions. The idea was that, at the end of the first fifty minutes, the students should regroup in new combinations, the cross groups, for another period of about fifty minutes. When he was a lecturer in London, a colleague had warmly recommended Andrew to try cross-group discussions, and they almost always worked well.

Andrew left the students to build groups as they wanted for the first period, and this went readily enough, the four young men who were inclined to giggle together immediately forming a group in the far corner of the lecture room. The master's students from abroad introduced themselves to the undergraduates, built the remaining groups, and happily discussed the problems together. Even the giggly group in the corner made some pretence of dealing with the problems, at least when Andrew walked over to them.

Fifty minutes later, it was time to rebuild the groups in new combinations. No problem, except with the giggly group who remained in their corner, peering sheepishly at the others.

Miranda, who was sitting in a group of four women, took the initiative. 'Bo-y-s', she cooed across the room, 'would one of you like to come and *play* with us?'

One of them walked over almost at once to Miranda's group, another joined another group, and master's students joined the remaining two boys. Apparently, cross-group discussions could work in Oxford, too.

* * *

In early December, with his teaching duties in England completed, Andrew set out on the long journey to Hanoi, which required three flights. His first plane took him to Frankfurt, where he had to wait for some hours for the next plane, bound for Thailand. He was happy to sit and read in the airport lounge, first a newspaper, later a novel. When lunchtime came, he found a Chinese place within the airport that had an informal buffet and a limited number of tables. A young Chinese woman asked if she could sit opposite him, to which he had no objection. They were soon chatting. She was studying in Britain and spoke adequate English. She was on her way back for a brief holiday to stay with her parents in China. Andrew was curious as to where in China she came from. It was a city well to the north of Beijing, not far from the Russian border and with a Siberian climate.

'Where are you going?' asked the girl.

'To Hanoi, in Vietnam.'

'Is Vietnam the name of a country? Where's that?' She had never heard of it, to Andrew's surprise.

He tried to explain where it was in relation to China; the two countries had a common border. The girl now seemed to recollect having heard of Vietnam.

'It's a small poor country in the south, isn't it?' Vietnam was apparently too far away from her part of China to have made any impression.

Andrew's impending journey to a faraway country, of which many people knew little, began to acquire an aura of romance. In the few years of their marriage, he and Antonia had liked travelling around Europe for short holidays. For Antonia, it was best with skimpily planned, impulsive trips with un-luxurious accommodation. Since losing his companion, Andrew had felt that much of the charm of travel had vanished. Some of it was returning in conversation with the Chinese girl.

* * *

Andrew arrived at the airport in Hanoi around breakfast time. He had not slept well on the plane. Two young Vietnamese women met him at the airport. One of them was from the department where the research was being carried out. The other was some years younger, an attractive slightly built girl of perhaps twenty. With them was a tall handsome European, an elderly Swede, whom Andrew took to be a diplomat of some kind without enquiring further.

A taxi took them into Hanoi along a busy main road through the countryside. Andrew, unshaven and bleary-eyed, nevertheless gazed fascinated at the tropical landscape, which included stately houses of exotic appearance built beside paddy fields. The road was busy with diverse traffic, not least masses of small motorbikes – often a young man driving, a young woman hanging on behind, and a child wedged between them. The taxi driver was constantly avoiding collisions by manoeuvring past them and, above all, hooting.

At the same time, the young Vietnamese girl was asking, in a good English accent, 'What customs do you follow at Christmas?'

The Swede gave a fluent and astonishingly detailed account of the intricacies of Swedish Christmas celebrations, delivered in a relaxed, pleasant voice with just a hint of the patronage of the elderly towards the young. He explained that they wrote some verse on the wrapping paper of each present, providing a clue as to what the present was. It should rhyme and be as long as possible, and the recipient should guess what it was before unwrapping.

'I must say, Christmas in Sweden sounds demanding,' commented Andrew.

'Not at all; all Swedes love every minute of Christmas enormously. If all else fails, we have Donald Duck on the television. I always watch it every year, after two glasses of *brännvin*, Swedish vodka, lovely and strong and spicy.'

This appealed to the young woman. Andrew wondered what her job was or why she was there. It emerged that, while the older of the two young women was an administrator at the medical department, the younger was her sister who was studying tourism, improving her English, and hoping to spend a year training in England. This was her opportunity to talk to native, or at least non-Vietnamese, English speakers.

'What is ripe?' she unexpectedly asked.

This came so out of the blue as to nonplus the elderly Swede, who didn't understand what she was talking about and was reduced to silence.

Andrew did his best to explain. '*Ripe* is often used of fruit; for example, one talks of an apple becoming ripe when it loses its sourness and begins to taste sweet. Or one can use the word metaphorically—'

'Metaphorically?'

Oh Gawd, thought Andrew. 'Metaphorically means…sort of loosely…imaginatively. One might say, "Vietnam is ripe for rapid technological change and economic advance."'

The elderly Swede was catching on. 'Or it can be used of people – a young woman ripe for love and marriage, if you don't think that's sexist.'

The girls giggled.

'Or a young woman ripe for university studies,' said Andrew and wondered, not for the first time, why he was making himself ridiculous.

They arrived at the hotel where Andrew was initially staying. He was thankful to have a long sleep in his room.

* * *

He woke in the early afternoon, dressed, and went out to find some lunch. It was warm, like a fine if humid summer's day in England, with the air heavily scented. He set off towards the street corner where the hotel girl had told him of a cash machine that would take his Visa card. Most of the way, the pavement was occupied with parked mopeds and motorbikes, so he was often walking in the gutter. At the street corner, he was hailed by men offering motorbike rides to wherever he wanted – Hanoi's main equivalent of taxi drivers. He turned them down. He was able to take out his Vietnamese money, after some puzzling and anxious moments at the machine.

From a map he had obtained at the hotel, he had picked out Hoan Kiem Lake, at the heart of the old city, as a place to make for. This confronted him with the need to cross a main street. He found a crossing for pedestrians, but the endless stream of motorbikes and cars in each direction had no intention of stopping for him. He waited, nevertheless, for a brief let-up in the flow.

A young Australian couple noticed him, and the girl explained, 'It's no good waiting. You must step out – the bikes will swerve round you. But don't stop walking, 'cos then it's dangerous. Come with us. We'll show you.' She hooked one arm round Andrew's waist and one arm round her boyfriend.

Andrew nerved himself to step out with them and discovered that the bikes were not going as fast as he had thought and indeed manoeuvred round them. But if the girl hadn't hung on to him, it would have been a test of his resolution not to stop in the middle.

'You'll get used to it soon enough,' said the boy when they reached the pavement, and Andrew thanked them.

'I was scared stiff at first, and he was too, 'cept he'd never admit it,' said the girl. 'Where are you off to? Like to tag along with us?'

'I was going to find somewhere for lunch and look round the lake,' said Andrew. 'I've only just come, and I'm still rather tired after the journey.'

'We had lunch down there; they're some nice places and not so expensive,' the girl said, indicating a side street. 'We're off to meet some friends. Might see you again, you never know.'

The young Australians left him to continue on his own. Two or three streets later, he was exhausted but had caught a glimpse of the lake. He decided to explore it after lunch. He entered a smallish restaurant, unpretentious but at least with wooden tables and upright chairs on the floor inside, rather than low plastic tables and stools directly on the pavement outside.

From the menu in English, he chose sweet and sour prawns; rice; and, after some consideration, a serving of spinach, which he often liked and was curious as to how it would taste Vietnamese-style. Inexperience with chopsticks made for an extended, preoccupied meal, and yes, the spinach was very fresh and tasty.

He crossed over a final broad busy street and was at the lakeside, in a sort of park. He began walking round the lake, which was pleasant enough. From his guidebook, he knew he was in the administrative area, with tree-lined boulevards and twentieth-century buildings from the French era. Several obvious tourists, young and of European appearance and carrying backpacks, were passing by, as well as Vietnamese people. After twenty minutes when he was halfway round the lake, he sat down on a bench, making him an easy target.

A couple of school-age Vietnamese children selling postcards accosted him, and after a short debate with himself, he bought some. The price was undoubtedly high, and he hadn't intended to write so many postcards. He would certainly send one to Toby and one to Janet and family and one to Hugh and Mark at Hereford, and perhaps the remaining ones would be mementos of Hanoi. Anyway, these were presumably children from a poor family, whom it was reasonable for a visitor from a rich country to assist. The money would go on necessities rather than drink or drugs.

He moved on and came to an open market. He was sufficiently curious to continue in and look around at what was being sold. As he gazed at an assortment of exotic fruits, he felt a tug on his elbow.

'Buy a T-shirt?' It was a Vietnamese girl, perhaps twelve years old, or a year or two more; it was hard to tell.

'No, thank you.'

Another tug on his elbow. 'I must sell something; I haven't sold anything all day. Take a proper look at this T-shirt. It's great.'

He reluctantly examined the T-shirts, which in any case he never wore. How to get rid of children selling postcards and T-shirts?

She showed him a white T-shirt with a picture of the lake he had walked round, with its shrine. '100,000 dong, it costs.'

It was, no doubt, enormously overpriced, like the postcards he had bought too many of. He probably ought to try to bargain with her, but he had always hated bargaining with children, even during harmless activities like playing Monopoly. Andrew felt a deep fatigue spreading over him.

'Here's 50,000 dong, but I don't want the T-shirt; thank you.'

The girl gazed fiercely at him. 'Do you think I'm a *beggar?*'

This was said with such outrage that he looked at her more closely; she had long black hair, which was what he noticed first, and a sensitive face and was slightly built by prosperous Western standards, but she clearly had a big personality. She was carefully dressed in a lightly coloured top and dark skirt – not like a street urchin.

He said resignedly, 'Oh, I suppose it's a good picture, and I can probably give the T-shirt as a present to someone, so I'll buy it and here's 100,000 dong.'

The girl brightened up strikingly; perhaps she had been genuinely desperate. 'Thank you. Now you've brought me luck for the rest of the day. Where do you want to go? I can show you the way.'

Andrew didn't really know where he wanted to go, and he didn't want to be accompanied by this girl. But he sensed that she wanted to do something, however small, in return for Andrew's absurd generosity. So he said he needed to get back towards the main street, the name of which he could just remember. She pointed the way and walked with him.

'Where do you come from?'

'From England. Or Britain or the UK, if that's what you call it.'

'What's your name?'

'Andrew.'

She repeated the name to herself, 'An-rew.'

He added, politely, 'What's yours?'

'Doan Vien.' A compound of two rather strange sounds he would find difficult to remember. She added, 'Foreigners call me Cathy, if that's easier.'

They walked on in silence. Then Cathy asked, 'Do you have any children?'

'No. My wife died in childbirth.' Andrew wondered why he was telling this to a complete stranger, a child in a remote foreign country. To change the subject, he remarked, 'I must say, you speak English well.' She had spoken fluently without noticeable accent.

'I can sell in English; I don't really know much.'

They had arrived at the main street. Andrew said goodbye and went back to the hotel.

He had arranged to meet Mary Stambrooke at her hotel, where she was on a brief visit. He arrived at the last minute, still carrying the T-shirt. Mary welcomed him warmly, and asked, 'Where did you get that T-shirt? It's not exactly your style. Is it a present for someone?'

Andrew explained about Cathy.

'If you see her again, you can tell her your friend, Mary, thinks it's good. Is your hotel okay? How much is it costing?'

Andrew told her that his accommodation was pleasant enough and not outrageously expensive, considering its position.

But Mary thought the cost per night was on the high side. 'I've got a friend who will rent out a flat, for about half that price if you stay there for the entire six months. It gets my seal of approval. I'd stay there myself, except I'm not here for sufficiently long at a time. Valerie, her name is. We can meet her. We'll have to move quickly before she finds someone else.'

'How does she come to own a flat she can hire out? Sounds like capitalism.'

'Vietnam has become more capitalist; that's why I'm here. Besides, Valerie knows the right people. I strongly suspect she's a *very* good friend of one of the housing officials. Don't ask her for details. I'll call her, if you like.'

Mary made the phone call and it was quickly arranged that the three of them would meet at Mary's shop the next day, after which they would go to look at the flat for Andrew's approval. In the meantime, later that evening, his department at the medical centre had arranged dinner for him.

* * *

'How do you like Hanoi?' the young Vietnamese scientist, Trung, was asking Andrew a while later. They were seated at the modest restaurant they'd come to for an evening meal. The department had assigned Trung to look after Andrew on his first evening in Hanoi.

Andrew's official job in Vietnam was to act as statistical adviser to medical research projects, mostly effects of drugs in animal experiments. The Swedish organization, SIDA, had initiated the programme as part of Swedish international aid, but under Sir Oliver Laine's influence, it had broadened into a combined British and Swedish undertaking, with Sweden dominating. Sir Oliver's firm contributed half of Andrew's upkeep, with a matching grant from the British taxpayer. In practice, this meant that Andrew was to advise on the design and analysis of experiments that Vietnamese research students carried out and assist the Vietnamese staff in supervising the students. Sir Oliver had, of course, dropped hints about the existence of additional, less official objectives, but Andrew, after discussion with Toby, had accepted these risks for the sake of visiting an exciting far away country.

Andrew was to be one of Trung's supervisors for his student project. Trung had enclosed Andrew's hand in both of his when they'd first met and shaken it warmly. In Vietnam, Trung explained, teachers were very special people; the relationship of student and teacher was of great importance. 'Are you getting used to the city? What do you find the most strange?'

Andrew said he'd found much that was exotic and exciting and much that he liked; he had taken easily to the food, and the people were friendly. He still had to nerve himself to cross the road, but he was slowly learning to cope with the traffic and expected to be at home with all the motorbikes in a day or two. He asked about the children selling postcards and T-shirts in the street; that was something you didn't see in England; were they helping out with the family income?

The young scientist didn't answer directly; he enhanced Andrew's impression that the better-off inhabitants of developing countries found the poorer people an embarrassment, not to be discussed with foreigners.

'You didn't buy anything from those children, did you?'

'Only some postcards and a T-shirt.'

'What did you pay for the T-shirt?'

Andrew reluctantly admitted to paying 100,000 dong.

'That's way too much. You must learn to bargain.'

Andrew had to agree that bargaining wasn't his strong side. 'As a matter of interest, where do you buy small everyday things? The hotel lady recommended a shopping mall in the street near the lake. Seemed to be mostly foreign tourists there.'

'Far too expensive. We never go there. We go to a supermarket called Intimex. I'll mark where it is on the map.'

The food, a series of dishes chosen by his host, arrived. Andrew battled with his chopsticks, slowly acquiring a degree of technique.

'When you get used to them, you'll find chopsticks relaxing.'

And indeed, Andrew soon entered into the spirit of reaching across with his chopsticks; picking up bits of fish, meat, and vegetables; and dipping them into the sauces. Dinner lasted almost an hour, after which Trung guided Andrew back to the hotel.

* * *

The next day at eight o'clock, immediately after breakfast, the driver of the departmental van, a man who spoke no English, arrived at the hotel and drove Andrew to the medical centre. Andrew spent the morning in brief introductions to various high-ups without getting any clear impression of them. He was jet-lagged, usually worse after travelling east rather than west. His hosts were sympathetic and had the driver take him back to the hotel at the end of the morning. He ate a light lunch and had a nap till the late afternoon.

He had arranged to meet Mary at her hotel, after which they would walk to the clothes shop she was helping manage. She showed him round the shop, which was called Mary's Eastern and Western Stores, and briefed him expertly on it. Then he sat outside in a plastic chair on the pavement while Mary dealt with some business matter. It was pleasantly warm. The people of Hanoi were going back home at the end of the day on their motorbikes, mopeds, and bicycles. A steady stream of young women rode with their often long hair flowing behind them.

Mary came out. 'How you doing?'

'Oh, I'm just sitting on the corner, watching all the girls go by.'

'Give it a whirl, give it a try, but it ain't much of an occupation,' commented Mary.

They chatted awhile, until Valerie arrived to take them to look at the prospective flat for Andrew. It took them about ten minutes to walk to an old house of five stories in a side street not far from the central lake. The flat was on the third floor. It consisted of a reasonably large living room, a small kitchen, a bedroom with only a double bed, and a small modernized bathroom. In the living room stood a generously sized sofa, two arm chairs with backrests, and a television set. The space was by no means luxurious but sensible and homely. He was glad to accept the offer.

Valerie was a woman in her mid-forties. A French Canadian originally, she was straightforwardly businesslike and spoke easily in English with an attractively French accent. She arranged for a taxi with which to collect Andrew's luggage, and the two women helped him move in straight away.

Chapter 12

Andrew woke early in his unfamiliar surroundings the next day and decided he was no longer jet-lagged; he'd slept enough to adapt to the moved-forward day. He thought the bedroom was pleasant, though minimally furnished; he could pin or Sellotape a picture on the wall to make it less severe – perhaps a Vietnamese print, to keep in character. In Hereford College, he had pinned up a Renoir reproduction he had seen in a Red Cross salesroom. (He had moved most of his possessions to a storeroom in London.) This thought reminded him that he was now remote from the comforts of an Oxford College. He would have to get used to not being spoilt.

He had not brought much food with him and went out in the semi-darkness to find breakfast. At a nearby street corner, he entered a small inexpensive-looking place, where a Vietnamese customer was being presented with what looked like a bowl of glass noodles with fresh vegetables.

'Could I have one of those, please?' he asked the lady behind the counter, hoping there wouldn't be a communication problem.

'Mien. That's name.' She indicated that he should sit down somewhere and wait while the mien was being prepared. Andrew succeeded in ordering a cup of coffee and took it to a little table outside on the pavement, where he could sit on a low plastic chair and watch the passers-by.

The noodles arrived and had a strong fishy flavour, identifiable as eel, in the broth. Together with the strong and spicy coffee, it made for an excellent breakfast. He returned to his flat, collected his briefcase, and walked to his former hotel, where the driver of the departmental car picked him up and took him to the medical centre. Given the driver's lack of English, Andrew could not explain about his change of address.

At the department, Trung showed him to the room that was to be his writing place. He switched on a huge air-conditioning machine with some ceremony, presumably a concession to foreigners from cool countries, as the offices for Vietnamese lacked air conditioning. The cool air would be much appreciated in the height of summer. But now in December, the temperature inside and outside the building was what Andrew was used to in an English summer, and Andrew asked Trung to switch the machine off.

Andrew set up his computer, which could be connected to the Internet, and opened his email. He wrote some replies to messages from England, and then he wondered how he would spend his work time in Hanoi. The various projects for which he was to act as statistical adviser would hardly amount to full-time activities, or so it seemed from the preceding day's discussions. He could continue with his own research.

He was interrupted by a knock at the door; one of his Vietnamese hosts came in with the same elderly Swede with whom he had travelled by taxi. His name was Lars. He wasn't a diplomat, as Andrew had supposed, but a biochemist involved in an aid programme loosely connected with Andrew's. Andrew was to share the room with him.

Andrew was embarrassed that they had not discovered they were attached to the same institute when they were riding in the taxi together. But Lars was only amused; he wasn't easily embarrassed. They were left alone and began to chat.

'The labs look very well equipped; I was surprised,' commented Andrew. 'Are things going well for the research students?'

'In many respects, yes. They spend roughly half their time in the department here and half their time in Stockholm. They get plenty done in Sweden, but it is a mystery what they are occupied with here. Obscure bureaucratic concerns, I suspect. And they're supposed to finish in four or five years, like their Swedish counterparts.'

'Do they manage that?'

'They have a generous supply of technical assistants whom they call their staff to help them here in Vietnam,' said Lars, 'but the staff are a mixed blessing in my view. My Vietnamese students would be better off if they didn't have technical assistants but were freed from bureaucratic duties so that they become practised in the lab work themselves. Later, they would be in an excellent position to train their assistants. Then I could really envy them – technical assistants have become a luxury in Sweden.'

Trung came in to tell them it was the time for the morning tea break. He took Andrew to the lunchroom, where there was an electric kettle and tea bags with the local green tea. They sat down at a long table with a group of men and women of varied age, presumably the usual departmental mixture of research students, technicians, secretaries, and lecturers, who looked at Andrew so that he felt welcome before they resumed chatting. Lars, who had lingered over his computer, joined them.

Trung said to Andrew, 'We are to have a meeting with Dr Thanh, the head of the department, in his room as soon as we've finished tea.'

'Have you got the hang of names here?' Lars asked Andrew. 'Can be confusing for newcomers. Dr Thanh's full name is Le Ho Thanh. Le is the family name, and Thanh the equivalent of our first name, but you say Dr Thanh, not Dr Le. And Trung is Mr Trung, formally. It's because there are so few family names, I suppose, taken after the sixteen royal families.'

Trung took Andrew to Dr Thanh's room, where two other young Vietnamese men were sitting.

'Dr Andrew, these are two of my students, Mr Tuan and Mr Luc. Together with Mr Trung, they will be coming to you for guidance on the design and analysis of their experiments.'

Dr Thanh gave the background to the experiments; a virus was causing childhood diarrhoea, and his department were developing vaccines they were testing in rats. They were also considering clinical tests.

'I have explained to Mr Trung and Mr Luc that it is very important to meet with a statistician like you and discuss from the start the experiments we propose to do. The design must be correct, so that we can analyse the results properly and draw reasonable conclusions. The same is true for the clinical tests.'

'I certainly agree,' said Andrew. 'Nothing worse for me than trying to clean up the results from a wrongly designed experiment. I suggest your students outline their proposals, and I'll see what advice I can come with.'

Dr Thanh closed the meeting politely but without ceremony.

Trung accompanied Andrew back to the room he shared with Lars. Andrew commented, 'Dr Thanh seems well informed. He can't be a purely political appointment, as people in the West sometimes expect about countries like Vietnam.'

Trung pulled a comically apologetic face. 'I'm a member of the communist party. So are Tuan and Loc.' He screwed up his face again.

Andrew didn't like to ask specifically about Dr Thanh.

Trung provided a document outlining his proposed project, along with some accompanying papers on rotavirus for Andrew to read.

'You will be jet-lagged still, so our driver will be taking you back early today.'

Andrew would have been prepared to walk or take a bus, but Trung arranging for the departmental driver to return him to the Old Quarter certainly made life easier. The Medical University was located in a busy densely populated part of the city, together with a big hospital, a mile away from the Old Quarter and the Hoan Kiem Lake. Andrew had now come to understand that the Old Quarter was the main tourist area, with hotels and a mass of shops and Andrew's flat nearby.

* * *

He stepped out from the departmental van into the hectic street activities, declined the instant offers of motorbike transport from the men waiting at the street corners, and ignored the constant hooting of traffic. The area was also called 'the 36 streets,' with each street named after the goods, such as clothes or fans, traditionally sold there. Andrew came on an entire block occupied by tinsmiths. No doubt the block offered intrigue, but now he wanted something calmer, and he set out towards Hoan Kiem Lake for a walk while it was still daylight.

Andrew was considering taking a traditional Vietnamese painting back to Britain and found an art shop near the lake where he could see, from the window display, that the prices were modest. He looked around inside and saw a print of people in traditional dress in a street scene that appealed to him.

'I like this one,' he said to the young man, perhaps in his middle twenties, who was sitting behind the counter. 'It's a print, I suppose. When was the original done?'

He had stopped asking young Vietnamese in Hanoi, 'Do you speak English?' because they usually did.

The young man, pleased to make a sale, chatted about the pictures and asked, 'Why you in Hanoi? Are you on vacation?'

'No, I'm here on a job, connected with an aid programme.'

'Are you Swedish? My name's Dien.'

'I'm British, but there's a Swedish connection with my job. I'm Andrew.'

'Can you come back in an hour's time, when the shop closes? I'll take you to my favourite place on my bike, and we can have coffee together.'

This came as a surprise, but Andrew couldn't see why he shouldn't agree to the suggestion. He looked at some more shops, read his tourist information book on public benches in the park, and returned to the art shop punctually.

Dien closed the shop and took Andrew to where he had parked his motorbike on the pavement. Andrew found himself hopping on to the back of motorbike and clinging on to Dien.

'You'll drive slowly, won't you? Or I'll be exceedingly nervous,' shouted Andrew. He hoped Dien wasn't the sort of young man who enjoyed showing off a reckless disregard for safety.

Dien moved off cautiously, and Andrew tried to relax, while continuing to hold on firmly with both arms round his driver. In one especially difficult episode, Dien drove slowly over a pedestrian crossing as if they were themselves pedestrians, with ten to twenty motorbikes approaching from each side.

They advanced down a boulevard past a massive Western-style building.

'L'Opéra. French Quarter,' called Dien.

After that, Andrew's attention was focused on motorbikes approaching from all directions until they arrived at a little café by a lake. They sat at a table in a secluded corner, and Dien ordered small cups of coffee. Both were happy to relax in silence for a while after the journey.

When their coffee was nearly finished, Dien said, 'Do you know how much I earn as an assistant in that shop?' He gave a figure in Vietnamese dong. 'It's enough to pay the rent and some food but not more.'

'How do you manage?' asked Andrew.

'My father sends me money every month, from home. He's a farmer.'

'Is he pleased that you work in a shop in town?'

'He wanted me to stay and help on the farm, but I'm not strong enough for farm work. So he agreed that I must find something else. The job here is until I find something better.'

As Dien had insisted on paying when they ordered coffee at the counter, Andrew offered to buy a second cup for each of them. But Dien insisted on paying again and collected the cups from the counter.

'You said you were working in a Swedish international project? SIDA?'

'I'm loosely connected with SIDA, yes.'

'Will you do something for me? Write to them, telling them about me, that I'm suitable for a clerical job with them. I speak and write good English and Vietnamese.'

Andrew was sceptical. 'I'll gladly give it a try, but I can't imagine a recommendation coming from me will have much influence.'

They rode back to the shop, and Andrew collected his picture and said he would contact Dien as soon as he had a reply from SIDA.

A few streets later, he encountered Cathy again; perhaps this was her standard pitch in the city, and he was almost looking out for her, to say, 'My friend liked your T-shirt. She told me to tell you it was a fine picture. Sorry if I was a bit unappreciative at the time.'

Cathy reacted to this at once. 'That's good. Today I've got some books. Come across the street, and I'll show them to you. Come on,' she repeated, seeing Andrew's reluctance.

She was earnest and persuasive. Andrew, reluctantly, but amused by her persistence, followed her across the street to a diminutive storeroom. Cathy pointed to a row of books on a shelf – cheap paperback reprints of standard classics. Andrew glanced at the titles and saw *A Quiet American*, a novel set in Vietnam he had often intended to read but had never got round to. Andrew assumed she was one of several children employed by the shop owner to hawk the books to tourists.

Cathy noticed him looking at it. 'You can have that for only three hundred.' Three hundred thousand dong – more than ten pounds – for a short, cheaply printed paperback. Andrew estimated this at about ten times the market price, but he was prepared to be generous.

'A hundred thousand dong.'

'For two hundred and fifty thousand dong, you can have that book and that one.' She pointed to *Pride and Prejudice*.

This came out deftly. Andrew felt that Cathy would be a worthy pupil of Mary. 'For heaven's sake, that's far too much, but I'm prepared to pay a hundred and fifty thousand for both books together.'

At this point, a Vietnamese boy standing beside them put in quietly and thoughtfully, 'Oh yes, I think that's a fair price.' He was a year or two older than Cathy.

Cathy pounced on him. It was unnecessary to know any Vietnamese to catch the general drift, something like, 'You stay out of this, you pig! Who do you think you are, anyway?'

Andrew sympathised. He knew what it was like to have your careful negotiations sabotaged by a supposed friend. It was time to end the encounter. He didn't want *Pride and Prejudice* but found another, longer classic and paid 200,000 dong for the two books.

He had made an impression on Cathy.

Later that day, he had a meeting with Valerie to make an initial payment and deal with other smaller matters. He took the opportunity to ask about the young salesmen. 'I see several young children selling things in the street – postcards, books, T-shirts. Why are they doing it? It can't fetch much money, and it can't be any fun for them. Are their parents so poor?'

'Many of them are orphans, apparently. Their mothers were teenagers living in the countryside who became pregnant and were forced to give up their children to an orphanage in the city. Unmarried mothers are not accepted in the countryside. The children are well looked after in the orphanages but not usually allowed to stay after the age of twelve or so. They move out and live cramped together in cheap flats in the city.'

* * *

Andrew wrote to SIDA, the Swedish International Development Cooperation Agency, recommending Dien as suitable for a junior clerical position. Twenty years earlier, Andrew would never have dreamt of giving a reference for someone he scarcely knew, but a lot of water had flown under the bridge since then. He had heard too many people from all walks of life say, 'It's not what you know; it's who you know that matters,' and had encountered too many examples of the truth of this, to feel any compunction about writing a glowing testimonial for someone he liked. He considered that everyone needs a break via a useful contact.

He began off, 'I am participating in a health programme connected with SIDA and, in the course of my activities, have met Mr Dien. Mr Dien, twenty-four years old, has an excellent command of idiomatic English in addition to his native Vietnamese and gives every impression of conscientiously performing his duties in the picture shop of high quality where he is employed.'

Andrew had learnt the hard way that, if a testimonial is wholly favourable, it is discounted as insufficiently critical, so he added, 'He is, however, of small stature and, while perfectly healthy, is not of the strongest physique.'

He enquired about possible jobs that Mr Dien might apply for and sent off the email to SIDA.

A reply next day informed Andrew that all job enquiries must be sent by the applicant himself, from Sweden. Furthermore, the current aid programme to Vietnam would end in two years' time and would not be extended, since Vietnam was developing rapidly and no longer required aid.

Oh well, he'd done what he could, and it had been a very long shot. He would inform Dien of the results by email.

But before Andrew got round to doing this, Sir Oliver Laine called him over the phone. 'How's it going, Andrew? Enjoying yourself in Hanoi?'

'It's been very interesting so far, but I have only just come.'

'I'm ringing you because I badly need your help. You remember Feelgood, the antidepressant our company is launching? We've been testing Feelgood Two on a limited number of American college students, and the group taking the real Feelgood feels better on average than the control group on the blank pills. Actually, between ourselves, we stopped the drug test as soon we were seeing significantly better results in the group on Feelgood.'

A classic wrong statistical procedure; the number of patients of the various groups should be fixed in advance. Andrew shuddered.

'Now we are proceeding to phase three,' continued Sir Oliver. 'We need to test a larger number of people, two or three hundred, for possible side effects over a period of months.

'The key word here is "outsourcing." We can save masses of money by running the tests in an emerging country, like Vietnam. Expressed in dollars, the currency of outsourcing, the cost of running the test in America is thirty thousand dollars per patient. To run it in Romania would cost a tenth as much, three thousand dollars per patient. It will be even less in Vietnam. The annual wage of a skilled Vietnamese worker is among the lowest in the world, only eight hundred dollars a year. We can easily afford to pay twice that much to each participant.'

'What do you want me to do?' asked Andrew.

'Rake up some Vietnamese to take part in the test – people you come across in one way or another, average citizens; they don't need to be depressed since, this time, we're testing only for side effects, not efficacy. They'll make a change from the usual test crowd, a mixture of impecunious American college students, migrant workers, down and outs, and alcoholics.'

'You don't mean I should find two or three hundred people?'

'Oh no, more like two or three. I've many contacts in Vietnam who are helping out in this matter.'

'What am I supposed to say to them?'

'You can ask if they would like to make a contribution to medical science, for which they'll be handsomely paid.'

'What about the likelihood of unexpectedly severe side effects?' asked Andrew.

'Good question. Side effects are very unlikely. Feelgood-Two is essentially a traditional herbal concoction that has been used for centuries on islands in the South Pacific without any problem we've heard of. Its only active ingredient seems to be a mixture of caffeine-like substances. It's no more harmful than Coca-Cola, to which the manufacturers always add caffeine. The proposed trial is a mere formality, to satisfy the controlling bodies.'

'Why not drink Coca-Cola, instead of taking Feelgood?'

'Another good question. Feelgood contains other caffeine-like substances as well as caffeine, and we're mixing Feelgood basic with a herb containing saffron. Saffron also has useful antidepressant effects. All that information comes from folklore; no need to carry out expensive research. Furthermore, saffron provides a pleasant taste and colour and enhances the vitally important placebo effect. You must truly believe in the healing power of the medicine if it is to do any good. Incidentally, there's no placebo effect with Coca-Cola, because people don't think of it as a medicine.'

'Would you be prepared to test Feelgood yourself?' asked Andrew.

'Of course. Indeed, I shall shortly be taking self-prescribed Feelgood from my store, to brace me for the horrors of Christmas with all the family – Feelgood together with a brandy. Incidentally, I regard outsourcing the trials of new medicines to emerging nations as an example of overseas aid at its finest, with benefits to both sides. The people of the emerging nation benefit directly in cash terms, no intervening bureaucracy, and at the same time, they provide a useful service to the donor country. Contact me when you've found someone.'

Sir Oliver rang off abruptly.

This gave food for thought around Dien. Andrew called back to Sir Oliver, saying that he had a possible candidate, and would Sir Oliver specify the precise sum of money on offer and how to proceed?

The next day, Andrew slipped off to the art shop. 'I've news of two kinds; I'll begin with the not-so-good.' He told Dien about the email from SIDA. Dien didn't seem surprised or particularly disappointed.

'The better news is that there may be a job for a limited period that at least pays well.' Andrew related Sir Oliver's proposal for service to medicine, including a fee of one thousand six hundred dollars, emphasizing that the element of risk in taking Feelgood was minimal. One dollar was worth fifteen thousand dong.

'One thousand six hundred times fifteen thousand dong?' Dien was wide-eyed with astonishment. 'Where's the catch?'

'That was my reaction to begin with, but I don't think there is one; it is much cheaper to run a trial of this kind in Vietnam than in most other countries.'

On returning to the department, Andrew emailed Sir Oliver. 'I have found a volunteer for the Feelgood test,' he write and supplied Dien's email.

The reply came almost at once. 'Splendid. I shall forward the address to Dr Lars Carlsson, who will take the matter further. Keep up the good work.'

Andrew could have guessed that Sir Oliver had further contacts with the Medical University, such as Lars.

Andrew soon had an opportunity to question his roommate. 'It seems we are both involved with Oliver Laine.'

'Only to a very small extent in my case. I sometimes help him organize a clinical trial, through my Vietnamese associates.'

'I thought you were purely academic.'

'I am really, but in Sweden, university researchers exchange with the medical companies. It's natural; it's a small country.'

'Do the Swedish companies exchange even with foreign companies?'

'The smaller medical firms have a short lifetime, until other firms, often foreign, acquire them. Not much point in probing into what's going on; the process is shrouded in secrecy.'

* * *

The next few days, he mercifully didn't meet Cathy again. He decided to be more economical in the future, buying only from the really deserving. From a middle-aged woman with only one leg, he bought *The Time Machine*, in a pirated old-fashioned edition. He vaguely remembered it from childhood and was curious to discover how it would seem now.

Before he walked away, the woman asked, 'Are you staying some time in Vietnam? I can teach you Vietnamese if you are.'

At first, Andrew did not feel ready for this and declined; then he changed his mind. The lady spoke grammatical, idiomatic, almost accentless English; she could well be a good teacher. She was unlikely to be expensive.

'On second thoughts, it could be a good idea. How much will it cost?'

'For an hour's lesson, fifty thousand dong.'

That was about two pounds, an absurdly low cost. Shameless to bargain, even if there was an is-the-price-too-much note in the woman's voice.

'Fine. My name's Andrew. I live just across the road over there, if it's better you come to me than I come to your place.'

'It's best I come to your place. My name's Hanh Phuc.'

They arranged to meet for the first lesson in two days' time, early after breakfast.

Two minutes later, a Buddhist monk held an ancient wooden begging bowl in front of him, and Andrew put some small coins in it.

The next few days he was fully occupied with work matters. He ate out once with Mary, and she had been similarly absorbed in her shop.

* * *

It was Wednesday and time for the first lesson with Hanh Phuc. Andrew had begun on a teach-yourself book.

'It's good that Vietnamese is written phonetically with Latin letters like English, rather than with thousands of picture characters like Chinese.'

'But, like Chinese, it's a tone language,' warned Hanh Phuc, 'so that words spelled with the same letters mean different things according to how my voice rises or falls. *Ma* can mean "ghost," but also "mother," "tomb," "horse," or "seedling" according to which of the six tones I use for the vowel.' She demonstrated this. 'We'll begin by practising the tones.'

Andrew had heard a Chinese demonstrate tones and thought that the sounds were pretty different and were not such a serious problem. (Even in English, the meaning of a phrase like 'This can't be praised too highly' can have its meaning reversed depending on the tone.) But Andrew found it more difficult to distinguish the tones in Vietnamese. The words with different tones had different accents in the written language, and this wasn't easy, either.

After a while teacher and student chatted about other things. Andrew, remembering the monk who had come with an ancient begging bowl, asked if there was a Buddhist monastery in Hanoi.

'They're a number of Buddhist monasteries in Hanoi. There's one not far from here. The most famous temple is about fifty kilometres away.'

Andrew suspected Hanh Phuc was a Buddhist herself.

Then she asked him abruptly, 'What is your religion?'

'I don't believe in the supernatural, but I agree with the general drift of the Sermon on the Mount and the parables in the Christian Bible. I don't see how society can function unless a large minority, or majority, of people think that they should behave decently to their neighbours, and they should consider that everybody is their neighbour.'

'Buddhism is the same.'

'But you're expected to believe in a lot of supernatural things, like reincarnation.'

'You don't have to believe in reincarnation or anything else supernatural, if it doesn't seem right for you. Or you can believe in it sometimes and sometimes not.'

'Don't you have to decide one way or the other?'

'Don't be so Western, Andrew.'

* * *

A week before Christmas, late in the evening, he went for his usual walk round the lake, past the old shrine. He caught sight of a small person sleeping out on a park bench wrapped in a blanket, head resting on a bag containing, presumably, a few clothes and other belongings. He had not before seen anyone reduced to sleeping out in Hanoi, a disturbing sight anywhere. He was curious to see what sort of person it was, a shrunken old man, perhaps.

He came nearer and saw it was a young person, not an elderly tramp, the face turned away from him, perhaps a boy who had been partying. He would eventually wake up and go off home. The weather in a place like Hanoi, even on a December night, was kind to the homeless, and Andrew need not concern himself. He resumed his walk but was sufficiently curious, after a few steps, to look back at the park bench.

The sleeper-out had turned so that the face was visible. It was a girl's face, which worsened things.

He considered attracting the attention of an adult Vietnamese, but no such person was in sight, and anyone passing was unlikely to appreciate a foreigner's intervention, particularly at this time of the evening.

He set out to continue his walk and forget the incident but impulsively turned back to the park bench for a closer look at the girl. Was it someone he would recognize among the sellers of postcards, T-shirts, and cheap paperbacks? He was wondering whether the face was familiar when the girl woke and sat up dazedly, and before she lay down again and seemed to return instantly to sleep, without taking in his presence, Andrew realized it was Cathy.

He emerged from his state of shock and, without further thought, stepped toward the bench and touched Cathy lightly on the face. She woke at once and looked at him, again in a daze, while he enquired, 'Why are you sleeping out here?'

It took a while for her to respond, 'Where else can I sleep? I've quarrelled with the others.'

'Why did you quarrel with them?'

'They don't like I'm making more money than they are.'

She'd probably boasted over how easy it was to sell things to him. Andrew doubted that it was all his fault but felt some responsibility. Without considering the consequences, he said, 'You can come home to the flat where I'm staying.'

Cathy looked at him suspiciously. 'You dirty old man?'

Andrew resented this. 'I'm a perfectly clean man in late middle age. But I hate to think of you sleeping out on a park bench. It's not safe.'

'The holy men will look after me.'

'The monks, if you mean them, are too busy meditating or sleeping to look after you.'

'Gautama, then.'

'The Buddha's dead; he can't help. Besides, it's not even warm. And it's nearly Christmas. People can't be left to sleep out at Christmas. They have to be found a room somewhere; there has to be room at the inn.'

'What do you mean, has to be room at the inn?'

But Andrew didn't have the energy to recount the Nativity to a Vietnamese orphan girl on a park bench late at night. 'I can't explain now. Can't you come with me?'

And to Andrew's relief, Cathy picked up her bag and followed. She plodded along without even a lacklustre attempt at conversation.

They climbed the stairs to the flat and entered. In the kitchen, Andrew asked, 'Would you like something to eat?'

'I'm too tired.'

'Perhaps some fruit?'

She accepted an orange. Andrew peeled it for her, and they sat down on the sofa while she ate it. She recovered enough energy for Andrew to enquire, 'Would you like a bath before you go to bed?'

'Suppose I could. Show me where.'

Andrew took her to the bathroom and pointed out which knobs to press or taps to turn to fill up the bath or get a shower and left her to it.

But after five minutes, Cathy called from the bathroom, 'Come and help. I can't do it.'

A small pile of clothes lay on the floor, and Cathy stood naked by the bath, looking disconsolately at the taps. Andrew could also be nonplussed by the complexity of baths in strange places and sympathized. He moved away from the shower, filled the bath to a modest level, and adjusted the temperature of the water. 'There you are!'

She was still disconsolate. 'Can't you get in with me?' She was tired and helpless, far removed from the fast-talking street kid.

'Oh, I suppose so.' He was indulging someone's little girl, perhaps a close relation's or a neighbour's. Andrew undressed self-consciously while Cathy looked at him with no attempt to disguise her curiosity. He climbed in, sitting at the back. Cathy followed after, and he directed her so that she faced forward. After a few moments she pressed back against him. He reached for the soap and offered it to her. She held it awhile but made no attempt to use it, so he took it away and began soaping her back. Cathy remained passive. He continued with her neck and the sides of her face. By this time, Cathy was making small appreciative noises.

'Take my front, too.'

He ignored this. It was a long time since he had been as close to a female; hardly at all since his marriage. He and Antonia had particularly liked fooling around in a bath. But Cathy was a bewildered little girl, furthermore undernourished and pathetic.

'Would you like to wash your hair?' To Andrew's surprise, most of Cathy had smelt reasonably fresh, even before she had been cleaned up, a possible exception being her hair.

'*You* do it.'

He reached across for the shampoo and wetted down her hair with the shower. Cathy remained passive, but the small appreciative noises continued.

He eventually got them both out of the bath and dried himself and then Cathy with the large towel. He found the extra sheets in the cupboard and made a bed for her on the sofa. Cathy climbed in and fell asleep more or less instantly. Andrew sat in his favourite comfortable chair and read for a bit, without much concentration, while he wondered what he was letting himself in for. Then he went to bed and slept soundly until the small hours.

Towards the end, he dreamed vividly. Antonia was back in his life, saying to him from close up, 'Andrew, love, you've become a bit hopeless, haven't you? You should have found someone else when I was gone, as the nurse at the hospital told you. I shouldn't have minded. I know you made some attempts to find someone, but you didn't push enough. You should have made things happen. I thought I taught you that. Now Cathy has come into your life – partly because of your own efforts; perhaps you learned something from me, after all. But what will you do? Will you go all passive again? You'll have to bide your time while she's growing up, as you had to with me. One good thing, even if I say it myself, she's like me, isn't she? I don't mean in looks, of course.' Antonia's voice was growing fainter; she was fading away; but she could add, 'Goodbye for now, Andrew. I shall be watching.'

He half awoke to find Cathy naked beside him, asleep with her arms round him.

Chapter 13

It was morning when he woke again. Cathy opened her eyes briefly, looked at him, closed her eyes again, and said, 'I'm dying.'

Andrew, slept out and relaxed, was slow to concern himself. 'What's wrong? You seem healthy enough to me.'

'Look.' She turned back the sheet to reveal bloodstains on the sheet between her legs.

After an initial shock, Andrew stopped being impressed. 'You're having your period.' Then it occurred to him, 'I suppose this is your first time. Women bleed like this every month. Didn't anyone tell you?'

'Yes,' Cathy said listlessly, 'but she didn't say it would feel like this.'

'How old are you?'

'I'm fourteen; that's what they say, but no one knows exactly.'

It was Saturday, and no one was coming from the lab to collect him. 'I suppose I can go and buy some of those things for you. Tampax; that's what they were called in my day. I'll go to Intimex; they're probably open already. They ought to have what you need.'

He dressed and went off to Intimex, where he'd been going for groceries and small purchases after Trung's recommendation. Even with the map, it had initially been hard to find, as it was on a side street. But it was a big supermarket, selling everything imaginable to a Vietnamese clientele. He was reluctant to search endlessly along the shelves, so he tried to find an English-speaking shop assistant to help him. He soon had two young women and an older one round him. The word Tampax meant nothing to them. He thoughtlessly began going through the motions of insertion, but quickly thought better of it and attempted explanations in simple language. 'Women …roughly once a month …blood.'

The ladies discussed the matter among themselves in Vietnamese, giggled, and returned with the right packet, to judge from the drawing. He thanked them and, feeling that now he was there, he might as well buy something else besides Tampax, explained to the women that he would now look around on his own.

He found two packets of milk and a packet of something resembling Ryvita and paid for the items at the counter. As he did so, he noticed that one of the two younger girls, who was replacing the articles on a shelf, had half turned towards him and was watching from a distance with a mixture of curiosity and polite wonderment. Andrew smiled at her briefly, and she responded with a sympathetic, understanding, and more prolonged smile.

Back in the flat, he found Cathy half-dressed but lying despondently on the sofa. Andrew said to her, 'Here's your package. The pictures are helpful.'

Cathy glanced at the packet. 'My head's awful.'

'I've got some aspirins.' He fetched his stock and two glasses of water. He took an aspirin himself and drank some water, in case a demonstration was needed.

'Do you need medicine too?' wondered Cathy.

'I'm getting a sort of sympathy headache.'

Andrew sat back in his chair and waited for her to recover. This took about half an hour. Andrew, feeling hungry, suggested that Cathy should finish dressing, and then they could go out and get some breakfast.

'Where?'

'We can have that breakfast soup at one of the cafes near here.'

'We can't both of us go to the same place so early. They'll think we've been sleeping together.'

'I thought we *had* been sleeping together.'

'I don't mean like that.' And as an afterthought, 'Silly.'

'Two cafes are next door to each other. You can go to one, and I'll go to the other.'

Andrew provided her with some cash. They sat down in sight of each other. Andrew glanced round occasionally, but Cathy ignored him. He chose the traditional noodle soup with beef called *pho* and ate unhurriedly and with satisfaction. Cathy, as far as he could see, was doing the same.

In due course, he strolled out of the cafe, and Cathy joined up with him down the street. She indicated briefly that this Saturday was to be spent like any other – in raking up customers for her T-shirts and book collection.

'When will you finish?' asked Andrew.

'About four.'

'I'll be by the door and let you in.'

He could probably get hold of another key if it was going to be needed in the future. He wondered if Cathy would really show up.

But sure enough, Cathy reappeared in the late afternoon. Andrew had bought some food for them, and in the evening, Cathy laid it out on separate dishes, Vietnamese style. Afterwards, while Andrew wanted to relax, she became energetic and took care of the clothes that were still in the bathtub where she had dumped them the evening before. They watched television awhile, Andrew dozing off in his chair. He awoke to find Cathy sleeping on the sofa.

Later in the evening, Andrew heard a knock at the door, and he opened it to find Valerie and Mary. They had come to see how he was getting on in the new flat.

'I like the flat. Actually, Cathy, the girl in the street I bought the T-shirt from, is staying here for the time being. She didn't have anywhere else to go. She's sleeping on the sofa. Can you talk quietly, and we'll have only the desk light on. I'll make some tea.' Andrew explained this rapidly and as quietly as possible.

He came with the tea and was met with considerable interest from the two women.

'She sleeps on the sofa, does she?'

'She begins on the sofa.'

At this point, Cathy half woke up and more or less sleepwalked to the bed, lay on it with one arm stretched out, and called, 'An-rew,' and then fell asleep again.

The women had watched with fascination. 'Does she usually run around in no more than a T-shirt like that?' enquired Mary.

'She has a limited wardrobe. She can't afford a nightdress; she's a girl of slender means.'

'I'll say,' remarked Valerie.

'I don't like to ask this, but isn't she a bit underage?' asked Mary.

'It's nothing like that,' answered Andrew crossly. 'She was sleeping on a park bench, and I thought she really ought to be somewhere inside and safe, and anyway it's nearly Christmas. You'll agree there has to be room at the inn at Christmas.'

'I suppose we'll have to accept that. Or what do you say, Valerie?'

'It sure is peculiar, but then Andrew *is* English.'

'Is he going to start a dormitory for all the stray children in Hanoi, do you think?'

'I haven't the funds for that, but I don't see why I can't help a particular person without a mass of ribald comments. There's no reason why I should have a bad conscience. It's like making a small contribution to a children's charity, as you've probably done in your time, except that I happen to be on the spot and can take in the child myself.'

'Have you given any thought as to what you are going to do with her?' asked Mary.

He had to admit he hadn't, really. 'Not so much yet. What do *you* think I should do?'

'You could find out why she isn't in school, for a start.'

That seemed a good idea. He had noticed a school in the neighbourhood and decided to take Cathy there and talk to the head – or at least try to. The three of them chatted for a while on a variety of topics before Mary and Valerie left, making final amused comments about Cathy.

Andrew climbed cautiously into bed without disturbing Cathy and decided not to switch on the bedside light and read as he usually did. He lay awake, irritated with the insinuations of his recent visitors and then carefully relaxed, conscious of Cathy's tranquil breathing.

* * *

In England, Andrew usually spent Sunday mornings reading the newspapers over a leisurely breakfast, followed by a miscellany of other activities – short walks, attending to mail, various kinds of reading, and tidying up. Now he was in Hanoi. How would the presence of Cathy affect things? He had no idea. Here was a teenage girl thrust into his life. He had no experience of long-term coexistence with children.

'What do you do on Sundays?' he asked.

'Sunday is my best day. I often sell enough things to get food for Sunday, Monday, and Tuesday.'

'You don't have to worry about food. I can buy for both of us.'

'That wouldn't be fair.'

'The cost won't be much greater.'

'One day, you'll go off. I must keep the business going,' responded Cathy.

But he wouldn't be able to go off; he was committed to her. 'I'll be here till after Christmas. I shall be in England for a few months after that. Then I shall come back here again. While I am in England, I shall go on paying for the flat in any case, and you might as well continue living here. You can keep the place going for me.'

'I could find a house and share the floor with other girls, as before,' said Cathy matter-of-factly. 'But it's much better here, not squashed up together with a lot of other girls.'

They cleared up the breakfast things.

Andrew looked at the sofa and said, 'Is there any point in having the sheets on the sofa? You always move into the bed sooner or later. You might as well sleep in it from the start, and we can keep the sofa for sitting in.'

Cathy, without comment, folded up the sheets and put them away in the cupboard in the bedroom.

Andrew sat in a corner of the sofa with the weekly newspaper from England he had managed to buy. Cathy sat down in the middle of the sofa, lay back contentedly for a few minutes, and then wriggled up beside Andrew. To get comfortable, Andrew put his arm behind her, after which neither of them said anything for a half hour. It was like a marriage in which the partners were perfectly happy in each other's company without feeling the need to converse.

Cathy stood up. 'I shall go out now.'

'Are you coming back for lunch?'

'Suppose I could. How shall I come in without a key?'

'I'll be outside the door at twelve o'clock. But it's silly not to have another key. I'll get one from Valerie, who owns the flat.'

'Will you tell her about me?'

'She already knows. She came late last night with Mary, someone I know from England, and they saw you run across the room.'

'Do they think I'm a sort of bad girl?'

'It did cross their minds, but I carefully explained why you were here. After some initial scepticism – I mean, after some discussion – Valerie seemed to think it was okay; Mary too.'

* * *

The next few days, Andrew was fully taken up with work matters. He had procured a second key from Valerie without much fuss, so Cathy came in when she pleased. For the first few days, he half expected to find the key and a short goodbye note indicating that she had packed up her few belongings and moved on. She would surely have tired of her existence with an elderly foreigner. But she had already returned when the departmental driver, whom Trung had instructed about the new address, had deposited Andrew in front of the house shortly before dusk.

He would find her busy preparing food or washing their clothes or meticulously cleaning round the kitchen sink or adjusting the air conditioner in the living room. Later in the evening, she'd relax and sit in the sofa beside Andrew, while he read or tried to understand the television. She was perfectly happy for at least an hour doing nothing more than sitting close up to him. Perhaps she was compensating for having missed the affectionate physical contact with parents that small children normally receive.

On Thursday, she pointed to a bowl on a small side table. 'I'll get the food each day. I know what it costs. I need you put hundred thousand dong in there, and I'll put in fifty thousand. That's fair. You eat twice as much as I do.'

On Friday, Andrew looked in on Mary and, while she dealt with items about the shop, recounted life with Cathy, including her food purchases.

'So she's taken over the household, has she?' commented Mary, drily. 'You'd better watch out. Have you made any progress in discovering why she isn't in school?'

'I'm working on it.'

Chapter 14

It was Saturday morning. Andrew and Cathy ate breakfast at one of the cafes and then walked sedately round the lake. Despite the early hour, some of the shops were open; a group of mostly older people played a version of racquets in the park by the lake; and another group engaged in a series of exercise dances, without partners, to music from a loudspeaker. A new lively tune was particularly popular among the twenty or thirty participants, many of them middle-aged women. Cathy soon joined the line of swaying, stretching, cavorting dancers, while Andrew remained an interested spectator.

'I love that tune,' she commented happily afterwards. 'It's great.' She told Andrew that hundreds of people took their daily exercise here every morning.

Andrew felt this was the moment to broach the subject of school. It was heavier going than he had expected; in his experience, teenage girls usually said they liked school. Cathy blocked any questions about her previous education or why it had ended.

Andrew tried with, 'They might have dancing like that at school.'

Cathy brightened up for a moment and then said she could get all that in the street.

But with some difficulty, he induced her to agree to look at the school later in the day, after she had finished her shift selling T-shirts and books.

She duly met up with Andrew, and they finally arrived at the school, late in the afternoon. Andrew had supposed that the place would be empty and they could look around it from outside and, perhaps, encounter a teacher who happened to be there on the weekend. To his surprise, a mass of boys and girls were leaving the school buildings. They were dressed in a

Western-style school uniform – white shirts, ties, and blazers – miles from the jeans and T-shirts the Vietnamese young wore in their free time; the attire was more like Andrew's idea of what proper middle-class Parisian schoolchildren would wear at a lycée.

A boy of about sixteen stood with his bicycle, waiting for someone.

'Could you tell me, please,' Andrew addressed him, 'why are so many pupils leaving school late on a Saturday afternoon; has there been some special event?'

The boy had no difficulty in understanding the question, despite the foreign language. 'Saturday is an ordinary school day; only Sunday is free.'

Andrew thanked him for the information. The school was rapidly emptying, presenting a perfect opportunity for Cathy and him to enter and meet a teacher. 'Come on!' he said and took Cathy by the hand.

'No,' said Cathy and stopped still. A complete and final Vietnamese no – like the one Andrew had encountered before, in a less extreme version, in the department where he was working. A 120 per cent negative. Her face was taut, her whole body rigid and stubborn. She might have made it clearer from the start that she had no intention of going to school again. Perhaps she had remained open-minded until she saw how her classmates would look. Andrew compared Cathy, despite recent grooming, still the quintessential street kid, with the neatly dressed boys and girls. He tried to imagine accommodating her to this ultra-respectable bourgeois school world and felt defeated.

He might discuss with Trung, or one of the staff at the Medical University, or Valerie, about how to get street children back into school.

In the meantime, an alternative idea occurred to him for at least a temporary measure. 'It will have to be Hanh Phuc, the lady with one leg who teaches me Vietnamese. She can teach you English. We'll get on excellently, all three of us. You've lost your mother; I've lost my wife; she's lost her leg. We may be able to find her by the lake; otherwise, we can talk about it when she next comes to the flat.'

He set off back to the lake, where he assumed they might find Hanh Phuc. Cathy gave a short laugh, and scampered after him. 'You do say funny things.'

'Funny peculiar or funny ha ha?'

Cathy could understand this. 'Both, but mostly peculiar. Anyway, I haven't lost my mother; I never had one.'

They walked on in silence, until Cathy said, in an everyday tone, 'If we were nearer the same age, we'd probably fall in love.' She glanced up at Andrew.

'Suppose we would,' Andrew responded briefly. He was not in a romantic mood. How did real parents endure their teenage children on a day-to-day basis? Emotionally, he had banked heavily on the school to get Cathy into life's mainstream. Now, Hanh Phuc remained as an unsatisfactory alternative. He hoped she would be on her usual pitch and they could settle the matter.

They walked on to the park bench beside the lake where Hanh Phuc had encountered Andrew before; she was there again. Andrew explained what they wanted.

'This is Cathy—'

'Doan Vien,' interrupted Cathy.

'Can you give her English lessons? Say, after me on Wednesdays.' One lesson a week seemed inadequate. 'And again on Saturdays, same time?'

Hanh Phuc was delighted at the prospect of a new customer. 'Same fee, fifty thousand dong for an hour's lesson?'

At which point Cathy started talking earnestly in Vietnamese. After a considerable exchange of words, Cathy reported to Andrew, 'Fifty thousand dong for you; thirty-five thousand for me.'

At the coffee break at work the next day, he brought up the subject of the street children. Were they around all the time? Did the authorities show any interest in them, did anyone arrange for them to go back to school?

A flicker of interest sparkled in Trung's eyes. 'When the My Dinh National Stadium was opened and the foreign visitors arrived, the police drove the kids away into the countryside so that they didn't upset the important visitors from abroad. But they were back again as soon as the closing ceremony was over.'

'Doesn't someone try to get them back into school? Then they would be off the streets as much as if they were driven away into the countryside.'

'The kids don't want to go to school.'

Lessons with Hanh Phuc seemed to be the best he could arrange.

Chapter 15

'What did you and Hanh Phuc talk about?' Andrew asked Cathy the following Wednesday evening.

'Causes of suffering,' Cathy said in non-committal tones.

'Unusual choice of topic, particularly for an English lesson.'

'She's religious. It's her leg. She said *you* brought up Buddhism.'

After a moment's silence, Cathy asked, 'Did you stop believing in God when your wife died?'

'No, of course not. That would have been ridiculous. All sorts of people have completely undeserved bad luck. It would be absurd to lose your faith just because *you* have bad luck. The point is, I never did believe in mysterious forces – not in God or the devil or ghosts or anything supernatural.'

Andrew wondered how much Cathy understood of this. Although he tried to keep his vocabulary simple, he had lapses. Cathy sometimes asked him what particular words meant and was not always grammatical, but she was otherwise at ease in the remote foreign language. Selling in the street was a hard and apparently effective school.

'Were you mad when they said your wife died? How did you learn? Why did she die?' Cathy sounded genuinely interested.

Andrew thought he might as well tell the whole story. 'The pregnancy was normal, except that the baby was turned awkwardly. I went with my wife for the delivery—'

'Where to?'

'The nearby hospital. I couldn't tell there was any problem, but after a while, the midwife, the nurse who assists at childbirth, called in the doctor. I heard the doctor say, "I think we'll ask the husband to leave now." A young nurse took me out of the room and said that my wife was going to be anaesthetised, given an injection to make her go to sleep, and that it was best I leave and come back in the afternoon. Nothing to worry about; just a question of moving the baby round.

'I looked into the room to tell my wife I was going to return a while later. She was obviously in pain, but that was usual enough during childbirth. She said "Goodbye for now."

'I wasn't alarmed that the doctor wanted me out of the way. It was something fairly new for husbands to be present at childbirth. I wandered in the hospital grounds for a while and then further into town for a light lunch. I decided to wait for about three hours before returning. It was a warm late-September afternoon, and sauntering around town was pleasant. I bought a bunch of flowers at a shop I passed.'

'That's what husbands are supposed to do,' said Cathy.

'I presented myself at the hospital reception. A middle-aged lady from the other side of the window said thoughtfully, "So you're Mr Carter? If you wait here a moment, I'll make a short call." She walked to a phone well inside the room, but I could hear her say slowly, "Mr Carter is here … Mr Carter." After a few moments, she returned to the window saying that the doctor would be along shortly.

'I thought her manner was slightly odd and said, "Everything's gone okay, hasn't it?"

'The lady said, "We're not allowed to discuss individual cases, and the doctor will be here very shortly. Why don't you sit down over there?" She began at once to look through some papers.

'I sat and waited longer than I expected. In fact, the doctor never came, but eventually, when I looked up, the same nurse as before was standing in front of me, a young woman of perhaps twenty-five, with a fresh face and a neat nurse's uniform. I still remember her name; it was Maureen. She said, "Mr Carter, we'll have a cup of tea and a little talk."

'She took me to a small private room, and I sat and watched while she made the tea. Then she came over, poured out the tea, and watched me taking the first sips. It was unexpectedly sweet, particularly as I don't usually take sugar in tea—'

'Hot sweet tea is good if you have a shock,' commented Cathy.

'Exactly. So I began to wonder if something was wrong with the baby – some birth defect, probably only minor.

'Maureen said, "Your little girl had a difficult time coming out, more difficult than usual. But she was a bonnie fighter, and we got her out all right, and she was soon breathing normally. We weren't expecting any serious problems, and then she stopped breathing awhile after birth; we aren't sure why. The doctor did all he could – he's a very skilful doctor – but he couldn't bring her round."'

Cathy was following the story with interest. 'What did you think when she told you this? How did you feel?' she asked, without inhibition.

'I felt sorry for this young girl who had been landed with the nasty job of having to tell me all this. I wondered why the doctor hadn't felt obliged to do it himself.

'Then I asked about my wife. Maureen watched me while I took another sip of tea, and said quietly, "I'm afraid I haven't any good news there either." In short, my wife seemed all right, but her pulse had weakened. The doctor at first hadn't thought it was serious, but it was the beginning of heart failure, and a while later, she died.

'Then Maureen said, "You mustn't mind what I shall say now. I mean, don't take this in the wrong way. You mustn't just give up and be bitter. Your life must go on. You must go out and find another young woman. You mustn't be like my cousin, who just sank into herself when she lost her husband. It was awful. It was such a waste of her life." She said this so forcefully. Earlier she was following a formal procedure; don't give bad news until the person is sitting comfortably and has taken the first mouthfuls of the soothing warm liquid. But now she was talking from some deeply felt experience. I began to think that the doctor had made a sensible, not a cowardly, decision in arranging for her to talk to me, instead of taking on the job himself.

'I asked the nurse if she had any use for the flowers. She took them and said, "Would you like to see your wife and be with her for a last time?" But I said no, I'd rather remember her as she was before.'

'But what did you *feel*?' asked Cathy.

'That several years of my life had vanished. I was back to square one. But I wasn't angry.' He couldn't reasonably enquire how Cathy felt about being abandoned by her mother, so instead he asked, 'How did you feel when the other girls chucked you out from the flat?'

'I'd show them that I was okay by myself. I was mad at them.'

Chapter 16

Hanh Phuc continued to come to the flat to give language lessons to Andrew and Cathy. Andrew was learning some everyday phrases and struggling with the tonal pronunciation. But some things he wanted to discuss in English.

'I am supposed to be finding people to take part in a test for side effects of a new medicine a British firm is producing, pills to take if you're feeling depressed. It is a very simple traditional kind of medicine, and it is almost certainly safe to take; the test is a formality to satisfy legal requirements. An advantage if you agree to take part in the test is that it is well paid.'

Hanh Phuc's eyes lit up at the sum on offer. 'It sounds as if you're offering me a gift. If it really is a gift, don't expect me to be grateful. We believe that the giver is blessed with good karma, so he benefits from the gift as much as the receiver.'

She sounded like Sir Oliver praising his favourite kind of international aid. Andrew noted her address and said that a doctor would be contacting her.

With Cathy, Hanh Phuc was sufficiently old-fashioned to want her to learn some poems by heart, in the first place "The Brook" by Tennyson – mercifully, only the first six verses. Cathy copied out the poem from a standard school anthology her teacher possessed. Then as a homework assignment, she should explain the meaning of a number of words Hanh Phuc had underlined in the text. Finally Cathy should briefly reply to three questions: Was it musical? What was the author trying to say? And was it a good poem?

Cathy consulted Andrew for help. The meaning of the words was easy to discover from the English and Vietnamese dictionaries they had acquired inexpensively from Hanh Phuc. Andrew's natural impulse was to find out what famous critics had written about the poem. The easiest way was to search the Web, so he took Cathy off to a nearby Internet cafe he had noticed.

It was full of children playing Internet games, so they had to queue until a computer became available. Cathy was initially disdainful of spoilt kids' games but lingered in front of one of the screens, succumbed to its charm, and hankered to play herself. But Andrew's parental instincts took over; homework should have priority, and he insisted on their both searching the web for Tennyson and 'The Brook.'

Thousands of hits on 'The Brook' came up in a fraction of a second. Cathy was fascinated. 'Let me do it.' She pushed Andrew's hands away.

So they went back to the Google point of entry; Andrew deleted 'The Brook' and 'Tennyson'; Cathy rewrote them, pressed return, and then went wild and clicked on everything in sight, randomly and at maximum speed.

'Getting the hang of it?' asked Andrew after five minutes, in resignation.

And, up to a point, she was. Images on the screen appeared and disappeared; a favourite picture reappeared after frantic clicking. Finally she turned up the first page of Tennyson hits, and a click led to the display of the poem on the screen. Cathy sat back in her chair, entranced.

They had still not found any critical comments of the kind Andrew hoped for. A new version of the poem appeared, this time in full, with the brook lyric interspersed among the rest of the poem relating a story, a kind of narrative. While the lyric was familiar enough to Andrew from school, the narrative was new to him; he revised his idea of the poem. After negotiation with the cafe attendant, Andrew watched the poem being printed out, while Cathy gazed at a computer game. Then they continued to search the hits and at last found a discussion of the poem that Andrew thought could be of use.

Their time at the computer ran out. They returned home and sat on the sofa. Andrew began reading aloud:

Here by this brook, we parted; I to the East

And he for Italy—too late—too late:

Andrew was absorbed into the life of the frail poet and his juvenilia. He read out:

I panted, seems, as I re-listen to it,
Prattling the primrose fancies of the boy,
To me that loved him; for 'O brook,' he says,
O babbling brook, says Edmund in his rhyme,
'Whence come you?' and the brook, why not? replies.

'Now it's you,' he said to Cathy, who was sitting against him on the sofa. And she understood enough to continue:

I come from haunts of coot and hern

'Whatever they are,' she interrupted herself, and Andrew wondered why she had been given such a difficult poem, even if it was standard school fare.

I make a sudden sally
And sparkle out among the fern
To bicker down a valley.

And so on with increasing confidence over the sound and rhythm of the words. She didn't seem to worry about the actual meaning.

For men may come and men may go,
But I go on for ever.

Then it was Andrew's turn again, and he continued to read aloud for a while. But he got absorbed in the plot where the narrator takes the excessively talkative father on the side so as to leave the lovers together.

'Why have you stopped reading aloud?'

'I was reminded of something that happened years ago.'

'That's like you, An-rew. You get lost in things ages ago.'

'Isn't it the same with you and everybody else? One can't avoid the past.'

'I avoid it. I live for now.' She read for the second time:

To join the brimming river,
For men may come and men may go,

She paused. 'That's true. Men keep leaving.'

But Andrew was busy recalling when he had come alive in the neighbourhood of Enby.

Cathy wanted to get her homework finished. She felt the terms of her assignment had been changed. 'I can't write about that little bit of poem, among all the rest. It isn't a proper poem anymore.'

'Hanh Phuc won't mind if you write about the whole poem instead.'

'But it's such a long poem. You'll have to help. You can begin by telling me what it was that happened to you long ago you were reminded of.'

Andrew explained briefly about the conspiracy to marry off Janet, how Fred talked endlessly about farming like the boring farmer in the poem, how the conspirators in real life had decoyed Mrs Morton away so as to unite the lovers as in 'The Brook.' He said, 'I don't see it's so difficult to write about the poem. You can begin by outlining the story. You don't even really need to say whether you think it's good, and if so, why, or why not.'

'It must be good because it puts you in such a funny mood – funny peculiar.'

The two of them eventually succeeded in writing nearly a page of critical appreciation of the poem, with some assistance from what they had gathered from the Internet. Andrew did not consider he had sabotaged Hanh Phuc's teaching efforts, since helping children with their homework was a time-honoured activity.

Chapter 17

Andrew had intended to go back to England for Christmas. But he had been in Vietnam for only a few weeks, and he had no relatives to stay with, both his parents being dead, apart from Janet and her family and Toby, who also usually visited there over Christmas. With them, he felt welcome, but this time he was happy to be elsewhere. Besides, he was preoccupied with Cathy. He learned that Mary was also spending Christmas in Hanoi, so he would have sufficient company.

Mary, a Catholic, always attended Midnight Mass on Christmas Eve and took it for granted that Andrew and Cathy would accompany her. Andrew half expected Cathy to switch on one of her 120 per cent negatives, but far from it, she was curious to go to a church service, particularly at midnight. They arrived in good time and looked round the large church. In one corner, exhibits reconstructed the Nativity, and these attracted Cathy's attention.

'Why's that woman having her baby among all those horses?'

'That's not *that woman*; that's Mary, mother of Jesus,' Mary informed her.

'Same as you?'

'She's the original Mary.'

'Is that the father? Or has he gone off as usual?'

Mary had fortunately moved out of earshot. Andrew pointed out Joseph as the rough equivalent of the father.

'What do you mean, roughly the father?'

Andrew didn't feel up to theological explanations. 'The best thing is if you look up "virgin birth" on the Internet sometime and, while you're at it, "immaculate conception."'

'Why's she having a baby in that place? It's so dirty.'

'Because there was no room at the inn —' Andrew began, but as "inn" was not likely a familiar word, he added, 'at the local hotel.'

'That's what you were saying before, weren't you, An-rew – no room at the inn? Anyway, why didn't they just stay at home?'

'They had to travel for … oh, some tedious regulations.' Andrew couldn't face explaining a census, either, so late at night on Christmas Eve.

They moved on to a sort of model Christmas tree, with candles. Some of them carried notes with inscriptions on them, tied round the metal support. Most of these were in Vietnamese, but two of them were in English, in memory of relatives. Cathy wanted to light a candle. Andrew placed some coins in a box nearby. Cathy broke off and said, 'I'd like to write a message. Have you something to write on?'

Mary produced an airways luggage label, ideal for attaching to a candle. Andrew fumbled for his felt-tipped pen. Cathy wrote, 'To Jesus and the Buddha,' in large detached letters over the luggage label, fixed it to the base, and lit the candle.

Mary, after initial shock, said to Andrew, 'The vicar is going to be in a quandary over that one.'

The service went off without incident; Cathy was entranced by the music and was too engaged for further potentially embarrassing comments.

On Christmas Day, Mary arranged a festive dinner at the room she was staying in, which had some limited cooking facilities. They exchanged a few small presents. Andrew had wondered what would be a suitable present for Cathy. What did a girl like Cathy want for Christmas these days? he had asked Mary.

'A nightdress,' Mary had stated unhesitatingly. 'Anyway, that's what I'm giving her.'

'Can't you make it a dressing gown? She might use that, but she's not the sort of girl who wears a nightdress, as far as I can see.'

Andrew had eventually asked Cathy what she wanted as a Christmas gift. This involved explaining about Christmas presents, apparently a novel idea for Cathy. She surprised him by saying she wanted a picture of him and her. He thought a photograph would be excellent, so they went to a kiosk with an automatic camera and took pictures of them both. After some consideration, they decided that photographs of themselves would be something to give Mary, too, mainly from Cathy.

Chapter 18

The weather warmed up considerably in mid-January and now offered something like the heat Andrew expected in the tropics, even if the Vietnamese regarded it still as the cool season. Cathy continued to be out most of each day selling postcards, T-shirts, and paperbacks. She appeared to take considerable pride in these activities, which could hardly have brought in much income; but she rarely asked Andrew for money apart from the weekly contribution for food. Andrew thought it was time she got a proper job. He approached Mary, without great expectations.

'Can you imagine giving Cathy some kind of part-time employment in your shop? Just mornings or, better, afternoons, so she can continue her lessons with Hanh Phuc, the one-legged woman? She can't go on selling postcards in the street indefinitely. Incidentally, her English is improving.'

Mary was surprisingly favourable. 'My Vietnamese assistant could help train Cathy, especially as she wants more time off. Actually, I'm curious as to how Cathy would shape up as a salesgirl in a proper shop. I'm willing to give her a try. I can come over one evening and discuss it with her.'

The next problem was how to present the proposal to Cathy. He was unsure how she would react; would she see the prospect as a step forward to a better life, materially and surely psychologically, or as a descent from freedom to domination by an older foreign woman? Would she be objective or mount an adolescent rebellion? The best approach might be to present Mary's visit as a negotiating opportunity, something she would enjoy.

'Where do you get the things you sell in the street – the T-shirts, books and postcards?' he asked Cathy one evening.

'From that shop I took you to one day.'

'Who owns the shop?'

'An old man.'

'Have you asked him for a job in the shop instead of in the street?'

'No; he's nasty old man. Be a bad bargain.'

'Mary may be interested in offering you a job in her shop. Can't you meet her here and bargain with her? She's no nasty old man.'

'S'pose I can.'

An evening for Mary's visit was fixed; and when it came, Andrew withdrew into the kitchen to leave them in private. From time to time, he heard Mary exclaim things like, 'For goodness sake, I'm not an old softy like Andrew.'

They eventually emerged into the kitchen.

'Each of us thinks the other has made a far better deal,' said Mary.

'Isn't that pretty much as it should be?' enquired Andrew.

'Possibly. Anyway, now we're off to fix Cathy's working clothes. You should come along too.'

Andrew sat on the low plastic chair in the shop, while Mary and Cathy occupied themselves in the room for trying on dresses. After two minutes, Mary came out. 'She's still a girl of slender means. Underwear needed.'

Half an hour later, they both sounded satisfied and came out to show Andrew. 'How does she look?'

Cathy was resplendent in a golden dress.

'Not half bad. Like a princess,' commented Andrew. 'Well, somewhere between a princess and a waitress in an elegant establishment.'

Noticing Mary's expression, he added hastily, 'But much more like a princess.'

Cathy looked at herself in the long mirror, initially with disbelief. 'It's not like me, but I'm good as a princess.'

Mary pointed out that the new clothes were for work only. 'But you can keep the underwear – a present from your employer.'

Cathy was to start the next day. Things always went rapidly with Mary, if they were allowed to happen at all.

At the end of each of the first few days, Andrew would ask Cathy how it was going and receive short replies. When an opportunity arose, Andrew put the same questions to Mary.

'She gets on well enough with the customers. She fingers them a good deal, while she helps them with the clothes. I was nervous for a while, especially after she patted an elderly male customer on the bottom affectionately, but neither he nor his wife seemed to mind. One thing; she needs to brush up on her math. Can you get her to add correctly? Perhaps even show her to percentages?'

Cathy was cool towards arithmetic. Andrew bought her a mini-calculator in an attempt to make simple addition palatable. She got the hang of decimals quickly enough. Percentages were more problematic. Andrew began, 'Mary pays you by putting money into your bank account, doesn't she?' (Mary considered paying wages in cash as hopelessly primitive.) 'The bank pays 2 per cent interest per year. How much will your money increase by if you don't spend your salary – whatever it is in dong?'

This aroused her interest, and eventually Andrew could give her ten straightforward problems to work out.

He looked through her answers. 'You've got seven out of ten.'

'Why haven't I got ten out of ten?'

'Three of your answers are wrong.'

'Only seven out of ten!'

'That's not bad,' said Andrew encouragingly. He was used to teaching less-than-brilliant pupils.

'Hanh Phuc says your Vietnamese is coming on better,' commented Cathy.

They were silent for a while, but Cathy had more on her mind. 'When you go off to work, what do you do?'

Cathy had never expressed any interest in Andrew's daytime activities before. Perhaps it was a side effect of having a steadier job herself.

'It's a medical department, attached to the hospital. Scientists study whether a certain treatment or medicine really has an effect. Deciding this can mean complicated maths, and I advise them how to do it.'

Explaining things to Cathy presented problems. In some ways, it resembled answering questions from a small child with perhaps an eight-year-old's limited vocabulary. You answered the questions briefly and oversimplified and waited to see how much he or she had understood in the light of his or her further enquiries, which were often peculiar. But Cathy was hardly a small child; she had been forced to grow up quickly; she had encountered a range of people, tourists from all sorts of places, and she was sophisticated in dealing with them. But her life had been vastly different from Andrew's, with consequences he could only guess at.

'Can I go with you to the hospital and look round some day when I'm not at the shop? Meet the sick people. I've never been in a hospital.'

'I don't myself meet the sick people, the patients. I talk to the doctors who are deciding whether the patients have got better.' He became involved in the niceties of explaining experimental and control groups – of how neither the patient nor the doctors may know which group the participant belongs to.

'But the sick person knows if he is swallowing a pill?'

'The patients in the control group are given a pretend pill that doesn't contain the medicine. It's called a placebo.'

'Take me there. It will be interesting.'

Andrew hesitated while he wondered how he would present Cathy to his Vietnamese colleagues.

Cathy said, 'If the doctors wonder who I am, I'll tell them I work at the shop of a friend of yours.'

* * *

The next Saturday, they took the bus to the department, a simple journey Andrew made on weekends; otherwise, the department insisted that their driver pick him up in the car. Andrew showed Cathy into the labs. She didn't say much, but her eyes lit up with astonishment at the elaborate equipment.

Soon, they met a young man who greeted Andrew warmly and looked curiously at Cathy.

'This is Luc. He's working with me,' Andrew told Cathy.

Cathy gave her Vietnamese name, Doan Vien, adding, 'Andrew calls me Cathy. I work at a shop where an American Andrew knows is chief.'

'Cathy wanted to see where I work,' said Andrew. 'How's the analysis going?'

'It's going okay. It will take more time. I'll be finished soon.'

Andrew asked some more questions. It soon became clear that Luc had fastened in some difficulty right at the beginning. Why couldn't he have said so days ago?

Later, they met Tuan, and much the same pattern emerged. Andrew glanced at Cathy to see if she was bored and turning her attention to objects in the room; but she was following the conversation intently.

Later, when they were back home, Cathy said, 'Those men expect you to tell them what to do.'

'They're supposed to be developing into independent researchers. I can't stand around giving them detailed instructions all the time.'

'They can't understand what you say, but they're too proud to admit it. When they say it's going okay, don't believe them.'

'What shall I do then?'

'Tell them to come to you as soon things go wrong. They mustn't wait for you to ask them about it. You don't mind being bothered.'

Andrew had more or less worked this out for himself but was grateful for a second opinion, even if it came from Cathy.

* * *

Andrew spent the next few days going through the students' projects. It was not clear what Luc was intending. Andrew found an opportunity to meet up with him and ask some orienting questions.

'How are you estimating the effect of the age of the mice?'

'I am following Dr Thanh's procedures.'

'What are those?'

'Standard procedures.'

'Which standard procedures?'

'The procedures Dr Thanh has told me.'

Some complicating factor – perhaps language problems – was clearly in play. Yet Luc's English seemed reasonably assured. Perhaps he was afraid of seeming disloyal to Dr Thanh or to some higher directive from a ministry. Or perhaps it was what Cathy had been saying, that Luc would not admit to failing to understand. Andrew could not do much about the first kind of problem but felt a direct approach might help with the second kind. So he said, 'This isn't an easy programme, so don't be surprised if you have difficulties. But you must tell me when something is unclear. And don't think you have to agree with me all the time; I am perfectly accustomed to disagreement. I like "Yes, but" discussions.'

This direct approach paid off. Andrew was soon hearing a genuine Vietnamese-English 'No' – that short sharp sound – when Luc thought that Andrew himself was failing to recognize some crucial point.

* * *

Trung took Andrew to Dr Thanh's office a second time. The meeting was even briefer than the first.

'Dr Andrew, we shall be delighted if you give a presentation on a subject of your choice for us at the department.'

Andrew agreed to do so.

Dr Thanh gave a date and time for the hour-long seminar. 'Now if you will excuse me, I have another meeting.'

After leaving the room, Trung said to Andrew, 'I shall be repeating each sentence in Vietnamese after you say it in English.'

Andrew considered this. 'I'd better cut the presentation to half as long, then.'

The younger people spoke good English, but the older staff were more at home in Russian or Chinese.

* * *

Andrew wanted to make the talk of broad interest, so he began with a very basic principle and then developed it by simple steps that everybody could understand, until ten minutes before the end, he had arrived somewhere near the research front; he had learned to do this from Joe Briesley.

Once or twice, he had second thoughts at the end of a sentence and trailed off into a lengthy qualifying 'although' clause, making Trung desperate.

'Dr Andrew, can you say again what point you are making?'

For the most part, Trung's sentence-by-sentence translation helped by further slowing down the pace.

Afterwards, Trung said, 'As thanks for your presentation, we're going to a seafood restaurant for dinner this evening.'

The departmental driver took Andrew, Dr Thinh, Trung, Luc, and Tuan to a restaurant near the West Lake specializing in Vietnamese seafood. Dr Thinh chose the dishes in consultation with the waiter, with comments in Vietnamese from the others. While they waited for the food to arrive, conversation proceeded in Vietnamese.

After a while, Dr Thinh, sitting opposite Andrew, asked, 'Do you know what we're saying? We liked your presentation; it was easy to understand.'

The first dish – crab which they dipped in what Trung explained was tamarind sauce, something new for Andrew and spicy – arrived. Later came fried squid with chips, very much to Andrew's taste, including the delicious chips, which he should call French fried potatoes, of course, unless it sounded too colonial. And further exotic dishes followed. The party was in good spirits; it was a happy treat for the Vietnamese as well as for Andrew.

The talk turned to films. 'We see a lot of foreign films,' said Tuan. 'I like action films.'

'Do you go to the cinema for them?' asked Andrew.

'No, watch them on my computer, in the room at the department with the Internet connection.' His boss had temporarily left his place.

Chapter 19

It was April, and Andrew was returning to England, as he was to give a more advanced statistics course in the summer term to the agriculture and forestry students, a continuation of the one in the autumn term. The idea was that he should spend roughly half his time in Oxford and half in Hanoi, but the arrangements should be kept flexible.

Cathy took the news of his impending departure badly. 'May come, may go; now you're going, and I'll never see you again.'

Andrew was touched by her response. 'It's only for two months. You know I am supposed to alternate between Britain and Vietnam. I have to do some teaching. You can stay on in the flat; I'm not giving that up, so you can see I'm intending to come back. You've got Mary if you need grown-up company.'

Andrew arrived at Heathrow in the morning and made his way to Oxford, a tedious journey by bus and train, as he couldn't bring himself to pay for a taxi. He walked with his luggage down the high street to Hereford College, greeted the porter at the gate, and took his suitcases up to his room. He had promised to write to Cathy on his arrival, so he unpacked his computer, connected it up, and sent a brief message and then went out for a walk.

It was a sunny April day, far from warm; he had almost forgotten what it was like away from the warm, moist Vietnamese climate. In particular, the air was thin, nothing like the heavily scented atmosphere of the tropics. But he appreciated the feeling of security, the orderly traffic, the ease of crossing the streets, the absence of men calling out to him and children selling postcards. He bought a few essentials at the supermarket and returned to the college.

His room was too bare. Something more needed to go on the wall, and he pinned up the photograph of Cathy. Later, he was looking at it thoughtfully when the medical man, Hugh, knocked and walked in without waiting for a reply. He immediately took a look at the wall; he had followed Andrew's glance.

'Who's the girl?'

'Someone I met in Hanoi.'

'She's a bit young, isn't she? Mind you, it's hard to tell with Asiatic girls. But she looks underage.'

'It's nothing like that.'

'Oh well, I suppose I'd better not ask what it *is* like.'

Andrew paid no attention; he was not in the mood for long explanations at that moment. They were soon chatting about other things. They had an easy, undemanding relationship that could resume where it had left off in December, like the reacquaintance of undergraduate friends after the long vacation. They discussed the courses each of them was preparing for, along with making more general comment on what they had been up to.

But Hugh was looking at the picture again. 'She's an intriguing-looking girl. How did you say you met her?'

'I didn't say. But I suppose I'll have to tell you sooner or later …'

* * *

Andrew met the rector, who indicated that he wanted a word with him in private. They went to the rector's room, a pleasant enough place with comfortable old furniture.

'Would you be interested in a more permanent fellowship at Hereford, possibly with the title of associated professor? We are anxious to enable a modest expansion of our activities in the scientific and technical direction.'

Andrew wondered to himself whether Mary had made further stipulations he hadn't been told about when she modified the conditions in her late husband's will, in addition to the requirement for more women fellows.

'Should I make a formal application?'

'No – no, not exactly,' replied the rector, vaguely. 'We shall have to feel our way tentatively in that direction.' His hands illustrated this with delicate, exploratory motions. 'It is sufficient for me that you indicate an interest. This is a small college, and I am sure you understand that personal qualities weigh heavily. We live in proximity to each other. A number of us are of the opinion that you measure up to these requirements excellently. You are on friendly terms with the medical fellow, who is somewhat out on his own, and the chaplain is simply delighted with you, with special reference to dinner time conversation. Please don't take offence if I say that, in a completely open competition, it might be difficult to make the case for the specialized nature of your academic accomplishments. We shall need to word the announcement of the position with great care. Recent overseas experience would be a merit, particularly in connection with an aid programme in the Far East, something like that. These things are left to the discretion of the head of the college, in this case me. Just one point – it might be necessary for you to reduce your activities in Cambodia …I mean Vietnam – how silly of me – but not in the immediate future. The fellowship is normally regarded as a full-time post, but concessions can naturally be made.'

Andrew said this was attractive, so long as the appointment was part-time for the immediate future. He remembered Joe Briesley's warnings about lingering in Oxford or Cambridge and thought that they didn't apply to elderly people in part-time appointments.

*　*　*

The weather warmed up the next day, and Andrew ventured into the college garden. He was sitting there one morning when Tom, the gardener, approached him.

'Back again, I see, sir. Nice to see you. How did it go in Vietnam? If you don't mind, I'll sit here, and you can tell me all about it.'

'It's a poor country, but things are developing rapidly. I liked the people I met; everybody's friendly. But I'm inclined to feelings of confusion.'

'I understand you met a girl there. Dr Hugh says there's a picture of her on the wall in your room.'

'Has Hugh told you about the picture on the wall?'

'Dr Hugh and I have an agreement. He tells me what's going on upstairs, so to speak, and in return, I tell him anything interesting that's going on downstairs. Don't worry, sir, we're both very discreet. We don't gossip. Our interest is perfectly friendly, nothing malicious. I really admire you for taking in the girl the way you did – sort of adopting her in an informal way. It's thoroughly Christian behaviour, if rather un-English. But I can understand you find it confusing, having a girl straight off the street moving in with you like that. She's a foreigner, too, so that means language problems, even if Dr Hugh says she speaks some English.

'That reminds me,' continued the gardener, confidentially. 'Have you heard the news? About Mr Clement Hargreaves?'

'Something sensational? Has he been appointed a cabinet minister or won the pools or something?'

'He's getting married.'

'Good heavens. Quite a surprise. I suppose it's not so remarkable really, but it's unexpected.'

'Exactly my reaction. I mean (begging your pardon, sir, anyway, you're not a bachelor but a widower, I hear), if Mr Hargreaves isn't a confirmed bachelor, who is? So it was surprising all right. I don't know any details. Perhaps you can find out and tell me – of course I don't mean that you sort of join the club with Dr Hugh and myself.'

* * *

An hour later, Andrew was saying, 'Congratulations, Clemmie! I hear you're getting married. What's the name of the young lady?' Andrew sat down opposite Clement Hargreaves at the college table set for lunch. They had both come rather late, and they were almost the only fellows present.

'Her name is Miss Dorchester, actually.'

If the name had been Susan or Frances or something similar, Andrew would have responded with 'nice name,' but 'Miss Dorchester' left him stymied. Eventually he said, 'I once came across a Miss Gloucestershire, similar sort of less usual name.' He wasn't sure how this was being received. 'Mark and Hugh don't seem to be around, but I'm sure they will be delighted when they hear, of course.' He resisted the temptation to add humorously, 'It all goes to show that fellows of Hereford College *can* get married.'

'I sometimes wonder what kind of influence Mark and Hugh have on you,' said Clemmie, very seriously.

'I feel I'm rather too old for them to have any overwhelming influence on me, but I like them both and think they're interesting people – they say thought-provoking and often amusing things. You like them too, don't you? At very least, you were happy watching *Columbo* with them on Mark's television.'

'Yes, but Mark and I enjoy *Columbo* for utterly different reasons. I admire how he solves the murders; Mark giggles at Columbo's raincoat and naive remarks. It's true that we get on perfectly well on a day-to-day basis, but Mark is far too anti-authority, to the point of childish irresponsibility. He disapproves of my attempts to ingratiate myself with people of influence. He calls it sucking up. But I go to a lot of trouble for the benefit not only of myself but of Hereford College folk in general, including Mark. You have to suck up to important people to get on, to get yourself and your colleagues heard and your opinions respected. Mark won't accept that elementary fact of life.'

'Mark could be more ambitious, I suppose.'

'He should have stopped thinking that people float up on merit to a safe pigeonhole. For the moment, he's safe with the rector's support, but that won't last forever. One needs constantly to be cultivating friends in high places. I've understood from schooldays the amount of work that entails. An important step was to become a school prefect, to demonstrate potential leadership qualities. For this, sporting accomplishments were required. I diligently endured all the discomforts of the rugby football field without complaint, eventually making it to the third fifteen. I was a forward.'

'Oh, very good! The third fifteen was quite something in my school – particularly as there was a fourth fifteen and even an extra fourth fifteen.' Andrew continued thoughtfully, 'I suppose "fifth fifteen" was too awkward to say or sounded euphonious in the wrong way. I agree that rugby is very uncomfortable, particularly in the scrum, but some people say they enjoy it.'

'Rugby football isn't for enjoyment. It's for character building. One must show one has the energy to use one's talents to the full, as exemplified by fondness for and success in sports. Of course, Mark would sneer at all that.'

They moved to collect coffee.

Andrew returned to Clemmie's fiancée. 'Is Miss Dorchester well connected, by any chance?'

'Of course. And it's not a matter of chance. Every step in life must be taken with a view to future consequences. At school, I specialized in the classics, Latin and Greek, because that was best for a career in the civil service. It got me a university scholarship but was intolerably tedious. I switched to law at the university. Naturally, I attended all the union debates until midnight, talking first off the paper and then on the paper, never omitting to congratulate other speakers on their fine performance, until I was made librarian. The combination of being librarian at the Oxford Union, plus prefect and member of the third fifteen at school, confirmed that I had the necessary leadership qualities to win a scholarship for study in America at an Ivy League university for a year. During this period, I practised writing three-hour essays on topics like "decadence" so that I could win a short-term fellowship at an Oxford college. I learned how to write much the same essay on whatever the one-word topic, to show the necessary breadth of vision and grasp of detail. So here I am with a fellowship, though admittedly at a run-down college. But the next step, into a fast stream in the civil service, is following almost automatically.'

Andrew was curious to know more about Miss Dorchester's connections.

'Her father is a successful businessman – very rich. He's close to the management of the Dorchester Hotel in London, among many other activities. He was invited partly because of the coincidence of the name. After we are married, we shall move into a small flat that is an annex of the hotel, at a nominal rent, an exclusive address in a fashionable part of London. In addition, the father is making available a house in the country for weekends and holidays.'

'I am sure that Miss Dorchester appreciates you as an up-and-coming man. I expect you'll be really happy in her warm embrace – when she'll no longer be *Miss* Dorchester, of course.'

'Naturally I've already checked that our biologies function correctly together. But to resume discussion of Mark, He goes down well with the undergraduates, particularly the young women in tutorials. They appreciate his straightforward opinions, however outrageous. What he won't see is that he sucks up quite as much as I do but to the young rather than to the influential. In his lectures, he is still anti-authority, but he is careful not to say anything that will really antagonize the relevant professor of theology; in fact, one could say that he sucks up to him, too. If he were more prepared to take responsibility, he would cheerfully suck up even more than I do.'

'It's true he avoids promotion and ensuing responsibilities, but I think he would say that this enables him to do things for their own sake, rather than because they are part of a calculation of how to get on.'

'The additional bothers are with Mark's religious views. How can he find the nerve to continue as college chaplain when he brazenly explains, at least in private, that he doesn't believe in God? He is liable to deprive people of the solace of religious faith.'

'He would probably ask you as a lawyer, presumably accustomed to take on apparently hopeless cases, to explain why wishful thinking is preferable to the truth.'

'Oh dear, I was afraid Mark was having a bad influence on you.' Nevertheless Clemmie smiled as he said this. 'The point is that it is far from clear what is truth and what is wishful thinking.'

'What is truth? Be careful not to sound like Pontius Pilate, Clemmie. Actually, I think the three of us have another thing in common besides affection for *Columbo* – we're all a teeny weeny bit cynical.'

* * *

Andrew returned to the garden seat for a while in the afternoon and was soon joined by the gardener.

'Have you acquired any further information on that topic we were discussing earlier, sir?'

'Her name Is Miss Dorchester.'

'Miss Dorchester,' said Tom thoughtfully. 'That's a funny name for a girlfriend, isn't it, sir? Perfectly fitting for a schoolmistress or the dearly loved companion of one's mother's maiden great-aunt, but a girlfriend? Most unusual.'

'Miss Dorchester is apparently very rich, or her parents are.'

'Ah! There you have it. Andrew, if you don't my calling you that, sir, I really appreciate the way you give me the critical information needed, without my having to ask for it directly as if I'm an old gossip. Let's keep it that way – in fact, you would be most welcome in our select group. What do you say? I shall have to confer with Dr Hugh, of course.'

'Well, thank you for the invitation, Tom, and by all means, call me Andrew, but I think it's best if I stay formally outside your select group, somewhere close to the periphery. One other thing you might like to know while I remember – Clemmie has checked that the biologies of the young couple function together correctly.'

'Ah! Now you've done it again, sir, Andrew I mean – told me what I want to know without my having to ask. It's perhaps sufficient that you *are* only on the periphery of our group, rather than inside.' Tom sat back and breathed in. 'It's a lovely day, and I must be attending to the garden. I love working with plants. They are so innocent, compared to all those animals you see on television in the nature programs. Those little beasts may be treasures of biodiversity, but they've no morals. They're forever copulating indiscriminately and eating each other, regardless of the pain they're causing.' He breathed in deeply again. 'Though mind you, plants are not quite as innocent as they look. Those fresh green leaves and succulent seeds are often full of poisons – alkaloids I think they're called – that finish off the careless or unsuspecting predator. That innocent appearance can be misleading.' He looked at Andrew.

'Tom, I don't think we are being especially reprehensible here. Clemmie gave no impression of talking confidentially to me; we're not being spiteful or even notably bitchy, and we are keeping the information to ourselves, aren't we, or at least within the group? I don't think we need worry about alkaloids.'

'I do agree, sir. See you again soon, I hope, perhaps in this same convenient spot in the garden.'

'One more thing before you go, Tom; can we look forward to any similar happy event involving Hugh rather than Clemmie?'

'I'm sorry, sir; the rules of our society are very strict; no discussion of each other's private life.'

Tom moved off.

* * *

Andrew was busy with his more advanced course on statistics for the agriculturalists and foresters. They were mostly the same students who had attended his earlier course, a mixture of undergraduate and graduate students.

'We learn a lot from the cross-group discussions,' commented Miranda, who was taking this course as well, 'even more than from the lectures, actually. And they're good socially. By the way, would you like to come to the departmental wine tasting? Friday's the next time, beginning at five o'clock with light food, so you probably won't need dinner. You'll find it in the tea room, in Agri. It's mostly middle-aged people like you who come – technicians, secretaries – also one or two research students, occasionally one of the lecturers. The gardener's holding it this time. It doesn't cost much. It's good fun, and you sometimes learn something about wine.'

Andrew decided to go to the wine tasting. He arrived a little before five and met a familiar figure extracting corks and adding ingredients to a salad.

'Ah, Tom, you must be the gardener organizing the wine tasting Miranda told me about.'

'Hope you enjoy this evening. Yes, I work part-time here, looking after the experiments in the departmental greenhouse.'

The other wine tasters arrived, twelve altogether, and Andrew sat down at a table with Miranda on his left and Christine, another young research student, on his right. Opposite them sat a middle-aged lady, the departmental secretary, who introduced herself as Mrs Riley.

Tom went round pouring out wine from bottles with concealed labels into the three glasses, marked A, B, and C, at each place. He addressed the company. 'This evening we are comparing three kinds of Cotes du Rhone. One costs seven pounds, one costs ten pounds, and one costs fifteen pounds. I'll tell you which is which at the end. You are to say whether you prefer A, B, or C. I'm not asking you to say which is the most expensive, only which you like best.'

The group of tasters helped themselves to the salad, sipped the wines, and tried to identify them by the written descriptions Tom had provided.

'"Inky purple colour; aroma of cassis, blackberries, liquorice, and fresh cream,"' Christine read out loud. 'Can anyone make anything of that? What's cassis, anyway?'

Andrew had no idea.

'Sort of blackcurrant, I think,' said Mrs Riley.

Miranda was reading the next. '"Ruby-red colour, with a nose of lively cherry, crushed coffee bean, and a hint of spice." Can't make anything of that. *Crushed coffee bean* for goodness' sake!'

'Perhaps it's easier to go on colour. Isn't wine A more inky purple than ruby red?' wondered Andrew. 'What about the third wine—'

'That's supposed to be red rather than purple, too,' said Miranda. 'I agree, A is the most inky purple. So we say that A is the one that tastes of blackberries and cream. While I think of it, what's happened to Paula? She usually comes to wine tasting.'

'Paula's depressed; the doctor told her to stay at home for a month. She's on pills,' said Christine. 'One of the research students,' she added for Andrew's benefit. 'She has supervisor problems.'

'Awful lot of people get depressed these days. Was it always like this?' Miranda asked Andrew and Mrs Riley.

'I suppose people got depressed, but they didn't see doctors and go on pills so often,' said Mrs Riley. 'You just accepted that you felt a bit low sometimes.'

'Drug firms must be doing nicely out of the pills,' commented Miranda. 'It's a good development for them.'

Andrew refrained from commenting.

They discussed which wine they liked best and filled in their forms. Tom collected them, added up the scores, and was soon announcing, 'Eight of you put the middle-priced as best, two thought the most expensive was best, and congratulations Christine and Mrs Riley, you liked the cheapest best. Makes life easier.'

Miranda wondered, 'Why didn't more of us like the most expensive wine best?'

'According to my husband,' said Mrs Riley, 'people don't store the expensive wines properly, so they don't come to their right.'

The talk loosened up. 'You aren't married, Andrew, are you? Were you ever?' asked Miranda.

'My wife died some years ago.'

'You should try computer dating, like us.' She leaned forward to talk to Christine across Andrew. 'How did it go in the great Deep South of America? Did your mum accept you were over there for a whole month?'

'In the end, but not before she said, "Whatever you do, don't come back pregnant by a black man."'

'Funny she's racist like that.'

'She worries so unnecessarily. She could have realized by now that I'm more into women, so to speak.'

Andrew had been following this exchange of remarks across him with some surprise, turning his head first towards the one girl and then towards the other.

'Anyway, how's it going with your latest?' Christine asked Miranda.

'Bill? Oh, he's all right, I suppose. But he keeps asking me to do things—'

Mrs Riley broke in with, 'Really, I think you ladies can spare Andrew and me the fascinating details. This is supposed to be wine tasting.'

'I suppose it is, really,' said Miranda. 'Actually Christine and I ought to be leaving now. I've enjoyed the evening a lot. See you all next time!'

They got up.

Andrew continued to chat with Mrs Riley, who remarked, 'Those girls seem to regard us as part of the furniture.'

Chapter 20

It was near closing time at Mary's Eastern and Western Stores. A customer, a tourist from Australia, had been fitted up in her newly sewn dress, with Cathy in attendance. She looked at a photograph pinned up on the wall and asked, 'Who is this?'

'It's an Englishman I've chosen as my father,' Cathy told her.

'You've chosen him as your father? Has he adopted you? Will he be taking you back to England?'

'No, it's not official like that. But I look after him when he's in Hanoi.'

A thoughtful look was noticeable on the customer's face, but she was in a hurry. Later, with the customer departed, Cathy closed the shop and went to the Internet cafe. She started on an email. She wrote out, experimentally, 'I want you.' After consideration, she altered the sentence to, 'I need you.'

* * *

In the middle of the same day in England, Andrew looked through his email. He was about to trash an obscure-looking message that the computer had declared to be junk mail but opened it at the last moment out of curiosity. As he looked at the message, a voice from behind read aloud, with some amusement:

Andrew
Come back soon
I miss you
I need you
Cathy

Andrew turned to find that Hugh had entered the room unnoticed. 'No wonder you've got that special moony look,' said the medical man. 'I'd have it too, with such a letter. Cathy is, of course, the girl whose picture hangs on the wall. You'll have to update me.'

Andrew wasn't ready for this. 'Now isn't a suitable time; it will take a while, and it's too close to dinner. Instead, you can tell me what you know of how the high-ups in the Church of England regard the chaplain.'

'He has quite a following among the liberal theologians, I'm told. The traditionalists regard him with deep disgust. The trouble began years ago with his thesis.'

'What was it on?'

'Primitive animism. The examiner was fetched in from Scandinavia somewhere and praised it highly. Apparently said it showed great analytical and imaginative perception. Then the theological faculty at the university, I forget which, in the north of England, dragged its feet. It said the thesis was unacceptable because it was written from an insufficiently Christian standpoint. He was in a nasty position. Hereford College rescued him by making him chaplain. The rector was certainly involved; he likes liberal theologians and loves teasing solemn people by making controversial appointments.'

They chatted on for a few minutes until, at seven o'clock, it was time for one of the more elaborate college dinners. Sir Oliver Laine, a friend of the rector, was to be guest. Andrew had not met him since the interview at the club.

Hugh and Andrew, dressed in their university gowns, moved towards the dining hall. In the anteroom, the fellows were assembling for sherry. A commotion indicated the arrival of Sir Oliver, accompanied by another elderly important-looking man, whose face seemed faintly familiar to Andrew.

'Good evening everybody,' boomed Sir Oliver in relaxed resonant tones. 'I've arrived with an uninvited guest, to add zest to things. Most of you know Effy Hacker, don't you? This is an historic occasion, because— I'll leave it to Effy to explain why.'

Sir Oliver and Effy Hacker had aged differently. Sir Oliver was benign and relaxed, in the manner of a child's favourite old uncle. Effy's face was taut, worn, and hostile, evoking a butcher's meat chopper.

'Thank you, Oliver,' he said without warmth and announced baldly,

'Today I have decided that my entire collection of historic sports cars, including all my Jaguar E-types …' He paused before adding impressively, 'will be given to the nation.'

'EFFY 1, EFFY 2, EFFY 3, and so on; you can read on the number plates,' amplified Sir Oliver. He caught sight of the college servant. 'Ah, George, are you offering me sherry? Stand by a moment. I have learned from the wine connoisseurs what they call the two-glass test. In order to appreciate a fine old sherry to the full, it is essential to drink the first glass rather quickly, preferably on an empty stomach. Then the second glass is delicately savoured in a state of meditative relaxation.'

(Clement Hargreaves was saying in a disgusted stage whisper to his nearest neighbours, 'Oh, good heavens!')

Sir Oliver emptied the glass. 'Kindly refill.'

George, the waiter, smiled and did as requested.

Sir Oliver was approving. 'Damned good sherry. I must say that if the Norrington evaluation of the performance of Oxford colleges was drawn up according to the quality and quantity of the drink served at high table, instead of how well the boys and girls do in their final examinations, Hereford College would move straight to the top of the league. No doubt about it.' His hand, initially held low, described an arc to illustrate the dramatic change in position; at the culmination, Sir Oliver was elevated on his toes in the manner of a ballet dancer.

'Thank you, Oliver,' smiled the rector. 'I shall take that as a compliment and pass it on to Francis, our steward.'

One of the fellows asked Effy where the E-types were going to be on view, now they were being given to the nation.

Oliver answered on Effy's behalf. 'When you are dealing with a man of Effy's calibre, the word *give* in the phrase *give to the nation* should be taken with a pinch of salt. The vehicles will be exhibited in Lord What's His Name's motor show, at a pretty stiff admission price. At the same time, they will be used to publicize Effy's new share release. There are limits to the idealism even of a man as distinguished as Effy.' Lowering his voice, Sir Oliver added, 'He wishes he could give his ex-wives to the nation and exhibit them in the same way, to help with the alimonies.'

Asked what had induced him to dispose of his cars, Effy said, 'A medical condition.'

This reduced the fellows to silence, while they wondered how serious the medical condition was.

'By *medical condition*,' explained Sir Oliver, 'Effy means old age. He finds it more difficult to concentrate nowadays. He suffered three minor but expensive accidents in as many months, after which his doctor strongly recommended him to give up driving, especially as he had made himself uninsurable. I'm having much the same problem.'

'I'm also making important contributions to established charities, of course,' said Effy.

'Effy is naturally concerned to dispel any aura of elitism associated with a large collection of expensive sports cars,' Sir Oliver enlarged. 'So he is making an anonymous donation to the Salvation Army. I'm lending a helping hand here. I've already written an unsigned column in the *Porterfield Morning Telegraph* announcing the substantial anonymous donation and will follow up with a signed letter referring to the news in the column and speculating as to who the anonymous donor is. The speculation will be further taken up in the "Peterborough" column of the *Daily Telegraph*, which will refer to my letter in the Porterfield paper. When sufficient interest has been aroused, I shall reveal the true identity of the anonymous donor in a leak to the parliamentary correspondent of *The Times*.'

It was time to move on from the subject of cars. Hugh, standing nearby, introduced himself to the guests. Effy Hacker responded somewhat coolly, to Andrew's surprise, 'Yes, yes, I know very well who you are. We've met before. I know exactly who you are.' Perhaps he was anxious to demonstrate that his medical condition had not affected his memory. He caught sight of Andrew. 'Rector, introduce us to this new chap.'

'I was just about to do so. As it happens, Oliver knows him well. Sidney, this is Andrew Carter, whom we were delighted to welcome to the college last year. He evaluates the role of genes on how we react to medicines. Not the sort of jeans we wear but the little things that make us what we are, in interaction with the environment, of course. Medical statistics.'

'Great Scott, what a topic! So why are you here, exactly?' Effy asked Andrew brusquely.

Andrew explained that he alternated between Hereford College and Hanoi in Vietnam.

'Why on earth Vietnam?'

'Effy, Andrew's with us in this international aid programme I told you about, as a statistical adviser,' intervened Sir Oliver. 'You must have forgotten.'

'Suppose I did forget. I can't possibly remember everything you go on about. This Vietnam caper is well intentioned, of course, but I doubt if it's a good idea. They're clever chaps there. Must be – first they showed off the French and then the Americans and finally the Chinese. They'll exploit any help we give them and then outcompete us on the world markets. That's how the Japanese and Indians got going in electronics – the Americans gave them a lot of help at a crucial time.'

'The economists say that Third World development will expand world trade and everybody will benefit,' said Sir Oliver. 'By the way, I should like to have a word with you later on, Hugh, about a little matter where I think you can help.'

Hugh nodded assent.

'Never trust an economist,' resumed Effy. 'They've no common sense. I saw a document one of them had written about the housing market the other day – packed with funny dots and tedious equations with stuff in brackets. Calculus even. Completely bonkers. You can't understand the complex psychology of the housing market with equations.'

'When Effy talks about funny dots, I expect he's referring to decimal points, aren't you Effy?' asked the rector.

'Is that what they're called, rector? Andrew, your line of country.'

'I expect you do mean decimal points. They're not too bad really, when you get used to them.' Andrew was beginning to feel that he had a walk-on role in a stage farce and was being wrong-footed; he needed help. 'What do you think about aid?' he asked the chaplain, who was standing nearby, listening with a polite smile.

'Professionally, I should say international aid is in total harmony with the spirit of the Sermon on the Mount. Love your neighbour as yourself.'

'For crying out loud,' exclaimed Effy. 'Why must you gentlemen of the cloth mix religion with politics? I'm inclined to think "Render unto Caesar that which is Caesar's, and to God that which is God's," should be your guide.'

'Rather than the Sermon on the Mount?' asked the chaplain innocently. 'Don't you love your neighbour?'

Effy was also towards the end of his second glass of sherry, and alcohol made him irascible, it seemed. 'Of course I love my neighbour,' he said in grim tones. 'But we must listen to the environmentalists. They tell us that, in nature, life is a struggle for existence in which the best adapted animals win and reproduce themselves faster than the less well adapted. That is how the race gets improved. We do well to bear that in mind. What is natural is good, the environmentalists are always telling us. Cut out sentimentality and indiscriminate aid handouts. Cruelty is the ultimate kindness, if you think big in evolutionary terms.'

Andrew was aware of the chaplain's distaste for social Darwinism, and wondered if he'd react. The rector, however, broke in, 'Oliver, last time you were here you told us that the environmentalists had gone bonkers, like the economists Effy complains of.'

'I suppose I did say something of the sort. Some wretched ecologists were trying to ban artificial fertilizer. We'd never feed everybody without artificial fertilizer. Anyway, it was bad for business. I'd still got some old ICI shares.'

'While on the subject of mixing religion and politics,' began the chaplain expansively, 'I noticed the photograph in the papers from a few Sundays ago where Sir Oliver Laine, MP, was piously emerging from church, beautifully dressed I may say, in the company of several other high dignitaries from the Conservative Party, including Sir Sidney Hacker.'

'That's different. One must set a good example to one's constituents,' said Effy, ironically Andrew hoped, but it was hard to tell.

Effy said, 'You're okay, chaplain, and I like you personally, but you're sadly unorthodox. You don't even believe in the devil. Young people, working-class chaps, and so on don't behave decently unless someone has frightened them with the devil.'

'Fear of the devil is like national service. Recommended for the young by the middle aged, something good for other people,' remarked the chaplain. 'But can I ask you, Effy, or Oliver for that matter, as we're all fond of each other, and I know you'll take it in good part, what deters you from shoplifting, say from a country shop with no surveillance cameras? It's not so difficult to get away with, and if you did get caught, you could easily talk yourself out of it. Are you afraid of the devil? Or do you think it's unfair on the shop owner to make off with things?'

Andrew was dying to hear their response to this. Sir Oliver had been opening and shutting his mouth, but before anything came out, the rector deftly summoned everyone into the dining room, shepherding Sir Oliver and Effy before him. The three of them sat together at the head of the main table, with Mark one place further down, while Andrew and Hugh landed at the bottom, out of earshot.

* * *

'Sir Oliver seems to be quite a pal of the rector,' remarked Andrew to Hugh. 'Difficult to see why.'

'They both like teasing people. Earlier, they baited self-important traditional conservatives; nowadays it's mainly earnest liberals.'

'There's more to it than that, isn't there?'

The two of them were now separated from the other diners because the nearest two had suddenly left, summoned by the college servant on important business.

'You're right. The rector wants to raise the college's standards, but we haven't got any money. He has to elicit donations from people like Sir Oliver. Actually, Oliver was prepared to contribute to my salary and research expenses but, inevitably, with strings attached.'

'What sort of strings?'

'Be careful who you talk to here. As you know, he's acquired shares in the medical company, A to Z Pharmaceuticals. He wanted me to provide clinical evidence in support of one of its products – not Feelgood-Two, an earlier concoction, much dodgier than Feelgood, which is more or less okay.'

Andrew laughed. 'He didn't expect you to fudge the results, did he?'

'More or less – at any rate, move into an extremely grey area ethically.'

Andrew's smile froze. 'You didn't go along with it?'

'No, I refused.'

'Was the rector involved? Fudging scientific results is a hell of a way to raise college standards.'

'He said that of course we should refuse, but from diplomatic considerations, it was better that the refusal came from me rather than him.'

Andrew, about to put a forkful of food in his mouth, removed it as a nasty thought came into his mind. 'Was I meant to be involved with the statistical analysis of this bogus trial?'

'No, no, no,' Hugh reassured Andrew. *Of course not* …no, no, no.' He paused and switched from a reassuring to a confidential tone. 'Well, actually yes, that was the idea at one point. You know how it is; the first thing you do with unsatisfactory experimental results is get a statistician to wave his wand over them – transform the data to reveal significant differences, that sort of thing. Of course I put a stop to that idea. My refusal to be involved naturally covered you, too.' He added, 'You're not supposed to know about this. As a matter of fact, I learned about the background only because I intercepted the rector's email.' He smiled vaguely and took a mouthful of soup.

'You intercepted the rector's mail?' Andrew, also engaged with his soup, put his spoon down, incredulous.

'Yes. This is a deadly secret, of course. You won't tell anyone, will you? Scout's honour?'

'I've never been a scout, but I suppose I can put my hand on my heart.'

Hugh was prepared to accept this. 'I act as the computer nerd round here, as you know. It is quite a lot of work. The elder fellows are hopeless if anything goes wrong with their computers, and my time spent teaching them what to do and correcting their mistakes is largely unpaid. The rector is particularly clueless. I thought it was only fair with a modest level of unofficial compensation. I fixed his computer so that his email was posted to me as well, together with his replies.'

'That's fantastic!'

'It was only for three days, in the first place.'

'In the first place?' queried Andrew.

'The rector's emails were *absolutely fascinating* – much better than the documents that are left lying around by the printer. The first one I opened began off, "Desmond darling, when you left last night it was as if a light had gone out of my life" – that sort of thing. Reminded me of the letters the Oxford Movement people wrote to each other in the 1830s. Pretty innocent, but not entirely so—'

'Do keep your voice down.' Andrew glanced down the table. The nearest diners were fortunately immersed in a loud and lively conversation.

'You understand, three days wasn't enough. My conscience extended the three days to a week and then to a month and then to three months …' He looked coyly at Andrew. 'Of course, you're not interested …'

Andrew sighed. 'Okay, I'm agog to hear more. Which Desmond was it?'

'That's what's so awfully interesting. Desmond Bingley. He writes local history, studies of northern England. He's much appreciated as a teacher. The rector's trying to get him to move from being a red-brick professor to a fellowship here. Sir Oliver is to fix a supplement to his salary, paid for indirectly by the Conservative Research Department. In return, Desmond Bingley is to write fulsomely on how much appreciated Sir Oliver was as a constituency MP.'

'Did darling Desmond agree?'

'After masses of emails, some of them really juicy, he accepted the deal so long as he could include the appreciation of Sir Oliver as a footnote, ascribed to the rector. I had just read the final exchange when I met the rector in the corridor. He was sitting on the sofa in the corridor with a glass of sherry, sighing to himself. He saw me, sighed again, and said, "The things I do for Hereford College. You've no idea. They are physically and emotionally exhausting, Hugh." He actually said that.'

'Touching.'

'I told him how much we all appreciated his efforts on behalf of the college. Then I rather lost my head. I said, jokingly, "As a doctor, my advice is, 'Lie back and think of England.' I must have been under the influence of those love letters. He gave me a funny look. I realized that I had better cancel the diversion of his email to my computer.'

'Did you do so at once?'

'Pretty much. Not absolutely at once because he was in the middle of an *absolutely fascinating* correspondence about university funding, but I stopped reading his emails less than six months later.'

The two diners returned to their places, so that further discussion was impossible.

The dessert arrived. The rector made a speech.

'It is my great pleasure to welcome Sir Oliver here today, and I should like to point out that it was on this very day forty-five years ago that he began as a member of Parliament. Congratulations, Oliver!'

All the diners, even Clemmie, applauded warmly.

Sir Oliver rose to his feet. 'Thank you, rector. And it's an immense pleasure to be here today. I ask myself, why do I like coming to Hereford College so much? Apart from the excellent food and drink, the answer is because I can say what I like to anybody here, for instance the chaplain, and he doesn't react as if I meant it personally.'

Chuckles were heard from the other diners, who seemed, Andrew felt, to be expecting further entertainment. Sir Oliver, now in his eighties, was notorious for singing after dinner. The gentlemen at the high table braced themselves for the inevitable.

'That was a wonderful dinner; thank you, Rector. Thank you very much, especially as I don't get invited to dinner as often as I used to. You could say I am more dined against than dining nowadays, as that fellow Bowra put it. Now if this were Scandinavia, we should all be joining happily together in a song at this point, but it's England, so instead I shall round off a *perfect* evening by reciting my favourite poem. My mother first showed it to me. She always had a good eye for poetry. She's in heaven now, at least I think so, though you can't be sure – the things she got up to on the side – God bless her. Reciting this poem will be a delight. It will make everybody *beautifully* nostalgic. You'll all join in the chorus, won't you?'

He was still standing and recited from memory, in a booming voice:

By the old Moulmein Pagoda, lookin' lazy at the sea,

There's a Burma girl a-settin', and I know she thinks of me;

For the wind is in the palm-trees, and the temple-bells they say:

'Come you back, you British soldier; come you back to Mandalay!'

Then Sir Oliver was signalling to the company, in the manner of an orchestral conductor, to come in with:

On the road to Mandalay,

Where the flyin' fishes play,

An' the dawn comes up like thunder outer China

'crost the Bay!

About half the assembled fellows joined in, with varying degrees of enthusiasm.

('What an imposition,' the medieval historian was whispering to his neighbour.)

An' they talks a lot o' lovin', but what do they understand?

…
I've a neater, sweeter maiden in a cleaner, greener land!

As the recitation continued, the fellows warmed up good-naturedly over the choruses, and Sir Oliver could end in triumph, sit down to warm applause, and announce in a voice dripping with sentiment, 'That's the finest poem – the absolutely *finest* poem – in the English language.'

One of the other fellows raised his voice across the table. 'I seem to remember you calling it a good bad poem in that newspaper article you wrote recently.'

'That's different – that was a newspaper article. You can't admit to liking Kipling *officially*. Besides I was short of time and took the material from an essay by George Orwell.'

'With acknowledgement, I hope?'

'Well – not actually, now I come to think of it. It was only the *Porterfield Morning Telegraph*; it would have been pedantic to give sources. Anyway, who reads George Orwell's essays nowadays?'

'What's this I'm hearing? Did you perpetrate a filch, Oliver?' asked the rector.

'Not a filch, in the strict sense – more a sort of absent-minded, gentlemanly …snitch. Like when you borrow a young man's umbrella that resembles the one you've forgotten to bring and it's raining hard. So not a full-blooded filch. But perhaps a leettle, sensu stricto, snitch.'

Andrew asked a colleague across the table, who was said to have political connections, 'Why didn't Oliver Laine have more of a career as a cabinet minister?'

'He was briefly Minister for the Arts,' explained the colleague, 'if you remember. The trouble is, although he seems to have plenty of money, no one knows quite where he gets it. Prime Ministers don't want to risk more financial scandals than they can easily avoid.'

'But he's still an MP.'

'Oh yes. He's sometimes called Father of the House. He's popular with his constituents, who say he understands their problems and takes a lot of trouble dealing with them. One or two of his stuffier constituency workers would love to get rid of him, of course, but they can't get him to step down voluntarily. They can't force him to, either, because he knows too much about them, or so it's said.'

On the way out, the chaplain, meeting up with Hugh and Andrew, commented, 'I quite like that poem normally, but having to chant the chorus, with him reciting in stage Cockney like that, I can barely describe my feelings towards Sir Oliver. I …I …wanted to …'

'Slosh him one,' suggested the medical man.

'Not exactly that, but I really nursed …nursed …'

'Murderous intents,' suggested Hugh.

'Well, I wouldn't put it like that—'

'Always within the constraints imposed by brotherly, Christian love, of course.'

'Exactly.' The chaplain relaxed.

'After all, Jesus Himself was prepared to use violence in the temple,' continued the younger man, equably.

The chaplain nodded wisely.

Hugh glanced at him. 'Mind you, I expect even Jesus harboured dark thoughts on that occasion.'

The fellows ambled out of the dining room in a relaxed mood. Andrew wandered off to his room in a daze, started up his computer, and wrote off an email:

Cathy,

I miss you too. I'll come as soon as I can.

Andrew

He got up and found that the medical man had somehow slipped into his room, unobserved again, and, to judge from his expression, had read the email over Andrew's shoulder.

'Stimulating chap, Kipling. Actually, I've really come in about the little word Oliver Laine had with me after dinner. He wants to find a key opinion leader to put his name on a paper describing the results of the Feelgood trial in Vietnam, the one you're involved in.'

'I'm not involved in it, for goodness sake; the most I've done is to induce two people to take part in the trial. They needed the money, and I was satisfied the risks were negligible and that I'd explained them properly.'

'Sure, Andrew, you're like me, snow-white. We drift a bit from time to time, but we can always blame people like Sir Oliver.'

'You're not writing *your* name on this paper?'

'No, I've got a much better idea for a key opinion leader – my old professor. I want you to come along and help me noose him. Your presence will be valuable support. Let me do most of the talking; just put in a word now and again. We need to get his professional approval of the trial – get him to agree, as a key opinion leader, that there's no evidence for Feelgood having side effects.'

'If you really want me around, I suppose I can come – collegial solidarity, and all that. Hope you know what you're doing.'

* * *

The following day, Hugh and Andrew were standing outside a door marked,

Horace P. Bradmore
Professor emeritus, Clinical Psychiatry

Hugh knocked on the door.

A voice from within, loud but quavery, responded with a final hint of questioning, 'Bradmore?'

They entered and sat down on the narrow sofa that the professor, dressed in suit and tie, indicated with a wave of hand.

'I normally have a waiting time of six months for a casual interview of this kind,' the retired professor was saying from his spacious armchair behind a broad and heavy-looking antique table in his office. Otherwise the room was small and cramped, with bookcase shelves loaded with files ascending to the ceiling. It looked as if the professor had retained his former oversized old table and chair after being obliged to move into a smaller room on retirement.

'Bradmore is a very busy man. But I made a special concession for Hugh, my former pupil. Bradmore has always had a soft spot for Hugh. And who is your companion, Hugh?'

'This is Dr Andrew Carter, who alternates between Hereford College and Vietnam, where he is a statistical advisor. He is acquainted with the trial that Sir Oliver Laine would like you to comment on.'

'As always, I am delighted to be of service, even if certain people think Bradmore is getting …what's the word I want?'

An embarrassingly long pause ended by Andrew asking, 'Elderly?'

'That wasn't the word I was thinking of … It begins with *s*.'

'Senior?' suggested Hugh.

Professor Bradmore's face brightened. 'Now it's come to me. *Senile* — that's the word I was engaged in remembering.'

'But you're full of intellectual vigour, Professor,' put in Hugh. 'Only somebody who really is senile could think otherwise.'

'That's right on target, Hugh. Actually it was Professor …Professor What's-his-name who was saying the other day, "Let's face it, Horace, we're both getting on in years, advancing dangerously close to senility …" He should speak for himself, silly fellow, not drag in Bradmore.'

'So you're happy to write a commentary on the trial in Vietnam?'

The professor's face clouded over again. 'It's not the mental effort that bothers me; it's the physical strain of standing on a chair to fetch down files from the bookshelves, collecting references from the library, writing tables, that sort of thing.'

'Sir Oliver understands that very well,' reassured Hugh. 'The scientists from his company, A to Z Pharmaceuticals, will carefully prepare a draft of the paper, complete with introductory background, methods, figures, tables, analysis, and discussion. You will read the draft, suggest any modifications of the text that they should make, and give your final approval.'

The professor relaxed. 'That sounds a very good start.' A concerned look reappeared. 'Does that mean that Bradmore will have to share authorship with a bevy of mediocrities from industry?'

'Not at all, not at all. Sir Oliver's opinion is that the paper will carry its proper weight, from a key opinion leader, only if you are the sole official author. The paper will appear in a renowned middle-ranking clinical journal that meets with your approval.'

'Splendid, splendid. Will this duty carry a modest fee? I did not enter this ancient profession for material reward, but the bank tells me my investments have not fared well in the recent decade, and naturally, I must think of the future, for my family's sake.'

'What fee would be appropriate?' asked Hugh.

'I would not normally undertake a commission of this kind for less than one thousand pounds.'

'Sir Oliver is considering a minimum of three thousand pounds.'

'Splendid, splendid; Sir Oliver is indeed a man of understanding.'

Professor Bradmore rose from his chair to indicate that the audience was at an end. He didn't escort Hugh and Andrew to the door, perhaps because the gap between the side of the table and the bookcases would have required an undignified shuffle on his part.

Hugh and Andrew conveyed their thanks, sedately left the office, and walked along the lofty corridor of the ancient building and down the first flight of stairs.

Just before leaving through the main exit, which was deserted, Hugh raised his hand in the air, and Andrew briefly clasped it – two footballers who had collaborated in the scoring of a crucial goal.

'We did it!' said Hugh, and they had a fit of giggles as they walked through the august doors.

'Will the editor of the renowned middle-ranking clinical journal have any problems with the arrangements?' wondered Andrew.

'I shouldn't think so. If necessary, Sir Oliver will provide a pecuniary inducement.'

'Does he dish out pecuniary inducements all round? Are you accepting cash payments from him?'

'Keep your hair on, Andrew! No, he's never offered me cash, and I should be suspicious and refuse if he did. But if you have any ambitions above the average, in medicine or many other professions, you can't avoid entering grey ethical areas. With Sir Oliver, it's impossible; you must have grasped that even before you took up with him. The thing is, don't cross over from grey into black. So far, you haven't. He may have helped to arrange your present job, but the money comes from wholly respectable sources.'

'I'm worried about Feelgood.'

'Don't. It's harmless small potatoes and can even be useful. You can feel good about it. And Horace Bradmore is basically sound, even if his memory isn't what it was – touch of vascular dementia. And he's only following customary procedures in taking payment for authoring an article that a drug firm has ghostwritten for him.'

'I suppose most doctors are cynical about drug firms,' said Andrew.

'Yes, and remember, life would be duller without Sir Oliver.'

They had left the Headington area where the hospital was located and were about to walk back to town past Magdalen College. There was a relaxed, vacation-time feeling and a lull in the traffic. Before them, nearest on the right, lay a splendid view of Magdalen's medieval tower in mid-afternoon sunshine and on the left the Botanic Gardens, with other ancient buildings in the background standing along the curve of the high street.

Hugh paused to look at this classic Oxford scene. 'Not bad, what?'

But Andrew regarded it with distaste. 'Oxford's okay in term time, with young people running around; now in the vacation it's creepy. I want some healthy normality.'

'Then I suggest we take a relaxed walk to Cowley and look at the car factories there. You'll get a good dose of normal life, and I'll see where some of my patients live. Could be interesting. Come on, back to the roundabout and off down Cowley Road.'

Hugh turned on his heel, and Andrew followed.

In Cowley, they came to the factory that BMW had taken over and saw the streets with rows of modest houses where some of Hugh's patients lived. They rounded off the trip by drinking warm draught bitter beer at a local pub. It was crowded, and they sat at a table close to customers who looked as if they might know from first-hand experience about the shop floor of the BMW factory. They began chatting, and Andrew asked his neighbour at the table what he thought of the impending new Mini.

'The shop floor's really modern and functional, and the new Mini will sell well, I expect.'

'Would you buy one yourself?'

'Actually, the dream of my life is to own a Porsche.'

Behind Andrew, a game was at a climax, with a dart missing its target.

'Fuck!'

'Language, Phil,' one of the few women customers reminded the player.

Shortly after this, Hugh said to Andrew, 'If you're restored to normality, let's get back to college, in good time for dinner in the hall.'

Andrew agreed; he was feeling restored.

Chapter 21

As it was mid-June and the start of the long vacation in Oxford and he had no more teaching commitments for the immediate future, Andrew flew back to Hanoi. From emails, he knew that Mary, who had disapproved of Cathy having Andrew's flat to herself, had insisted that she move in with her. Mary's room, which included a simple stove for cooking, was not large, and Andrew would not have been surprised if the two of them had gotten on each other's nerves. But Mary said disputes had been limited.

Cathy, though she continued to look in at Andrew's flat every two or three days, liked having company in the evenings; Mary was glad to have help with meals and cleaning. Cathy came with few possessions and was not in the way. But the result, as Mary admitted reluctantly, was that Cathy gradually took over the household almost as much as she had in Andrew's flat. Nevertheless, Cathy took it for granted that she would move back to Andrew's flat as soon as he returned, and when he arrived there, he found her reinstalling herself.

They fell back in their old relationship, and the ménage settled into cosy stability. Cathy did much of the food shopping, some of the cooking, and all the washing, which they both considered covered her part of the rent and upkeep. She was independent of Andrew in the daytime. In the evenings, Cathy happily did household tasks or the dress adjustments that were part of her job with Mary. Andrew was often preoccupied with his own work or other reading, or he sat in the sofa watching those programmes on television that he could understand. In pauses from her other activities, Cathy was inclined to shuffle up on the sofa close beside him, catlike, without saying anything.

'You don't mind when I sit next to you like this, do you?' she asked one evening.

'No, but I'm surprised you want to.'

'It's nice; there hasn't been anyone before. Isn't it nice for you, too? Mary thought we should sit apart in our own places.'

'Don't you miss having all the other young people around?'

The answer was a heartfelt 'No! It's heaven not having them around all the time. It's luxury. It's as good as to know when the next meal's coming.'

But Andrew thought her life too limited. 'Have you been outside Hanoi ever?' he asked her one evening.

Perhaps once, years ago – on a bus trip organized by the orphanage. Not far out; it had made hardly any impression.

'I think we should make a trip to central Vietnam, to Hoi An and Hué. I want to visit these old cities in any case, and you might as well come too.'

'Mary won't be pleased if I miss work.'

'Mary can come along with us. It will be over a weekend. The other lady can take over on Saturday.'

'Mary doesn't like holidays.'

'She's American about holidays, but I think I can get her to come.'

And by planning their excursion to overlap with an American public holiday, Andrew induced Mary to make the arrangements and travel with them.

'Where are we going to stay without spending a fortune?' Mary had asked.

Andrew had initially been surprised that Mary was so cost-conscious. Perhaps this was how the rich stayed rich. 'Can't we behave as a pseudo-family and stay in one room with three beds in an unpretentious hotel? We can tell the management that Cathy is the daughter of a friend, if they wonder.'

'Suppose we could. Make sure Cathy takes her dressing gown.'

* * *

They were to go by train, a long journey. At the station, Cathy watched, enraptured, as the train pulled in, standing so close to the edge of the platform that Andrew had to pull her in abruptly.

Mary was half amused, half irritated with Cathy. 'This is like travelling with a toddler who needs constant attention. Surely even you have seen a train before?'

'Not that close.'

'You see a train that close only once, so Andrew had to act quickly.'

Once on the train, Mary placed Cathy by the window and sat beside her so she couldn't stray unnoticed; Andrew sat opposite. Cathy gazed out of the window, entranced and largely silent until they were some distance from Hanoi.

'Is England like this, too?'

'You mean the countryside?' Andrew could only say that it wasn't like England, and it was more mountainous than Andrew had expected. Hills like pinnacles emerged abruptly from the landscape, alternating with expanses of forest, with few signs of humans.

'How do people live with nobody around?' wondered Cathy.

* * *

It was a long overnight train journey to Da Nang in central Vietnam, after which they went by bus to Hoi An, which proved to be a fine place for tourists. They looked at the old Japanese bridge and at a magnificent Buddhist temple and at the exceedingly pretty view across the river.

Mary asked Cathy what she thought of Hoi An.

'It's beautiful. It's out of a storybook.'

'Do you prefer it to Hanoi?'

'Hoi An isn't for ordinary life.'

'But you're pleased to have come and seen it?'

'Yes, but I don't want to live here; it would be like living in a dream.'

By now, even if they had managed to sleep quite well on the train, they needed some respite from examining ancient monuments. Mary and Andrew sat down on a park bench, and Cathy inserted herself between them.

A Vietnamese girl of about Cathy's age or a bit younger, dressed in a dishevelled blouse and tatty shorts, walked in front of them. Cathy regarded her with distaste. The girl was carrying a small package and paused when she caught sight of the three tourists.

'Buy postcards?'

Cathy was clearly hating this episode; she was covering her eyes with her hands. She was presumably being agonisingly reminded of the life she had miraculously escaped. Andrew glanced at Mary, who was deciding that it was best to get rid of the girl without fuss.

'Let's have a look at the postcards.'

She selected three and bought them at half the price being asked. The girl was delighted and moved off.

Cathy removed her hands from her eyes. 'How can that girl think of being dressed like that when she's out selling postcards? What will the customers think?'

Andrew had to reinterpret Cathy's behaviour. She wasn't horror-struck at the wretchedness of the girl's poverty; rather she regarded the girl's dirty blouse and tattered shorts as a disgrace to the profession of street seller, in which Cathy took great pride. This precluded any feeling of sympathy for a poor country cousin. Cathy's own clothes were inexpensive but kept impeccably clean.

Mary said, 'C'mon, it's time to look at the shops.'

* * *

While they browsed round the town, Mary noticed that one of the restaurants gave cooking lessons and read the notice about them in the window.

'This is something we should try! It works like this; we choose a dish, the cook shows us how to prepare it, and then we eat it. Not all that expensive, either.'

Mary hustled the others inside the restaurant, and they were soon receiving instructions in the kitchen. Mary, full of confidence, chose an elaborate Vietnamese seafood dish for the three of them; Andrew was happy to cook spinach as an accompaniment.

Cathy was less than thrilled. 'The good thing with a restaurant is that somebody else does the work.'

She agreed to help Andrew with the spinach – in which case, Andrew thought, they could try the more ambitious variant, spinach with peanut sauce. Cathy was soon chatting enthusiastically in Vietnamese with the chef, with a running translation for Andrew. A quick boil of the spinach and then toss it into a frying pan with oil, garlic, and black pepper. Then she turned her attention to the more complex tasks of Mary and her chef. A Vietnamese kitchen was home ground; Cathy took over.

'Not like that, Mary! Easy, natural, like this.'

She was luckier than Mary had been in attempting to toss chicken in the pan. The chef, amused, nodded approvingly.

Mary protested only mildly. 'This dish is *my* cooking lesson, Cathy. Yours is the spinach.'

They sat down at table, tasted the food, and pronounced it delicious.

A party of Australians – all men, most of them in advanced middle age but a few much younger, around twenty – entered the restaurant. Mary and Andrew speculated about what they were doing.

'When it's all men, it might be some sporting group, Australian football or something,' said Andrew.

'But then you would expect the majority to be young men, plus a few more elderly.'

The men were strikingly proper and well-behaved. Beer was the strongest anyone was drinking; some were on Zingo or other soft drinks. Conversation was polite and orderly. Mary and Andrew decided that they couldn't be football players. Finally, Andrew went over and asked one of them, a man of about fifty, what they were doing together in Vietnam.

'We were in the same platoon in the Vietnam War, and we're meeting again thirty years later, for the first time since the war,' related the man patiently. He seemed to be the group organizer, and was perfectly prepared to talk to Andrew. 'Some of us have come with our sons, to try to explain to them what it was like. We have a naughty box, and if one of us swears, even if it is only in fun, he puts money in the box and it goes to a charity in Vietnam. Every now and again, I put in some coins on some pretext even if I don't swear, and the rest of us do the same. We've talked a lot together and relived a heap of events, and our sons are beginning to understand what the war meant to us. It's great to visit the country again when it's peacetime and see how things have changed.'

Andrew returned to Cathy and Mary and passed on what he had been told. 'Hanh Phuc ought to be here.'

'Why?' asked Cathy.

'She probably lost her leg, like lots of other civilians, because of a mine left behind from the war. These former soldiers are in effect saying to people like Hanh Phuc that they're sorry.'

'It's not their fault. They were doing what they were told,' was Cathy's reaction.

* * *

One evening after they had returned to Hanoi, they were sitting at home, Cathy sewing clothes for a customer and Andrew reading a draft one of the students had written for a paper to publish his results.

'What are you thinking about?' asked Cathy, noticing that Andrew had laid aside his papers for a while.

'How happy most people round here seem to be.'

'Why shouldn't they be?'

'They're so poor, by Western standard. Or take Hanh Phuc. She's never self-pitying about her leg.'

'It's the Buddha looking down over her; she's religious. She meditates every day.'

'Perhaps a lot of people in Hanoi meditate, and it changes their attitude about things and calms them down.'

Andrew decided he needed the same experiences. He should begin with lessons in meditation from some qualified teacher. He raised the subject with Hanh Phuc, who told him to contact a Buddhist monastery on the outskirts of Hanoi.

'Do they speak English there?'

'One or two of them do, probably.'

'Can you go with me? It would make things easier.'

She agreed; and they decided on a suitable time to visit the monastery, which adjoined an ancient temple. They reached it by taxi. The temple was exotic to Andrew but was of modest size. Andrew entered it shyly with Hanh Phuc. The main room was decorated with woodcarvings of dragons, a Chinese influence, but they were friendly rather than hostile dragons.

Hanh Phuc took him further to a small complex where they encountered a monk. He indicated an anteroom to the temple, with an open door, where an older man was working with some papers. Hanh Phuc knocked discreetly and Andrew followed her in. She talked quietly with the monk, a scholarly-looking man of about fifty, who glanced at Andrew but made minimal comment. Andrew could not tell how he was reacting.

Then he looked up and said abruptly, 'If you want to learn meditation, best start now.'

Hanh Phuc discreetly left the room to wait outside.

The monk got up from his chair and sat on a small carpet beside the table, assuming a lotus position. He signalled to Andrew to take up a similar position opposite him. Andrew eventually managed to manoeuvre his legs in the preferred way.

'Good! Important to begin in the right way,' commented the monk.

They sat for about five minutes, with eyes half closed, while Andrew wondered what was supposed to be happening.

The monk said, 'That was good. I want you to sit like this for ten minutes each day. Lean against the wall if it is easier. You will meditate on the question, "Where is the location of the thoughts?" Come back at about this time next week and tell me what you have found the answer to be.'

He smiled at Andrew and returned to the seat at his desk and to his papers. Andrew thought it was improper to say anything, and he withdrew to Hanh Phuc, waiting outside.

'Should I have offered to pay something?' he asked Hanh Phuc.

'Put something in that wooden bowl there.'

Andrew lay in the same as he gave Hanh Phuc for his language lessons.

In the evening, Cathy asked, 'How was it at the temple? Did you fix your meditation lessons?'

Andrew explained that he had been told to meditate on the location of his thoughts. 'Have you any idea what the answer ought to be?'

'How should I know?'

'You live in the place. Somebody might have discussed it with you, perhaps at the orphanage.'

'No, I don't know. The head or the heart.'

Andrew conscientiously meditated as he was told. At the end of the week, he felt none the wiser. He told the monk, 'I don't know where the thoughts are located.'

The monk smiled. 'Good! That is the right answer. You can't tell where the thoughts are located.'

'Don't some people think their thoughts are located in the head?'

The monk didn't answer that directly. 'If you ask small children in Vietnam, the say, in the heart.'

He got up from the desk and adopted a lotus position on the mat. Andrew again sat opposite the teacher.

'Now I want you to practise thinking of nothing,' said the monk.

They squatted for a while in silence. Andrew tried to blot out his thoughts, but they jumped from one subject to another. He felt obliged to tell the monk that it wasn't proceeding well.

'What are you thinking of?' asked the monk gently.

'The taxi trip here, for example.'

'In your mind, let the taxi grow larger and larger. It will disappear.'

Andrew found that he could do this and have a sensation of thinking about nothing. At least his thoughts stopped moving from one thing to another. He eventually told the monk this.

The session ended.

Andrew was told, 'It is progressing well. Some people think that meditation must be something wonderful and complex. You let it be simple and natural. It is better so.'

But Andrew wasn't wholly happy with the pursuit of nirvana; it was too negative. 'It's Mahayana Buddhism in Vietnam, isn't it?'

'That is correct. The Great Vehicle. We do not strive to attain nirvana for our own sake. Our good actions are for the benefit of others, not for ourselves. Mahayana is like Christianity.'

Andrew returned home. Over the next week it was difficult to find a time before very late in the evening when he could meditate undisturbed by the presence of Cathy. He felt too self-conscious in front of her. The best place for meditation was in bed. There, he let his thoughts grow big and fell asleep shortly afterwards. He felt it was inappropriate for him to continue with his lessons.

He explained the situation to the monk.

'The time is not ripe for your meditation. Never mind; you will come back to me when you are prepared.'

* * *

'Your meditation began well. How is it going now?' Hanh Phuc asked Andrew, in Vietnamese, at one of his lessons.

Andrew could understand the question and tried to reply in Vietnamese but soon reverted to English. 'I don't feel I want to spend so much time so inactively. At least I have some insight now into what meditation means. The monk understood my attitude.'

'He realizes you are very Western still. You will take years to change.'

Chapter 22

Andrew was still concerned that Cathy's personal contacts seemed to be confined to two people much older than herself. In the evenings, she was too preoccupied with running his household for her own good, even if she appeared content enough with her life.

'Do you see the people you shared the flat with nowadays?' he asked her. 'Have they got over your selling successes? Are they talking to you again?'

'They talk to me a bit now and then, when we meet in the street. But they don't want to hear about how I live now.'

'Did you have a best friend when you were in the orphanage?'

'Yes, but she left Hanoi and disappeared.'

Andrew had another try. 'How about that boy who interfered with your negotiations over the books I was considering buying, what seems ages ago?'

It took a while for Cathy to work out whom Andrew meant. 'Oh, Kien. I talk to him sometimes. He's all right; actually, he spoke up for me against the others.'

'I thought he was intriguing. He was reasonably at home in English, too. Can't you invite him here sometime, say in the late afternoon, so I can see him, too?'

'Suppose so.' She showed no particular enthusiasm.

Nevertheless, a few days later, she announced, 'Kien can come, not tomorrow, the day after.'

* * *

Kien was appreciative of the flat. 'You've got it comfortable.' He sat down on the sofa, trying out various positions and then breathing out contentedly. 'Not bad. And it's real quiet here.'

He asked Andrew what he was doing in Vietnam and then about his life in England. It was a lively and sympathetic interest, which Andrew felt was genuine.

Kien said he had a job with scooters and motorcycles. His ambition was to open his own shop and be his own boss.

'Then the customers become the boss,' Cathy told Kien.

He and Cathy began to discuss the merits and demerits of their current bosses. Cathy was open and direct about Mary; Mary knew the business (even if she needed Cathy's help on some local customs), she was prepared to explain what she was doing, and she was fair, but she was exacting. Kien listened attentively and made several comments.

Andrew felt they should have a chance to talk with each other in their mother tongue, so he told them he was going out to do some shopping and that he would see them later.

He walked out into the tropical heat; shopped; and, to pass the time, went to Mary's shop. She was examining the accounts while the other assistant took care of the customers. Mary and Andrew sat outside on the corner at the shop entrance, and Andrew related about Kien.

'You haven't left them alone to smooch on the sofa?'

'I wanted them to have an opportunity to talk together in Vietnamese, instead of English as they have to when I'm there. Anyway, they're too young for the relationship to be smoochable is my impression.'

'Andrew, you're too trusting, at least of Cathy.'

A few days later, Mary was asking, 'Were they smooching when you came back?'

'No, they were having a snack in the kitchen. Spinach, as it happens.'

* * *

Kien was in the flat on subsequent occasions over the next couple of weeks.

'How do you find Kien nowadays?' Andrew asked Cathy.

'Oh, six out of ten.' Cathy was languidly looking at some magazine she had got hold of in the street.

This was an unexpected kind of assessment. 'He seems solid and reliable,' observed Andrew.

'That's part of the six.'

'Do you find plenty to talk about?'

'He has plenty to say about motorbikes and how to sell them.'

'But he's interested in other things too, isn't he—what you're doing, for example?' persisted Andrew.

Cathy didn't look up. 'Funny you say that. When you left us alone that day, suddenly walking out, Kien thought you were fixing our marriage – as a kind of father – letting us meet for half an hour first. Later he tried to find out what you earned, to see if he could expect a large marriage gift—'

'Dowry?'

'I had to explain to him that you're far too Western for that. Kien gets some things really messed up.'

* * *

Mary's friend, Valerie, was kept abreast of events and continued to show interest. 'I saw Andrew and Cathy strolling arm in arm the other day. They're quite affectionate nowadays, all within the family, so to speak. It seems to be a genuine case of adoption.'

'It would be a fairly simple case of adoption,' explained Mary, 'except that Cathy has an adopting tendency too, at least as much as Andrew. Each has adopted the other.'

'I wonder who Cathy's real parents are and what they would think about it.'

'The real *father* is Andrew, as I see it. He's not a perfect father; he's too permissive. But he's unquestionably the real father and some of the time, I feel like the real mother.'

'Entering into the spirit of complex cases of adoption, does Cathy feel she's Andrew's real mother?'

Mary considered this. 'No, I think it's more she has a sense of responsibility towards him – someone the daughter has to look after in his old age.'

Chapter 23

Andrew was back for another period in England. Before leaving, he had discussed the situation with Mary.

'Cathy had better move in with me. She'll get into mischief if she has your flat all to herself.'

'Isn't your room too small for two?'

'We'll manage.'

* * *

Andrew was visiting his in-laws, Janet Arlington as she now was, and her family. He had arrived in the late afternoon, having driven up from Oxford. Janet and Fred had a family of five children spread over twelve years. The oldest was a married woman of nearly thirty, who had recently provided a grandchild. The three youngest children still lived at home. Andrew parked in the yard of the large farmhouse, where there stood four other miscellaneous vehicles. Before he could ring the bell, Janet and the youngest boy opened the door and warmly welcomed Andrew into the house. In the hall a huge bookcase contained an ancient edition of the Encyclopaedia Britannica, an assortment of paperback romances, albums of Donald Duck, and back numbers of *Farmers Weekly*. Covering the opposite wall were pictures by the children at various stages of their growth.

Andrew glanced in at the living room, with its jumble of furniture. On one wall was an enormous unframed picture of Fred's favourite cow, which Toby had painted for his brother-in-law. Opposite hung a voluptuous Victorian picture of a naked Susanna innocently taking her bath, viewed by the two elders – a family heirloom, inherited from Fred's father. His deeply religious parents had insisted on a biblical picture in the fine room, and his choice had been a protest against their interference.

They went into the kitchen, with its old round wooden table in the middle. The refrigerator was covered with notes held on with magnets. Numerous photographs of family and friends were pinned on the walls.

This was the background to a constant movement of the three children who were still living at home, plus their friends, neighbours, and assorted cats and dogs. Furthermore, older relatives, in-laws, and friends of the family frequently stayed overnight at the farmhouse, to the point where it was sometimes known as The Arlington Hotel.

They had a simple meal in the kitchen. The two boys soon got up from the table and began fighting affectionately in the corridor, accompanied by loud barking from one of the dogs.

'Stop it, you two!' called Janet from the kitchen. 'You're driving Pickwick crazy – us too.'

The two boys moved off good-naturedly, without protest, and Pickwick followed, wagging his tail.

The kettle had boiled for tea and the table had been cleared when there was a loud, theatrical knock on the door. The twenty-year-old daughter ran out of the kitchen to investigate, and a moment later was exclaiming, in thrilled tones, 'Jimmy!'

Her elder brother appeared soon afterwards in the kitchen. He was a merchant sailor, turning up on an unexpected leave, and his family fulsomely welcomed him home. For the next forty minutes, he recounted in detail numerous adventures of life at sea.

In the first years, when the children had been small, Andrew had gladly visited the house with Antonia, savouring the life of a conventionally happy family – the contrast with Andrew's own experience, as an only child in a quiet home, had been immense – and equally glad to depart a while later, exhausted. He was beginning to feel exhausted again now. Janet probably noticed this; she organized the younger boy to take Andrew and the dog Pickwick out for a walk.

His nephew was an easy-going relaxed young man who chatted amicably while showing Andrew around with a great sense of personal involvement in the neighbourhood. Andrew could also relax in his company. He remembered how he and Antonia had concluded that two or at most three children, plus at most one pet, were optimal and were what they should have. The Arlington life was idyllic, but an outsider was inclined to exhaustion.

Andrew and his nephew arrived back at the farm and encountered Fred, who was back home after managing the day's farm work. He and Andrew sat and chatted in the living room opposite the picture of the cow, until Fred was clearly impatient to escort Andrew on a personal trip round the farm.

* * *

Andrew retired to bed wondering to himself, again, whether he and Antonia would have achieved a similarly idyllic, but preferably less demanding, family life.

He slept well until he was woken up at six o'clock the next day, in half-light. Farm life began unconscionably early. Janet insisted on visitors sharing this but softened the impact with a cup of tea she brought to the bedside along with a scone. The visitor was then allowed to recover for a while before taking part in the family breakfast, during which items from the newspaper were read out and commented on boisterously. Fred was around briefly for breakfast, before bustling off to attend to the farm. Janet presided deftly over the household, with its mixture of human and other animals; marriage had transformed her. Andrew reminded himself of his own part in securing this transformation; it was intimately connected with memories of Antonia and an activity of which he was proud.

He was reluctant to leave the neighbourhood without having a look at Enby Hall. He wanted to look at it together with Janet, to discuss it with someone who had known it in the old days. He took this up with Janet during a relatively quiet period after breakfast.

Her manner altered abruptly. It was not that she reverted to the passive apathetic Janet, who had been transformed by a marriage that Andrew had helped scheme to bring about; rather, she became angry, for the first time that Andrew could recollect. 'I have no happy memories of that place, and I make detours to avoid seeing it from the car.' She put some kitchen items away. 'Hearing the name of that place makes me feel headachy, so I want to take two aspirins and lie down, as I used to do all the time back then. Can't understand why *you* want to look at it either.'

* * *

So Andrew drove over alone to look at Enby Hall, partly out of nostalgia and partly to see what had happened to it since it had been sold off outside the family. Seeing the building from a distance made him curious to investigate further, partly because it was different from what he remembered but why he couldn't decide – perhaps a change to the roof. He entered the grounds and parked on the gravel in the driveway. The scrunch under the wheels evoked the complex feelings he'd experienced when he would arrive longing to see Antonia while dreading Mrs Morton's hostility.

The last time he had been there, Mrs Morton had taken her leave of him with the words, 'If you remarry within the next ten years, it will be an insult to Antonia's memory.'

Mrs Morton had already made it clear that she blamed him for his wife's death.

He climbed out of the car and walked towards the main door. His spirits revived when he saw a sign in the drive that read, 'Your Laine Mail Order. Submit over the Internet. Sir Oliver supplies all your needs.' A large photograph of the man himself, smiling in welcome, accompanied the message. *All rather absurd*, thought Andrew.

Inside, the old entrance hall was still recognizable. At first there was no sign of activity, but eventually a young man appeared, to whom Andrew introduced himself.

'My name's Andrew Carter. I used to know the family that owned the hall in the old days and often visited the place. Could I have a quick look round?'

'Of course, Mr Carter. Pleased to meet you. I'm Christopher Ryegate. Actually, do you mind if I walk round with you? There's not much to do late on a Friday afternoon. Everybody else is away for one reason or another, and I've been left holding the fort. You can tell me how the place used to be in the old days.'

Andrew had not bargained for this; he had expected to walk through the house by himself, taking his time at certain places and evoking and laying to rest certain memories.

'I'll bet it's changed a lot here, on the ground floor, hasn't it,' Christopher was saying.

In the entrance hall stood the plaster cast bust of the founder of the family, moved down from the junk room, with a placard relating how he had brought gas to north Lancashire. The old drawing room and dining room were now offices with various functions, which Christopher took his time explaining.

'The house has become institutionalized, needless to say,' commented Andrew. 'I'm not altogether sorry. When I knew it, the place had a much stronger personality, not entirely pleasant. It was sliding downhill in a series of small steps, owing to money problems. The owners had placed a bucket under a hole in the roof.'

'They really had a bucket there? You may have noticed the roof's been redone.'

'The appearance isn't improved, but I suppose the new one's easier to maintain.'

They went upstairs. The big bedroom was now an archive. Toby's old room was what looked like a store for office accessories, stationery, plastic mugs, and the like. Janet's room was converted to a workshop, with a prominent mounted drill and a lathe. The door to Antonia's room was closed.

'I have strong memories of that room,' Andrew told Christopher. 'I suppose it contains computers or something now.'

'Perhaps you're in for a surprise.' Christopher looked pleased with himself. He opened the door triumphantly for them both.

It was virtually as Andrew had first seen it, a young girl's bedroom. He felt as if he were entering a museum, whisked back to the remote past.

'We've kept it as a sort of quiet room, to lie in if you're not feeling well or just want a rest for a while, get away from things. Smashing view, isn't it?'

They both looked through the window over the splendid river valley to the hills behind, a perfect north England landscape. To get a better look, Andrew sat down in an easy chair by the wall. Christopher followed his example and sat in one of a pair of upright chairs on the other side of the room.

'Lovely old picture, too.' Christopher pointed above Andrew's head.

It was the watercolour of the young lovers. For one reason or another, Antonia had left it in place. Their first tiny flat lacked a suitable wall. The subsequent unfortunate turn of events precluded moving it, as intended, into the new house they acquired.

'My favourite place in the whole house, sitting in this comfortable old chair, opposite that picture. You won't believe what I shall tell you now; I came here one day in the lunch hour with a girl I liked. She worked here. We sat together and had a chat. We discussed the picture for a bit and then she put her hand in mine; and one thing led to another, and the next day, we were engaged.'

'Actually I can believe it,' said Andrew. 'I hope it worked out all right.'

'Oh yes. We got married last year. We've had our first child two months ago. Was the picture around in your time?'

'Yes; curiously enough, I bought it.'

'How on earth did you come to do that? Must have set you back some?'

'It was a birthday present for the younger daughter of the house – a bit extravagant, perhaps, but not so awfully expensive then.'

'Sir Oliver – if you've heard of the Tory backbencher, Sir Oliver Laine, an amiable scoundrel – wanted to sell it. He bought the house. When he saw the picture, he told everybody that if it was properly restored and the colours brightened, he could get a packet for it.'

'I heard the family sold the house to Sir Oliver. I didn't know he wanted to restore the painting. Why didn't he?' asked Andrew.

'His wife put her foot down. She said that he could do what he liked to the roof, but if he did anything to the picture, she'd murder him.' He added thoughtfully, 'She's tough like that.'

'But it appears that Sir Oliver, whom I've come across, let her have her way and didn't get murdered. And they apparently stay married.'

'Yes, he didn't make any fuss. He married her for her money when he was an ambitious young Tory MP on the way up and a good catch, and she was the Honourable Agatha Something, so it was an entry into aristocratic circles. They didn't pretend to be in love; at any rate, he didn't. They both have affairs the whole time, apparently. I'm not a gossip, but I like to keep up to date with where celebrities are getting off.'

'Have you seen her?'

'Yes, she comes here occasionally to look at the house.'

Andrew, feeling he should comment, said, 'Weird thing, top people's marriages.'

'Despite everything, Oliver and Agatha look happy and relaxed when they're together in public.' He added, 'The house may be bit of mess architecturally, but I'm surprised the family could bear to part with it. Anyway, the old lady passed away, and the children weren't interested in keeping it up. What's your connection with the family, by the way?'

'I was married into it for a while, ages ago.'

'Oh cripes, you must be the Mr Carter who married Antonia. I heard about it from some people around. Awful business, her sudden death. I'm really sorry; you shouldn't have let me ramble on like that.'

'Not at all, you told me many interesting things. And the worst happened many years ago, and I've got over it.'

They returned downstairs to the entrance hall.

'What goods are you selling by mail-order?' asked Andrew.

'A big range, with an emphasis on the electronic – CDs, computers, mobile phones, that sort of thing. I'll show you Sir Oliver's current favourite, an advanced mobile.'

He took Andrew to a display desk at the side of the hall, on which stood a huge computer monitor, which Christopher switched on. Soon, Sir Oliver appeared on the monitor, holding a small rectangular tablet and saying, 'This is the Stellarphone. Voices, messages, and pictures shoot through cyberspace to the silver screen that fits your pocket – cost wise, too.'

Then Sir Oliver called to someone from his Stellarphone, 'See you soon, hugs and kisses.' Soft music. A zoom towards the tablet to display a written message, 'I'm in love, I'm in love with my Stellarphone. And my Stellarphone just loves me.'

'He's emphasizing that the Stellarphone is user-friendly,' Christopher explained for Andrew, unnecessarily.

Time for more music. Sir Oliver was joined by a small man wearing spectacles with unusually large round lenses, carrying his own Stellarphone. To the tune of 'Me and My Teddy Bear,' they went into a song-and-dance act:

Me and my Stellarphone
Have no worries, need no loan
Me and my Stellarphone

(They clasped their Stellarphones to their chests.)

Just play and play all day

'Extraordinary; it's Freddie,' said Andrew, looking at Oliver's companion, easily recognizable after all those years. 'What's he doing there, still in his goggles?'

'Do you know him? From what I've heard, he and Joe Briesley, the television guru, met at the bar one evening during a conference. The first hour they spent swapping irreverent stories about a common acquaintance, a Cambridge don with a peculiar name—'

'Alaryck Tomlinson?'

'That's the one. When they were thoroughly warmed up, Freddie said he was into mathematical modelling of the mail-order market and how to make it work. Joe repeated, "Mathematical modelling of the mail-order market? All those *M*'s. I'll tell Oliver Laine; he'll like that." One thing led to another, and the upshot was that Oliver Laine wanted to open his own mail-order business, and he bought Enby Hall off Toby Morton for the purpose. Then Joe Briesley went over full-time to his television programmes. He never finished his ideas for Stellarphone, which was his baby, really.'

'I used to work with Joe Briesley, and I know he was intrigued by mobiles,' said Andrew, 'but I have less contact with him nowadays. I moved back to London to be closer to my elderly parents when Joe said he was leaving Stephenson University to concentrate on television.'

'Now I remember hearing that you were in Joe Briesley's department. Were you surprised when he went over full-time to television?'

'Not really. He liked teaching at the department, and he at first thought Oliver and his firm, Northern Lights, was fun to be with and would back the commercial development of Joe's ideas. But he didn't like how they tended to sell off the patents to the big players at an early stage, before there was a finished product. Also Joe wasn't impressed by the businessmen. He used to say, "You hear constant complaints about how long it takes academics to make up their minds, and admittedly we can dither awhile before we come to a decision, but then we usually stick to it. But these business people! They tell me, don't develop this, develop that, all very decisive, straight from the shoulder. Then two weeks later, they say there's been a change of plan; go back to the first idea. Another two weeks later, they say, on further reflection, you should focus on the second idea; it's more in line with the state of the market.'"

'These tissues of relationships,' reflected Christopher, 'with separations and new connections. Often, a muddle is all that comes of them, but every now and again, something quite creative results, like this mail-order business. And Stellarphone. Even after Joe dropped out, Sir Oliver and Freddie loved the idea of it and fooled around making this video together.' He added, 'Apple is further ahead with their version, so Stellarphone, if it ever appears, will have to compete on cost.'

Andrew drove away from the house in an elated mood.

'Enby Hall doesn't bother me anymore,' he told Janet later that evening. 'It's much healthier under its new regime. You'd like it now. The ghosts have moved off elsewhere.'

'For the most part, it stopped bothering me as soon as I left it all those years ago. I largely forgot it; I was too busy with my new life. I'd say there's nothing to exorcise, really. But I get a headache if someone goes on about Enby Hall for more than a minute or two.'

* * *

Andrew wanted to talk about Enby Hall to someone who might listen, so he rang to Toby, who had moved from the neighbourhood but was still living with his old partner. Toby, like Janet, hadn't the least nostalgia for Enby Hall and had not visited it since it had become a mail-order store, but unlike Janet, was curious to hear all about it from Andrew and share memories. Andrew related the afternoon's events in detail, and Toby interrupted with comments and questions, until both were satisfied.

Then Toby asked, 'Have you come to any conclusions as to which is more exotic, Hanoi or Hereford College, Oxford?'

'That's not an easy question. The Vietnamese I meet are friendly and easy to get on with so that I feel at home, even if the climate is utterly different; and as individual people they seem sensible enough even when their customs differ from what we are used to. The inhabitants of Hereford College are also friendly, but no one seems quite normal.'

'As caricatured in numerous novels?'

'I wouldn't say that. The ones I talk with most aren't complacently self-satisfied. Nor do they show off with clever remarks. They're rarely bitchy about each other. But there's a clergyman, the college chaplain, who is weirdly unorthodox, and a psychiatrist who is always trying to read one's private letters and emails and an ambitious, young fellow who is everybody's idea of a faintly pompous emerging senior civil servant. And most surprising of all, we constantly have mealtime conversations about the meaning of life as if we were still students – undergraduates, I should say.'

'I wonder what effect this is having on you? I met Oliver Laine the other day, and he says that, reading between the lines of what he's heard, you are living in Hanoi with a very young native girl you've picked up from the street, whose professional name is Cathy.'

'Where did he get that from?'

'He's been sounding out a gossipy don or gardener or someone. I told him he's probably got it all wrong, misreading between the lines, because it sounds utterly unlike you.'

'He *was* misreading between the lines. Was he disapproving?'

'Can't say he was. He was with Effy Hacker, who was a bit sniffy and saying something about conduct unbefitting a university teacher who may need to act in loco parentis. But Oliver said, "Come off it, Effy, you know you and I'd do just the same in his position. Not to mention all those seriously religious geysers in Graham Greene novels; they're all sleeping with native girls. Good for Andrew, I say.'

* * *

After his short holiday in the north, Andrew was in Oxford for his teaching duties. He and Cathy continued in email contact.

'Heard anything from your young friend?' Hugh would ask at frequent intervals.

Andrew had accepted that keeping Hugh informed was the path of least trouble. Hugh fell into the routine of knocking on Andrew's door fifteen minutes before dinner on the days when Andrew notified him that Cathy had written an email and listening while Andrew read it out aloud. He had just begun reading to Hugh the latest message, unusually long, when he heard another knock at the door, followed by the entry of Tom, the gardener.

'Mind if I join you? Hugh told me you've had an email that promises to be juicy.'

'Okay, Hugh will tell you anyway. But I don't think I need to repeat the opening bit, just routine sentiments. She continues, "By the way, Mary has moved into our flat while you're in England this time. She now thinks it's more comfortable than having the two of us in her room. She told me to tell you. She says, 'A young girl like you shouldn't live by herself, even if her employer keeps an eye on her at work.' But her real bother is Kien. She's deeply suspicious of his intentions – quite unnecessary. I like Kien; I'm even quite fond of him. But he's a late developer, not like me, and he's more interested in bikes than girls. It's good you like Kien, so we can work together on him. The best thing is if you ask Mary to an evening meal with us, which I can help to make, and I tell Kien to drop in just by chance on some good excuse. Then they will meet, and Mary will see what sort of boy he is and perhaps start chatting about business. They are both equally boring (not all the time) when they get stuck on business, so they should get on fine. Mary might even help him get started up. (But I have better ideas than they about the *real* needs of the customers.) This will distract Mary so that she will get off my back, and I can awaken normal healthy feelings in Kien, which I'm sure are there but embryonic (I looked up that word myself, I didn't get it from Hanh Phuc). It's for his own good, really.'

'Quite a letter,' commented the medical man.

'I must say, Cathy's English has come on enormously, much bigger vocabulary, more verbs,' responded Andrew warmly. 'Hanh Phuc must be a good teacher.'

'Fine adjectives and adverbs, too, I should say,' said Tom, 'not to mention complex sentence construction, but that's not what Dr Hugh meant, I should think.'

'Anyway,' responded Hugh, 'grab your gown; it's time to proceed troughwards. Grub's up by now. Pity we can't continue with Cathy's schemes, but they're not really suitable for high table conversation, except alone with the chaplain. We'll have to talk Cathy some other time, perhaps with Tom, in a secluded part of the garden.'

* * *

After dinner, Andrew went to the common room to read the newspapers and met Clemmie, who immediately put down his newspaper.

'Ah, Andrew, we have a matter to discuss. I know that you have been married and that your wife died in unfortunate circumstances. I have never considered that this would adversely affect your teaching activities with female pupils. But reliable sources have drawn my attention to your interactions with a very young Vietnamese girl. Personally, I have no doubt that your relationship is of the utmost propriety.'

'Thank you, Clemmie.'

'But you should not be engaged in it. You should be helping to shape the destinies of nations. I appreciate that you are unsuitable for a high administrative post—'

'I've no wonderful leadership qualities, like you.'

'But you analyse the efficacy of new drugs that can affect an entire people's well-being. This should be your preoccupation, not picking up a stray girl off the street.'

'It was Christmas.'

'An inadequate reason.'

'Wouldn't you have done the same? You're one of the most religiously observant people in the college, and providing room at Christmas is what Christians are supposed to do.'

'As a busy devout Christian, one delegates. I donate to a number of charities, including Amnesty, Médecins Sans Frontières' (articulated in a perfect French accent) 'and sometimes the Red Cross. Not the Salvation Army, because I like to distinguish between the good and the undeserving poor.'

'But shouldn't Christians attend even to the undeserving poor? I seem to remember an ancient prayer for all sorts and conditions of men.'

'If you are shaping the destinies of nations, time and money barely suffices even for one's own children. Miss Dorchester and I are almost ecstatically in love, and we intend to have at least two children to perpetuate the line. But we agree that children should not clutter the place up – not crawl around vomiting on the carpets. When they are small, au pair girls will look after them in a separate part of the house. As seven-year-olds, they will be off to boarding school. When the term ends, it's skiing in the winter, pony trekking in the spring, and camping in the summer.' His voice softened. 'We shall bestow our love and affection at all times, if from a distance.'

'Perhaps that's easier if they're not around all the time. But you're saying that simple kindly actions aren't easy to combine with the responsibilities of leadership.'

'There are no easy answers as to how to reconcile the Christian virtues with the demands of everyday life. I consider such matters every Sunday and agree with those in ecclesiastical authority. Bishops are not so silly as to give all they have to the poor. And matters pertaining to personal faith should accord with the accumulated wisdom of the Church. One does not question the divinity of Christ, as our chaplain does.'

'Perhaps he wants to think for himself?'

'He should first practise obedience.' He leaned forward. 'As you know, I am concerned about his possible influence over you. I am appalled that you can let a street urchin upset the planning of your life.'

'Thank you for your concern, Clemmie, but I can't junk Cathy now. And I've rather given up planning my life, as things never proceed according to plan, in my experience. Isn't it the same for you?'

'Plans are often disturbed by events, but they are necessary for better focus.'

'I don't think I can agree. But anyway, best of luck to your plans for you and Miss Dorchester.'

Chapter 24

Andrew's teaching commitments at Oxford were over until the next term, and he had recently returned to Hanoi and his empty flat. One morning shortly after his arrival, he looked in at the shop to see if either Mary or Cathy was around. Neither of them was; the shop was in the charge of a middle-aged Vietnamese lady. Andrew looked idly at the photographs on the wall. One was of him – the picture they had taken in the kiosk the first Christmas. Pinned beside it was a picture of Kien, looking thoughtful and responsible, much as when Andrew had first met him. Cathy had indeed intrigued successfully, with Andrew's assistance, to reconcile Mary to Kien. Cathy and Mary appeared, and Andrew was too engaged with them to enquire further about Kien.

The following weekend, Andrew wanted to make some excursion in Hanoi and suggested the three of them visit a nearby lake. It was too far for them to walk, and Andrew was curious to try one of the scooter taxis – that is, to be driven on the back of a scooter by one of the innumerable men who stood on the pavement calling to any new arrival who might want to travel somewhere. Cathy had nothing against this; Mary was horrified.

'Have you any idea how dangerous it is to ride those scooters?'

As it happened, Andrew had an excellent idea; it had been a topic of discussion at his department. The traffic accident rate was about ten times higher than in Britain or Sweden. But it was not so bad for professional drivers, Andrew pointed out, and he attempted to persuade her to proceed with them for what was only a short journey.

'Can't you try it one time?' Andrew persisted, egged on by Cathy.

Eventually, Cathy squashed between Andrew and the driver on one scooter, and Mary, grumbling, clambered onto another. Andrew was now used to scooters in Hanoi; the driver was skilful, and Andrew was happy to relax in his professional care. He could feel that Cathy, after a tense start, was loving the ride. He couldn't see how Mary was taking it.

They arrived at the lake without serious incident; Andrew thought the experience had been relatively tame.

Mary was pink in the face but paid up, including a tip, without comment.

Later, she said to Andrew and Cathy, 'I was out of my mind, letting you talk me into us riding those scooters; completely crazy in that God-awful traffic and without helmets even. One thing's for sure, we're all returning by taxi. I don't mind how much it costs.'

They strolled by the lake and returned by taxi. Later in the afternoon, they met up with Valerie, who asked them what they had been doing.

Cathy explained which lake they had been to.

'That's a long way. You didn't walk, did you?'

Mary, tight-lipped, said, 'No, we didn't walk there. Andrew and Cathy, the wretches, talked me into riding on a scooter. Appalling traffic, no helmets. We are lucky to be alive. Why isn't it required to wear a helmet?'

'It's so hot and damp here. Helmets are very unpopular; they're known as rice cookers.'

'I'm not saying they're comfortable; I'm saying they're necessary. Can't you use your contacts in government circles to make helmets compulsory for riding scooters and motorbikes?'

'I can enquire what's going on. You're not alone in your views; there've been some demonstrations. You could join one of the next.'

* * *

Cathy and Andrew were sitting on the sofa after dinner. Cathy had been busy altering a dress for a customer at the shop but had finished and was now lying back thinking about something. She often did this, and Andrew now accepted that she regarded doing nothing much as luxury rather than boredom. She enjoyed sitting in the quiet doing nothing. As she had told Andrew, this was the first time in her life she could sit in comfort, free from a bustle of young people constantly around her. This evening she had a notebook beside her, in which she wrote from time to time.

Andrew asked what the notebook was for.

'I'm writing a story,' she said contentedly, 'in Vietnamese.'

'What's it about?'

'That's a secret. It would spoil the story to talk about it before it's written.'

Andrew was curious. He sensed he was in the story and wasn't sure he wanted to be. For the moment, he continued reading. From time to time, Cathy had bursts of activity in which she wrote at high speed in her notebook but with frequent crossings-out and rewriting.

Later in the evening, she said to Andrew, 'Sometimes I have to explain to myself or other people what you and I are to each other.'

'So do I. What other people?'

'Kien or people in the shop. I don't say everything to them, of course. But I knew you and I were close that first night. I was tired and confused and fell asleep on the sofa at once. Then I woke up in this strange room and found my way to your bed and lay close to you. I could feel my body against yours, and it was special. And you felt the same about me, didn't you? But if I told people we love each other, they would get the wrong idea. Instead I say that we look after each other when you're in Hanoi.'

'The first night you were a confused helpless little girl, young enough to be my grandchild. I was touched that you trusted me.'

'You could give into your feelings more often, but then you wouldn't be you.'

Andrew was inclined to see advantages in inhibitions. 'If people were always giving into their feelings, society would break down. Inhibitions are healthy.'

'I explain to myself that you and I are not lovers because we don't sleep together properly. And we aren't like father and daughter, even if they're supposed to love each other because you're not bossy enough to be a proper father. And we're certainly not like brother and sister; our ages are too different, and we don't quarrel most of the time. So do you know how I explain our relationship?'

'Can't imagine.'

'We've come together because a giant has collected us.'

Andrew tried to adjust to this idea. 'What does the giant look like?'

'I don't know because he's invisible. He doesn't really belong to our world. He's a sort of spirit-giant. But he's a kind, friendly spirit-giant; he watches over us and sees we don't come to any harm. And in return, he uses us as socks, sort of, because he suffers from cold feet.'

'Are his feet cold even here in Hanoi?'

'It's not always warm here. And his head and body are high up where it's cool.'

'How does he get his feet into us? He doesn't wear us, does he?'

'No, we're not that sort of sock. We lie along his feet and warm them up for him.' Cathy smiled happily; she clearly enjoyed this picture.

She picked up her notebook and wrote some more. Then she continued, 'The trouble is that we are so unlike each other. Even if the spirit-giant doesn't put his feet into us and he doesn't wear us out, we can't go on for a long time as a pair of socks because we aren't sufficiently similar. Sooner or later, he'll want socks that match better, and he's trying to find a more suitable partner for each of us. He's thinking of what's good for us as well as for himself.'

'Has he got two pairs of feet?'

After some reflection she said, 'He has a twin brother. He'll pass on one pair of properly matched socks to him.

'He accepts that I shall move on, sooner or later. I think he guesses that I shall join up with Kien. He's probably right. Kien has possibilities, even if things move awfully slowly. The spirit-giant is also concerned about you, his other sock. He's not in a hurry, but he's looking for somebody suitable for you, too. He's pretty sure he'll find somebody for you sooner or later.

'And talking about odd socks, you've seen that Hanh Phuc has a special sock for her wooden leg.'

'Yes. It's sad looking at it,' said Andrew.

'She gave me something to read that was written ages ago, in old English, but put in our own English on the next page. One of the lines is "And gladly would he teach, and gladly learn." Hanh Phuc said that was like you.'

Andrew couldn't help feeling flattered.

'By the way, can you remind me how you work out which days of the month a girl is fertile? I saw it on the Internet when I did a Google on immaculate conception, but I didn't note it down.'

Andrew, disillusioned, nevertheless thought he should reply, 'Two weeks before the start of her next period. The safe period is the rest of the cycle excluding thirteen to seventeen days before the next bleeding. And you can't know for certain when the next bleeding comes, and do leave Kien alone.'

'Now you're talking like a real father. Don't worry about Kien; he's far too young for the time being. But a little knowledge is always a good thing.'

'If you think that, why not start school again?'

'I don't have to go to school to learn things. I'm already educated – highly educated. I learned to sell things in the street, and in a foreign language, too. Being with Mary I've gotten good at explaining for the customers all the stuff we have in the shop. You've taught me percentages, and Hanh Phuc has taught me English and religion and poetry, and if I need to know anything more, I look it up on the Internet. What more do I need? It wouldn't be better if I'd gone to that school you dragged me towards.'

* * *

Andrew recounted this conversation to Mary on the next occasion she enquired what Andrew was doing to get Cathy back into school.

'Cathy says she doesn't need any more formal education because she's already a first-class honours graduate of the Open University of Life.'

'What did she really say?'

'That really was the sentiment, even if the words are those of Dame Edna Everidge.'

'And you left it at that?'

'I don't see what more I can do.' But he added, 'She's writing a story, even if it's a secret what it's about, so she might be induced to read more. I'll see if Hanh Phuc can come up with something at the right level of ambition – perhaps *Pride and Prejudice*.'

'Surely she wouldn't be interested in that. A few villagers in a faraway country, nearly two hundred years ago, with nothing ever happening.'

'The book sells hugely in India.'

'I suppose you can give it a try. She can't go on standing in the shop most of the day and then sitting with you in the evenings with nothing better to do than dream of an extended smooch or worse with a largely apathetic Kien.'

*   *   *

Andrew could subsequently report that Cathy had devoured *Pride and Prejudice*, in a Vietnamese translation Hanh Phuc had lent her, in two extended sittings. She had then asked for more by the same author.

*   *   *

A few days later, Andrew was working at home in the flat one Saturday afternoon when Cathy arrived with Kien. They went into the kitchen for a while.

Then Cathy emerged and announced to Andrew, 'Kien needs a bath. The one where he's living isn't working. It's OK if he has one here, isn't it?'

Andrew could see no objection at this point.

'Kien likes to eat something about this time, so I'm doing some food for all three of us.'

In the evening, after Kien had gone away, Cathy, reclining in the sofa, remarked to Andrew, 'I'm upgrading Kien. Before I thought six out of ten. Now I rate him' – she considered for a while – 'six and a half out of ten. Even a tiny bit more, so I can round up to seven out of ten, as you've taught me to do.

'While I remember, Kien will probably want another bath in a few days' time. He likes it here; he likes the quiet and the comfort, in the same way I do. He may ask if he can live here with us. If so, you must say no, firmly. Don't give any reasons; don't argue. It's fine having him here for a bath and some food, but it will spoil everything if he's hanging around the whole time. The apartment's too small.

'Another thing – don't talk about baths with Mary. She wouldn't understand, and it would upset her.'

Chapter 25

Mary was still concerned with helmets when Andrew met her next. Mary had intended spending roughly half her time in Hanoi and half in America, she told people, but she had no fixed schedule; she moved according to needs. Helmets was a cause that currently held her in Hanoi. She had persuaded Valerie, who spoke Vietnamese reasonably well, to take her to a pro-helmet demonstration.

'The demonstration was a triumph. And now Valerie's highly placed contacts say that it won't be more than a few months before there's a law compelling everybody to wear helmets when they ride those frightful machines. It almost reconciles me to communist dictatorships.'

'You'll soon be able to forget about helmets.'

'You're joking. The real work is just beginning – getting the helmets into the shops and making them available to the public.'

'Helmets in Hanoi absorb your attention much more than Hereford College, in spite of all the money you donated to the college.'

'The gentlemen of Hereford College are an engaging lot, certainly gifted and reasonably achieving, and I'm happy to meet them and hand over Hiram's money. But the college was Hiram's thing, not mine, and mainly affects a few privileged people. Helmets are a bigger matter altogether. They will benefit millions of people. It's my kind of cause.'

'Have you any idea what Kien and the owner of his shop think about helmets?'

'Kien says his boss is showing no interest. He hasn't grasped what a business opportunity is staring him in the face; in fact, Kien understands the situation better than his boss. I'm impressed with him.'

'You're sounding like Cathy. She's been upgrading him, too.'

'I'm setting up Kien in an independent business. Of course, I'll be his manager at first.'

Andrew was afraid that helmets had affected Mary's brain. 'Do you know enough about the motorbike business in Hanoi? You don't even like motorbikes. People need clothes, too; can't clothes shops be your cause?'

'Nothing wrong with clothes, but helmets save people's lives. I can learn enough about the motorbike business to keep Kien on a sensible path, and anyway I shall concentrate on the helmet side of the trade, at least to begin with. Kien will stockpile them over the next few months. I'll make sure he does it sensibly, but I am confident that he will. By the way, what do you mean when you say that Cathy is upgrading him?'

Andrew was anxious to avoid tricky ground. 'She's like you – she thinks that Kien is maturing.'

'She's right about that. If Kien shows up at your flat, he can be allowed the occasional smooch with Cathy on the sofa, but not for more than fifteen minutes at a time and with you keeping me fully informed of what's going on.'

Andrew still thought that Mary was underestimating the difficulties in operating a motorbike shop. 'Who's going to help with the language? What's Kien like as a salesman? Can he talk to the customers?'

'Valerie can deal with documents in Vietnamese, when I don't get much sense from Kien. Right now, she's finding a retail space for us, and we'll be opening shortly. For helping to sell helmets, I shall enlist Cathy part-time; she can move between shops.'

* * *

Andrew was preoccupied with institute affairs for the next few days, during which time Mary pushed developments forward rapidly. She and Valerie found premises for selling motorbikes and accessories in the same neighbourhood as her clothes shop. Mary and Kien had begun ordering helmets, a process into which Cathy had been drawn. Cathy's involvement led to problems, as Mary explained to Andrew when they next met.

'I showed Cathy pictures of various kinds of helmet, some of them made outside Vietnam, and asked for her views about them. I thought it was a good way to arouse her interest, and she had strong ideas about what kind of people would want to buy each type. Unfortunately, Kien thought she was being naive and girlish and made patronizing remarks, whereupon Cathy unleashed a flood of contemptuous remarks. Sadly, I could understand only the general drift of her reply; it was all in Vietnamese. She was furious, and it's plain she's an instinctive feminist.'

'I must say helmets are a surprisingly loaded issue, with major repercussions in all directions. Did Kien apologize?'

'Not really, and Cathy stalked off. I spent some time reasoning with Kien, and he finally agreed to come to your rooms with a peace offering – candy of some sort. You can leave them on the sofa for longer than usual, say around thirty minutes, so that they can make it up.'

* * *

Kien duly came to the flat with a peace offering. Cathy received him coolly, after which Andrew left them together. After the prescribed thirty minutes, Cathy was in a better mood, but even so, Kien departed early.

Andrew, curious as to how things stood, decided on an oblique approach. He asked Cathy, who by this time was busy writing in her notebook, 'What does the spirit-giant think of Kien nowadays?'

'He thinks Kien is childish and says too many silly boyish things.' Cathy continued writing without looking up.

'He doesn't want you to give up meeting Kien completely, does he?'

'He says Kien could be a lot worse.'

'You could remind the spirit-giant that you're not sixteen yet.'

'But I'm nearly sixteen, and time is running out.'

'Sixteen is nothing, and you're not living off the street anymore; you're a shop assistant.'

'I want to feel safe, settled.'

An area remained where Andrew would have liked more information. 'Does the spirit-giant say anything about whether you're in love with Kien?'

'He says that, when I begin to grade Kien eight out of ten, then I may be in love with him. By the way, Kien will be coming again later this week.'

* * *

Andrew returned late to the flat one day the following week and found Cathy back in her usual good humour.

'You know what happened today? Kien turned up when I was writing one of my stories. When I was on my way to the kitchen to make tea for us both, he asked if he could read what I had written. Normally I wouldn't have let him, but I had nearly finished a story that was really good, I thought, so he might as well read it and I could see if he had any feeling for, you know, literature. I spent a long time in the kitchen so that he could read it properly. When I came back, he looked solemn and thoughtful, and said he had no idea that I could write so well.'

'So he has a highly developed literary sense?'

'Enough for me to feel funny all over, all warm towards him, something new for me. Suddenly he was eight out of ten. I was going to suggest we had a bath together, something the spirit-giant disapproves of nowadays. Then he pointed out some spelling mistakes and what he thought were weak bits, but he's still almost eight out of ten.'

'Must you take his comments so personally? Can't you discuss your story with him?'

Chapter 26

Andrew was sauntering after work in the last hour of daylight on his way to the clothes shop to relate for Mary the reconciliation of Cathy and Kien. He took a shortcut through the market, walking rapidly to avoid interaction with the salespeople. But close to the exit, the press of people slowed him to a halt, and he couldn't avoid a young woman, taller than average, about his own height. She carried the usual set of postcards and T-shirts. Unlike the other street sellers of Andrew's experience, her expression was tired and resigned; also, she was older than the usual street children, perhaps around twenty.

'Like some cards?'

'I've already got masses, thank you.'

The initial hope in her eyes changed to desolation. It was pathetic to see.

'On second thoughts,' said Andrew, 'I'll buy this lot of six. How much?' The price was reasonable, even without bargaining; he handed over the money. But he had earned the right to ask further questions.

'May I ask, why do you have to sell postcards in the street? Can't you get a job in a shop?'

'I was in a clothes shop; it closed down.'

Andrew looked at her. 'Have you been standing out here every day for weeks since then?'

'Sometimes it goes well,' she said listlessly.

It was her depression that meant he wouldn't forget her; he couldn't face the prospect of remembering how he had abandoned her.

Impulsively, he said, 'Can you be here for another fifteen or twenty minutes? You could sit on the bench over there. I may have another customer for you.'

She made a grateful reply.

Andrew impressed on her, 'When I come back quite soon, you will be here, won't you?'

She nodded, listlessly.

Andrew dashed off, almost running out of the market along to the clothes shop. At this time of day, both Mary and Cathy were usually working there. He should persuade Mary to leave the shop with Cathy in charge.

He must decide on tactics. He shouldn't present the girl as an object of pity; rather, he should emphasize the business opportunities the girl provided.

He arrived at Mary's Eastern and Western Styles and found Cathy occupied with a customer; Mary was going through the accounts. He outlined the situation to Mary with appropriate enthusiasm.

'Now that Cathy is going to divide her time between two shops, won't you need another assistant, especially while the relationship between Kien and Cathy is settling down? I've come across an experienced shop assistant, a young woman of about twenty who is currently between jobs. Can you come and look her over? She's waiting nearby. I was struck by how suitable she seemed to be.' He thought it wise to add, 'But of course you're the best judge of that.'

'I suppose I could humour you by walking along and taking a look at her,' said Mary magnanimously, 'but don't expect me to be thrilled to bits.'

Andrew did what he could to hurry Mary off to the market. It was a relief to find the girl still there.

'I'll leave you two to discuss matters,' said Andrew. 'I'll go back to the shop.'

* * *

A while later, Andrew was delighted to see Mary return, together with the girl. He watched while Mary deftly arranged for Cathy to introduce the girl to the shop, saying to her, 'This may be our new assistant. Tell her about the shop; make some tea and sit with her outside and answer all her questions. She wants to know if she'll like it here.'

Mary and Andrew sat down at the till. Mary began, 'When I saw that girl, I thought, now Andrew, that old softy, is thrusting another Cathy on me.'

'But Cathy has made excellent progress, hasn't she?'

'She's turned out well, but it was a frightful gamble. Anyway the new girl – she's told me her name, but I'll never remember it (I shall be calling her Cathy-Two for the moment) – she's older and more experienced than Cathy the First, and the two of them can complement each other. So I thought, okay, I'll humour my old softy but on certain conditions.'

'Such as?'

'First, notify Hanh Phuc that she has a new pupil, to be paid for by you; she'll have a lot of work to do on Cathy-Two's English.'

'No problem there; it doesn't cost much.'

'And you'll need to do your bit with her arithmetic.'

'There shouldn't be any problem there, either.'

'Furthermore, Cathy-Two has nowhere decent to live, and she will be moving in with me.'

'That will be cramped, won't it?'

'Exactly. So I shall be arranging with Valerie to find me a larger apartment. I am expecting you to pay half the extra cost.'

Andrew took a moment to consider this. 'If the extra cost is within reason, I can manage that, too.'

'Fine. The problem with old softies like you, Andrew, particularly when you're employed by the state, is your penchant for being good with other people's time and money – particularly if they are business people. It saves you having to say no.'

'I'll bear that in mind.'

'That's all I have to say on the matter for the time being. I shall shortly be taking Cathy-Two home for showering, delousing, and disinfection; we can confidently expect her to take the job on offer. Then we'll return to the shop and fit her up with new clothes. You and Cathy are welcome to be here and approve the results.'

Chapter 27

'How's Cathy-Two making out in the shop?' Andrew asked Mary at the first reasonable opportunity a week later.

'She's come on a lot. She lacked self-confidence to begin with, but I worked hard at building up her self-esteem, and this is paying off. I must say Cathy-One helped greatly too.'

'In what way? I was worried that she would regard the new Cathy as an intruder.'

'So was I, so I made them talk together from day one. What they say is usually in Vietnamese, but they give every impression of being on good terms. It's partly that Cathy-Two stimulates Cathy-One's premature maternal instincts. Cathy-Two looks dazed, confused, and helpless, and Cathy-One moves in decisively and takes her under her wing.'

'How do you find living with her?'

'She was so grateful at having somewhere to lie down in peace that my heart melted. Actually her soft side goes down well with some of the customers, particularly middle-aged women who are losing their figures. They find her sympathetic. Cathy-One is better with the younger, tougher women customers and the men, who continue to appreciate being stroked and patted when they're trying on their clothes.'

* * *

Andrew wanted an early morning stroll round the lake and persuaded Cathy to join him. They walked past the men playing racquets and headed towards the exercise dancers, watched them for a while, and discussed the new assistant at Mary's Eastern and Western Styles.

Cathy said, 'It's awkward with two Cathys around the place, and saying Cathy-One and Cathy-Two sounds crazy; I can't understand why Mary couldn't choose something else. She's not completely stupid. Someone has to do something about it, and it will have to be me. So I've decided to change my Western name. I Googled on English names and found one I liked, and now I wonder what you will think of it.'

'I don't know until you tell me. Whatever it is, I expect I shall get used to it after a while.'

'My new name …will be …' She paused for effect, for what struck Andrew as an unnecessarily long time, even for those inured to winners being announced on television entertainments.

'Antonia.'

She noticed Andrew's reaction and asked, disappointed, 'Don't you like it?'

'It was my wife's name.' He was chilled; the conversation was unreal. While he felt suspended outside the everyday world, the new Antonia's expression blossomed from disappointment into rapture.

'An-rew! Don't you see what this means?'

'Not really; does it mean something?'

'It means that, in my previous life, I was your first Antonia. I was Antonia-One; I'm her reincarnation.' She did a brief ecstatic dance on the path. 'If you don't believe me, ask Hanh Phuc.'

'I may have told you my wife's name.'

'You never told me her name. I'm certain.'

She had probably started with the *A*'s, the scientist in him reminded Andrew; the chances of her picking the name by chance weren't remote.

The new Antonia, out of breath after the dance steps, said, 'You're too Western, An-rew, but the spirit-giant understands perfectly. I expect he knew all along.'

She took a few more dance steps and then asked, 'Besides, aren't I like your first Antonia? Do you know the meaning of my old Vietnamese name, Doan Vien? Happy Reunion.'

'You're like her in personality,' Andrew admitted. 'Not so much in looks.'

'It's personality that counts.'

From the loudspeakers came the sound of the exercise dance that the old Cathy had found great. Exultantly, the new Antonia joined one of the lines of swaying, jumping, hopping women.

* * *

It was the hottest time of year in Hanoi. Andrew had bought some flowers that had caught his eye from a street stall and thought he would give them to Mary, and the two of them were sitting outside the shop on the pavement in the gathering dusk. They watched the passers-by on their motorcycles and mopeds. It was different now; no girls with long hair flowing behind them. All were wearing helmets.

'Andrew, there's something I've been meaning to say for some time and have never got around to it till now. It must have been the flowers that reminded me; it was almost romantic: Thank you for the children. They're a goddamned nuisance but a great blessing, and I wouldn't have missed having them for worlds. It's all thanks to you.'

'I should thank you for them, too; you're heavily involved.'

'I will miss them when they move on,' continued Mary, wistfully. 'A year ago, I never dreamed I would think that.'

'Antonia, as she wants to be called now, is slowly moving closer to Kien, but Cathy-Two isn't talking of leaving you, is she?'

'Not at the moment, but she'll move on sooner or later, probably sooner. A young Australian keeps coming to the shop for no particular reason and doesn't ignore an opportunity to chat with her. She brightens up as soon as she sees him.'

They sat in relaxed silence for a while, watching the flow of motorcyclists.

Mary asked, 'Aren't you going to miss someone calling to you, "Anrew!"'

'Yes, up to a point, but it's natural for her to grow up and leave home, and I wouldn't want it otherwise. I hate to see parents hanging on to their children and calling them by some ridiculous nickname suited to a six-year-old even when they're in their late teens or early twenties.'

'So you're happy to live on your own?'

'I've got one silly suggestion, if you have the patience to hear it.'

'Andrew! I'm fascinated.'

'That we move in together, at least when we're both in Hanoi. Valerie ought to be able to fix something we both like.'

'Well I never! Andrew! Again, almost romantic, especially coming from you. It's a great idea! Antonia will soon be moving in with Kien, and we don't have to wait for Cathy-Two to move out; she can have a room of her own with us.'

Mary kissed him warmly.

* * *

Andrew ascended the last bit of the narrow staircase to his room at Hereford College and was surprised to find Hugh and Tom sitting there, waiting for him.

'Welcome home, Andrew, and Tom and I have an important announcement for you.'

Andrew laid aside his suitcases, took off his coat, and sat down with them at the table.

Hugh stood up. 'As you know, Tom and I are members of a society, which we now call The Hereford Society for the Improvement of Natural Knowledge of the Human Species. The rules of the society do not exclude unnatural methods for obtaining the knowledge, and all proceedings are conducted in the utmost confidentiality. You have preferred to stay on the periphery of this exclusive society of two, and we have respected your decision not to be a full member. The important announcement is that we have elected you to be a corresponding member of the society. This is a great honour that we are convinced you will not decline.'

'It is a great honour indeed, and thank you very much, sirs.'

'To celebrate the occasion, I have bought a bottle of well above average wine.'

Hugh poured out the wine, and the three of them tasted it in appreciative silence.

'Now what's the latest about Cathy and Kien?' asked Tom, two minutes later.

'There have been further developments. Kien told her (she's called Antonia now, not Cathy) that he needed her, and Antonia was quite touched by that. But what really pleased her was that Kien said that he wished she'd say that *she* needed *him*. She thought that was real progress. She told him that she'd needed him for ages but that he hadn't been ready. Then she discussed the matter with the spirit-giant, who said that, now that she rated Kien eight out of ten for longer than five minutes at a time, she should consider moving in with him and helping with the shop full-time.'

'Are they getting married?'

'Yes indeed; the spirit-giant has become much fussier about proprieties. By the way, why haven't you asked Mark to be a member of the Society?'

'We were afraid that membership was incompatible with the dignity of the cloth,' said Hugh, and Tom nodded.

'Even when the wearer of the cloth is Mark?' asked Andrew.

'Even in the case of Mark. So when is the young couple getting married?'

'As soon as Valerie has Antonia's papers fixed, using her contacts. Kien's papers show he is over sixteen.'

'Who's giving Antonia away? You or the spirit-giant?' asked Tom.

'The spirit-giant is unfortunately invisible and inaudible, so it will have to be me. He'll be a witness, along with Mary or Hanh Phuc. No one else will be there, as far as I know, so it will be a quiet wedding. Are there any developments regarding Miss Dorchester and Clemmie?'

'Clemmie deposited printed notes in everybody's pigeonhole informing us that the bride's parents would love to welcome all employees of Hereford College, including kitchen and garden staff, to what the papers are regarding as one of the year's most important society weddings, but unfortunately the size of the hall limits the number of guests to one hundred and fifty, and an invitation can be extended only to the rector. Clemmie is super at having it both ways.'

'Banish cynicism and bring back hope,' said Andrew. 'I am sure we shall be delighted in the future to say that we were all seriously considered as guests at Clemmie's wedding.'

'You mentioned Mary,' said Tom. 'Is she still preoccupied with her shops and helmets?'

'She's as economically minded as ever, so I'm helping her save money. Cathy-Two, Mary, and I are sharing a flat these days,' said Andrew. 'Valerie found a nice one for us, just the right size and reasonably central. But members of the society don't discuss each other's private lives; Tom told me that very clearly.'

'Does that rule extend to corresponding members of the society?' Tom asked Hugh.

Lightning Source UK Ltd.
Milton Keynes UK
UKOW05f2134060913

216674UK00001B/1/P